Pleasure's Daughter

Amelia could only guess what her aunt and uncle must have thought when she had entered the church dressed like a whore but, judging by their shocked expressions, they, like her, had thought the attire unsuitable for a bride. As soon as the priest had declared the Marquess of Beechwood and Amelia man and wife she could have sworn that but for the presence of the guests and clergy her new husband would have taken her there and then.

'I own you now,' he had said, smirking. 'You are mine to do with as I please.' She knew it was only a matter of time before she would have to confront that which she most feared: her desire for him.

Pleasure's Daughter

SEDALIA JOHNSON

Black Lace novels are sexual fantasies.
In real life, make sure you practise safe sex.

First published in 1998 by
Black Lace
Thames Wharf Studios
Rainville Road, London W6 9HA

Reprinted 2001

Typeset by SetSystems Ltd, Saffron Walden, Essex
Printed and bound by Mackays of Chatham PLC

ISBN 0 352 33237 9

Chapter One

The carriage lurched forward, jolting Amelia awake. She caught her breath, drawing in scents of perspiration and newly fallen rain. Stretching her arms high above her head until her fingers touched the roof, she glanced briefly at her fellow passenger, a ruddy-faced woman balancing a basket of eggs on her lap, before sliding down the window and thrusting her face out into the startling morning air. The cool, moist breeze which caressed her skin did much to soothe her burning cheeks, but it couldn't take away the overwhelming frustration which enveloped her every time she thought of her father's passing.

She settled back against the seat and sighed as she remembered how, after months of watching the life drain out of him, she had prayed for death to come and release him from his suffering. Well now it had and, all sorrow spent, she was left with only a sense of annoyance for she knew that her life would never be the same again. A fact borne out by the summons she'd received from her aunt, Lady Margaret Boughby, just a week ago.

Departing the house which had been her residence for the last twenty years didn't trouble her that much; it had ceased to be a home long before her father fell ill. What did bother her, however, was that she would be leaving

1

the one thing which had kept her alive during those frantic days and lonely nights: Tom, the stablehand.

Amelia shivered as she remembered the first time she'd seen him. He was tossing hay in one of the lower barns on the estate. Naked to the waist, his blond hair flowed over his shoulders like a golden river, the ends darkened by the product of his labour.

Sensing her presence, he'd stopped what he'd been doing and blatantly stared at her, his topaz eyes blazing. As her gaze had met his, she had experienced an intimate stirring, the like of which she'd never known before; a feeling which drove her to seek out his company whenever life at home became unbearable.

The rhythmic motion of the carriage pushed Amelia's legs together and she shifted uneasily as she thought of the smoothness of his back, his trim waist and his lean but powerful thighs. How she longed to be enclosed again in those muscular arms, to feel his nose toying with her little pleasure-bud while his confident tongue explored the succulent folds of her sex.

A groan escaped her lips as a throbbing rose in her groin, sending waves of longing throughout her. Just thinking about Tom caused wetness to spring again in that secret place and ooze down on to the tops of her thighs, while her nipples hardened to press painfully into her stiffened bodice. She furtively clenched and unclenched her sex under the layers of her petticoats, trying to recreate the rapture Tom's tongue could bring.

Amelia flicked open her fan in an effort to quell the fire which was burning its way over her, moulding her coarse chemise to her body, and caught the concerned glance of the woman opposite. Amelia forced a smile in her direction and closed her eyes, preferring to savour the vivid memory of Tom's magnificent penis.

Amelia remembered the first time she'd seen it, how it had brought a gasp to her lips as it sprang free of his breeches and stood between them like a slightly arced club. She also recalled the moment when, taking him deep into her mouth and brushing him with her tongue,

2

she'd realised that his erection was no monster to be afraid of, but a pleasure-giving tool, an expression of his love for her.

It was during these brief but exquisite moments that Amelia began to sense there was much more she could experience, heights she had yet to reach. Now she would never know what they were, leaving him as she had back in Steeple Ashton, while she took this journey to a new, daunting life among her noble relatives.

Amelia's thoughts were interrupted by the carriage rolling to a halt and the door being dragged open.

'We're at the crossroads, miss.' The driver leered at her and held out his hand. Ignoring this gesture, Amelia picked up her valise and clambered out into the brilliant sunshine. While her eyes grew accustomed to the sudden glare, the desire which had possessed her only moments ago began to fade, ebbing away from her until all that remained was a dull ache in the pit of her stomach.

She blinked and, tightening the grip on her bag, went inside the posting inn. The sour smell of alcohol and stale tobacco assaulted her as she walked into the bar. She was grateful that there were no drinkers in residence for she knew that no respectable woman would dream of entering such a male-dominated atmosphere, but she was thirsty and wasn't about to wait shivering outside for her connection when she could be enjoying a warming cup of chocolate in here.

Amelia looked round and, seeing no one behind the counter, moved towards a doorway on the left.

'Hello? Is anyone about? I'd like some service if you please!'

Receiving no reply, she put down the valise and tentatively stepped into the hall. Silence surrounded her as she walked along the passage, pausing now and again to peer into equally quiet rooms along the way. It was only when she reached the foot of a flight of stairs that she became aware of muffled conversation drifting down from the floor above.

Gazing upwards, Amelia contemplated shouting her

request again in that direction but thought better of it and, grasping her skirts, started to climb the stairs. As she approached the landing, the noise gradually crescendoed into the heated tones of an argument.

Amelia paused, wondering if she should really be wandering about a strange inn on her own, but then decided that as she'd come this far she might as well carry on. She approached the nearest room with caution, peering round the door just enough to see what was going on inside.

Two people, one a burly, middle-aged man in a worn linen shirt and breeches, the other, a gentleman in a fine suit, stood by the far window quarrelling.

'You owe me. I won fair and square, so when are you going to pay up?'

The gentleman sniffed, raising his chin defiantly. 'I'll pay you when it pleases me, not before.' He turned to leave but the shorter man caught his arm.

'You'll not leave until I have my money!'

'How dare you, sir.' The gentleman's fingers toyed with the handle of his sword. 'I should demand satisfaction for this outrage.'

At that moment, a woman Amelia hadn't noticed before stepped from the shadows and insinuated herself between the two of them, wrapping her arms around the burly man's neck.

'Give it a rest, will you. He said he'd pay up didn't he?'

The middle-aged man withdrew from the woman's arms, then looked at the gentleman before pulling on a battered tricorne hat. 'Mark my words, your Lordship, or whatever your name is. I'll get my money – either on my own or with a friend. You wait and see.'

He picked up his frockcoat from a nearby chair and stormed from the room, avoiding bumping into Amelia by mere inches. She scooted as far back against the wall as she could, praying that he hadn't noticed her as he left.

'See what a little feminine charm can achieve?' the woman giggled.

Amelia then made out the sound of their footsteps approaching and, gasping, pressed her hands flat to the wall, trying her hardest to remain still and undetectable. Out of the corner of her eye, she observed the couple come out on to the landing, the gentleman pausing to plant a brief kiss on the woman's cheek before guiding her towards a room in the other direction.

Amelia let out a sigh and started for the stairs, only to stop dead in her tracks when she heard the unmistakable groan of a bed, swiftly followed by raucous laughter.

A familiar fire ignited between her legs at these telling sounds, forcing her to lean against the banister. She squeezed her thighs together and, delighting in the ripple of pleasure which shot up her spine, turned round and blinked in the direction of the distant room. She knew that even to think about encroaching on someone else's privacy was wrong, but the sudden opportunity of this situation filled her already stimulated senses with a yearning so strong she could not deny it.

Swallowing hard, Amelia grasped the banister and guided her shaking body along the rest of the passage until she stood on the threshold of the room in question. However, despite the urgency she had felt a few moments ago, it was several seconds before she actually managed to muster enough courage to look in.

When she finally did, her eyes were greeted by the sight of the woman she'd seen earlier reclining naked on a bed, her light brown hair fanning out like a blanket behind her. Her legs were raised almost level with her hips while her fingers traced circles around the base of her full breasts.

Amelia blinked, her eyes drawn to the area between the woman's legs where her glistening, swollen lips lay parted. She had never seen her own genitals before, let alone another woman's and her eyes lingered there, taking in the subtle beauty of the rose-pink folds.

She blinked twice as the woman moved her hands

away from her breasts to that enchanting orifice and dipped two fingers into herself. A wave of heat engulfed Amelia while she watched her scoop up a small amount of her creamy excretions and begin to massage it into her clitoris.

Moving into the centre of the doorway to gain a better view, Amelia sank down on to her knees, her own pleasure-bud beginning to stir and press against its protective hood of flesh, while her hands urgently sought the hem of her gown. Her fingers easily slipped underneath her skirts and, lightly skimming the surface of her silk stockings, soon came into contact with the bristly reaches of her pudenda. Easing her fingers into the swollen creases of flesh there, she sought her own climax.

Amelia glanced up, as if to seek instruction from the woman's movements, and was confronted by the partially clad form of the gentleman towering over her with hands on hips, a grin stretching his lips.

She guiltily withdrew her fingers, before staring up at him with flaming cheeks.

He was a most striking man. He had shiny, chestnut hair which was swept off his forehead and loosely caught in a ribbon at the base of his neck. His lightly tanned face was dominated by a sharply chiselled chin which supported a pair of full, expressive lips and a slender, hooked nose. But it was his eyes which really caught Amelia's attention. A dark brown, they were two perfectly shaped almonds with heavy, half-closed lids which added a lazy, almost weary expression to his countenance.

The man raised his eyebrows and held out a hand to Amelia. She didn't move but bit her lip as she fought to control the fluttering in her chest, aware all the time that those eyes were watching her every move.

Amelia fell back on her haunches, breathing heavily, and finally managed to break from his gaze. No man, not even Tom, had inspired such a sense of awe in her before and she struggled to think of what it was about him which had caught her fancy. She glanced at him

6

once more, taking in the rest of his finely honed body. He was naked to the waist and she noticed that his torso sported the same sun-kissed glow as his face and consisted of a well-developed chest, an impossibly firm stomach and the narrowest of hips, barely concealed under a pair of skintight chamois breeches. She noted too the bulge which strained between his muscular thighs, creating a taut line across his pelvis.

'Madam,' he growled, his commanding voice resonating throughout the room, 'I haven't much more patience.' He shook his hand in front of her face.

Amelia accepted it with hesitation, unsure of her ability to stand, and shuddered when she sensed the strength of his grasp. Giving no resistance, she finally allowed him to pull her to her feet. He was a good half foot taller than her own average frame and, she guessed, in his mid-thirties.

'Well now, what shall we do with this little voyeur?' He glanced at the woman on the bed while his grip gradually tightened around Amelia's wrist. 'I think she needs to be taught some manners, don't you, Fran?'

The woman nodded enthusiastically and, forgetting about her self-stimulation for the moment, raised herself on to her hands and knees in order to get a better view of them.

Fear gripped Amelia's heart when she looked up and caught sight of the man's determined expression. 'Please sir, I –' She stumbled, at a loss for words.

'Please?' he mimicked, jerking her nearer until only his excited manhood stood between them. 'Please what, my dear?' He raised a hand to her neck, his fingers leaving a trail of goosepimples as they moved up to her face. 'What is it that you want, child?' he asked, forcing her to look at him. Amelia's bottom lip trembled as she stared deep into the dark eyes and drew in the musky, masculine scent which rose from him. At the back of her mind, beyond the wall of fear she'd constructed, she realised that she wanted more than anything else to be possessed by this stranger. The longing she felt for him now far exceeded even that all-consuming need which had driven her to seek out Tom's embrace in the first place.

'I, I –' she managed at last, only for the words to die in her throat when she heard the distinctive clatter of a carriage, her carriage, drawing up outside.

Panic surged through Amelia, blotting out the desire which only seconds before had filled her, as she came back to the present and the reality of the situation. She attempted to pull away from the man, only to be squeezed even tighter to him by an arm encircling her waist. She pushed her hands against his chest, her fingers disappearing into the thick blanket of reddish brown hair there, while she felt his hardness pressing into her through the layers of her petticoats.

'Oh no, my dear, you will not escape your punishment so easily,' the man whispered hoarsely, pushing a finger between her rigid lips. As Amelia felt him probing the moist contours of her mouth, anger, combined with a feeling of helplessness, enveloped her, quashing any desire left. Without thinking, she bit down on his finger as hard as she could and, when the man cried out and sharply drew away, she made the most of her freedom and ran from the room.

Collecting her valise downstairs, she caught sight of herself in a nearby mirror. Her once-tidy raven hair had fallen free of its restraining lace cap and hung in ringlets about her shoulders, while her shapely breasts pushed at the boundaries of her stays, threatening to spill out over the top of her dress at any moment.

Despite this dishevelled appearance, it was the wantonness in her emerald eyes which truly shocked her. It was as if she was staring at an impostor, someone who both frightened and stimulated her.

The sound of heavy footsteps above snapped Amelia from her contemplation. She cast a glance in the direction of the stairs, before clutching her bag tightly to her chest and hurrying out of the inn into the fresh May air.

* * *

8

Lucas turned away from the window, a faint smile at the corners of his mouth as he walked back to the bed.

'Well, she sure gained the better of you,' Fran chirped, raising herself up, her large, unfettered breasts wobbling with the effort. Lucas scowled at her and flexed his sore finger. She was right of course; he just didn't want to be reminded of it. Why, just thinking about that sable-haired creature made the anger rise within him.

Seeing the tension in his face, Fran placed her hands on Lucas's shoulders and began to massage them with the tips of her fingers. He turned round and clasped her pendulous breasts, kneading them until their nipples grew hard. A sigh escaped Fran's lips and she collapsed against his chest, pulling him on to the bed with her. She slid her hand down to the springy fabric of his breeches where his penis strained, and slowly undid the drawstrings.

'You must not be so hard on yourself,' she whispered, her fingers lightly stroking his cock. 'After all, you can't have every woman.'

Lucas smiled to himself, delighting in Fran's knowledgeable touch. At least this one knew her place – unlike that chit. Well, if she thought she could elude him so easily, she was sadly mistaken. Now that he knew where she was staying, having recognised the crested coach immediately, he was determined to use every opportunity to show her just how futile it was for her to try to deny him again.

Amelia mounted the marble steps with a sense of dread. She knew that the initial impression she gave would be crucial in determining how she was received into her new family. At least she'd been able to tidy herself when the carriage had paused to let a farmer and his cows cross the road. If only she could erase the memory of that stranger's determined gaze as easily as she had toned down her high colouring with a liberal use of powder.

A solitary footman awaited her in the lavishly

furnished hall. Having taken her valise, he led her towards a small anteroom at the side. Amelia took a deep breath, trying to slow her racing heart, while he opened the door and announced her.

She sank into a deep curtsy, raising her eyes as she did so in order to take a look at the figure draped across the settee. Sporting the same dark features as herself, her aunt was decorated from head to toe in silk and diamonds, her fully panniered skirts spanning the width of the couch.

Amelia straightened up and caught sight of Lady Boughby's look of disdain. 'So, you have arrived at last,' she sighed, snapping her fan shut, 'and it seems that what I've heard about your father's lack of, of respect for his position – is reflected in your dress. Where on earth did you get it?' Amelia silenced the retort which immediately flew to her lips while she self-consciously toyed with her unstructured skirt. She spied a cup of tea on the table in front of Lady Boughby and realised she was thirsty.

'Aunt, I –' Lady Boughby clicked her fingers and a footman stepped forward.

'Show this ... child to her room and make sure she's suitably attired for dinner this evening. God's truth, I can't let my lord think my niece is a complete bumpkin.'

'Madam, Aunt, some tea ...' Amelia trailed off as she felt tears prick her eyes.

'A servant will bring some up to your room. Surely you do not expect me to receive visitors with you here, attired thus? I have my reputation to think of.'

Amelia knew that if she stayed to argue her case as her spirit demanded, she would only embarrass herself even more before this aggressive woman. So she meekly dropped another curtsy and, biting her lip, joined the footman at the door.

Once in her room, Amelia threw herself on the bed and buried her face in the pillow. How naive she'd been to think that she could actually fit in with her privileged relatives.

Even after the passage of nearly 21 years, it was obvious that Lady Boughby still hadn't forgiven her father for bringing shame to the family by eloping with a governess. Amelia realised that it must have been a great scandal at the time, but she knew that if her aunt had tried to understand the love her parents had had for each other, before consumption separated them, then perhaps she would have been able to understand why he'd been forced to take such a drastic action in the first place.

Amelia remembered the day they buried her mother and how, looking into her father's sorrowful eyes afterwards, she had instinctively known he'd never recover from her death.

She shivered and sat up, wiping her eyes in the process. It was a memory she had no desire to dwell on, not now that she had far more pressing things to think about – namely, what type of life she was going to have in a household where she clearly wasn't wanted.

Amelia was so caught up in her own thoughts she hardly noticed the door quietly open and another figure enter the room. It was only when she felt a waft of cool air strike her burning cheeks that she looked up and was confronted by the vision of a startling blonde girl swathed in powder blue silk. Three, maybe four years Amelia's junior, the girl's high cheekbones and full, pouting lips gave the impression of great beauty to come.

Amelia's eyes travelled over her fashionable dress with its wide skirt and tightly laced waist and guessed that this delicate-looking female must be her cousin. She held out a trembling hand, praying that her eyes weren't too puffy. 'Constance, isn't it?'

The girl smiled and lowered herself on to the edge of the bed. 'Everyone calls me Connie, including mama, who I assume is the cause of your tears.' Amelia looked away, biting her lip. 'Come now, no need to be ashamed.

I am the first one to admit that she can be a bit prickly at times, but that's only because she doesn't know you. I expect in a day or two you'll be the best of friends, just as I hope we can be.'

Amelia caught her breath and looked at her cousin. 'I should like to have someone I can talk to. It is something I have missed of late. Perhaps I'm just a bit sensitive, having had to leave my home and –' She stopped short of saying his name, feeling herself colouring as she did so. Would it be so shameful to tell the girl about her liaison? It would certainly help to get everything out in the open.

'You've had to leave your lover?' Connie chuckled and patted her arm. 'Living here does not mean one has to become a nun, you know. I too have a secret which even mama isn't aware of. Perhaps I'll tell you about him one day. What I'm trying to say is that you need not worry about confiding in me. I won't tell a soul.' She leant forward and, taking Amelia's hand, brought it to her lips. 'I would like to hear about him. Perhaps talking about it would make you feel better.'

Amelia looked into her blue eyes and saw such a depth of honesty in them, she instinctively knew Connie could be trusted. 'Very well, I will tell you, but only if you promise you will not repeat any of this.'

Connie nodded and made the sign of the cross, before plumping further on to the bed so that the two of them were sitting side by side. 'Tom was his name, he was a labourer on the estate, and the moment I saw him I knew we were going to share something special, although at that time I knew not what.' Amelia cast Connie a glance and, satisfied by her expression of concentration, continued.

'When my father grew ill and it pained me greatly just to look at him, I took to going for long walks in the evening. One such night I was walking in one of the fields and I heard a rustling on the other side of the hedge. Curious, I peered over and saw Tom stuffing some dried hay into a muslin bag to make a pillow to go

12

with the blanket he'd already laid out. When I questioned him as to why he didn't sleep in the barn with the other workers he told me that he preferred to spend his nights outside under the stars and would be honoured if I joined him. All my commonsense commanded me to refuse him, if only for my reputation's sake and yet, despite this, there was a part of me which wanted nothing more than to spend the night with him just savouring the subtle sounds of the slumbering countryside.'

Amelia smiled. 'I remember the first time he touched me that night. I was lying beside him, enjoying his warmth, his closeness, when I began to feel something moving, crawling up my leg. I thought it was an insect and made to brush it away only to find that it was Tom's hand moving under my skirts. He must have seen the fear in my eyes for he laid me back against the blanket and kissed me, his tongue exploring the soft depths of my mouth, while his hand continued to move deeper between my legs.

'Then, when his fingers touched my secret place, parted my already swollen, slick lips, tracing the lightest touches around their edges, I couldn't help but bury my face in his chest and nuzzle closer to him. Without realising what I was doing, I began to rock back and forth, pressing my mound against his wrist. He pulled up the back of my skirts, the cool air tantalising the burning skin of my buttocks, and slipped his other hand under me.

'I remember him pulling me up and manoeuvring me on to his lap so that I was sitting astride him. How I gasped when, using his legs, he started to bounce me up and down on his thighs, his fingers easily slipping into the entrance of my maiden sex. As he began to push them further and further into me, I found myself leaning forward so that my already excited bud rubbed against the bulge in his groin and created a sensation so strong within me, I couldn't control my actions.

'I thought I would surely go mad as something burst

within me, making my thighs quiver. I wrapped my arms around Tom's shoulders, and delighted in the feel of his tongue as it snaked over the domes of my breasts, his nose buried in my cleavage.

'I continued to move long after this wonderful feeling ended, wanting Tom to experience it too, but he suddenly pushed me away from him and staggered out of sight.

'I cannot understand why he did that, why he didn't continue and satisfy himself, like he did me. When I questioned him afterwards, he told me that my quim was sacred and his penis would never corrupt it.' Amelia smiled ruefully and looked at Connie. She was shocked to find her cousin's hand toying with the strings of her bodice. Amelia questioned the younger girl. 'Why wouldn't he satisfy himself?'

Connie didn't answer but slid her slender fingers inside and cupped one of Amelia's breasts, her icy touch creating goosepimples on the delicate flesh. She sighed as her fingers closed around a nipple and teased it until it hardened and pressed into her palm.

'Don't worry about that now. Just relax.' Her voice held an urgency Amelia hadn't noticed before and she tried to protest. 'Hush, it's all right,' Connie whispered, withdrawing her hand and placing a finger against her quivering lips. 'There is nothing to be afraid of. I was simply trying to help you remember that night with Tom. Perhaps you can tell me more when you've settled in.' She rose and went to the door. 'Come, the moment has arrived for you to choose one of my gowns for dinner this evening. I think an emerald silk will suit, don't you?'

Chapter Two

Descending the stairs, Amelia had to admit that her cousin had impeccable taste. The gown she's chosen for her suited her figure admirably. It clung to the ample swell of her breasts, emphasising her tiny waist, before billowing out over panniers. Connie had also applied rouge to Amelia's cheeks and a light dusting of powder to the rose-pink skin of her chest to give it a soft glow.

Glancing in a mirror at the base of the stairs, Amelia knew that she looked an equal to her cousin who was resplendent in a crimson damask, and for the first time since she'd arrived she felt able to meet her aunt and uncle with the confidence she would need to move within their circle.

Amelia ran the palms of her hands over her skirts, smoothing out an invisible wrinkle, before sweeping into the drawing room behind Connie.

Amelia watched her closely as she sank into a deep curtsy before her parents and then stepped back for her to do the same.

'I see that our niece shares your beauty, my lady,' Lord Boughby announced, taking Amelia's hand and drawing her to her feet. She was surprised to find that her uncle was nothing like she'd imagined him to be, but a stout, greying man in his early fifties.

'It is pleasant to see her finally attired as one in her position should be. I trust that you have recovered from the journey, Lady Amelia.' Amelia felt her aunt's eyes roving over her and she straightened up, holding her head high, knowing that the middle-aged woman wouldn't be able to find any flaws in her appearance this time.

'I have rested well, thank you.'

'Splendid,' boomed Lord Boughby, 'then allow me to introduce you to a dear friend before we partake of a glass of ratafia. I present Lucas, the Marquess of Beechwood.'

Amelia dipped into another curtsy and raised her eyes to the man who stepped forward. Her smile died as she recognised him.

He was dressed in a suit of aquamarine silk interlaced with silver thread, his throat and wrists decorated by falls of crisp, white lace, while his auburn hair was covered by a delicately powdered wig. Her gaze lingered on his slim hips and the gleaming sword secured against one of them while she took a deep breath and pulled herself up.

Amelia's heart thundered in her chest and she sensed her breasts straining at her stays when the marquess took her hand and raised it to his lips. As his lips brushed the soft tips of her fingers, she had an urge to snatch her hand away and fear swept over her. But already her mind was racing, reminding her of what she'd felt for him only a few hours before, forcing her to confront the desires she had experienced at the time.

She squeezed her quivering thighs together as she felt herself grow wet at the recollection of the feeling of his chest under the pressure of her fingers, the vision of his excited tarse throbbing and pushing against the ineffectual constraints of his breeches.

She raised her eyes slowly to meet his and, seeing the thinly veiled anger in them, bit her lip and looked sharply away.

'Are you unwell, my dear?' her aunt enquired, opening her fan and flicking it in front of Amelia's heaving chest. 'You look rather flushed.'

'I suspect –' the marquess smacked his lips and smiled at Lady Boughby '– that she's simply in need of some refreshment.'

Ignoring him, Amelia allowed Lord Boughby to put his arm around her shoulders and guide her towards the sofa. A few seconds later she realised she was shaking when Connie sank down beside her and gave her a glass of liqueur.

'Judging by your reaction, it seems that I'm not the only one who thinks Lucas attractive,' she whispered.

Amelia stared at her cousin in disbelief. 'I, I don't know what you mean. I simply felt faint. It's the corset you lent me – just too tight, that's all.'

'Of course it is.' Connie smiled knowingly and then left her in order to talk with the marquess who was leaning against the mantelpiece.

Amelia sipped the chilled liquid while searching for a way out of this impossible situation. It didn't take her long to realise, with a sinking heart, that the only option open to her was to act as normal as possible and pray that Lucas was gentleman enough not to say anything to her aunt and uncle about their previous meeting.

Amelia cast her gaze towards the fireplace and caught her breath when she saw how blatantly her cousin was flirting with the marquess. Connie fluttered her eyelashes and leant forward so that he had a perfect view of her cleavage while she absentmindedly toyed with the lace at his throat.

Amelia blinked and glanced at her aunt and uncle and saw that they were engaged in their own conversation and hadn't noticed how outrageously their daughter was acting, just a few feet away.

Returning her gaze to the mantelpiece, Amelia saw how easy Connie seemed in his presence and shuddered. Was Lucas the secret lover she had spoken of? Had she learnt her forward ways from him?

Amelia was almost relieved when her aunt announced

that dinner was being served and, though she had no stomach for food, she was grateful for the distraction – that was, until she realised that Lady Boughby had seated her directly across from the marquess.

Amelia tried to keep her eyes on her plate during the meal, knowing that if she could achieve this half the battle would be won, but no sooner had the main course been served than she felt her vision wandering in the marquess's direction.

Lucas lounged in his chair, one hand toying with his fork while his other supported his chin. He looked up and met her glance with a broad smile, his pearly teeth gleaming in the candlelight. He picked a stalk of asparagus from his plate and lifted it until it hovered above his mouth. Amelia watched, mesmerised, as a few silky beads of butter collected on its tip and then dripped on to his lips. Lucas snaked out his tongue and ran it over them, sliding it across the greasy contours, savouring every last drop, before pushing the asparagus stalk deep into his mouth.

Amelia swallowed hard when he slowly drew it out between pursed lips and then plunged it back in, his tongue lovingly circling its base. She knew she should look away, focus her eyes on anything other than this suggestive action, but she couldn't. She was as much caught up in its meaning as the marquess, a fact which caused perspiration to break out above her top lip.

Lord Boughby addressed him then, drawing his attention away from her. Amelia flopped back in her seat as far as her stays would allow and slowly dabbed her moist chest with her napkin. Though they'd only just met, the marquess seemed to know just how to get to her and, what was more, he seemed to enjoy seeing her squirm. She sensed that part of this haughty attitude was his way of getting back at her for the injury she'd caused him that morning, but there was something else which she couldn't fathom, an unknown reason behind his behaviour which sent her pulse racing.

'Come, ladies, it's time we retired to the drawing room,' said her aunt.

Amelia dutifully followed her aunt and cousin out of the room, her eyes briefly catching those of the marquess as she passed him.

For the next half-hour, Amelia silently listened to her aunt and Connie discussing their plans for her new wardrobe. She tried to match their enthusiasm, to voice preferences as to the colours and styles of her new gowns but, even when it was announced that the dressmaker would call on her the next day, she was only able to produce a fleeting smile, her mind still preoccupied by what had taken place at the dinner table.

The door opened and Lucas entered the room unaccompanied, Lord Boughby conspicuous by his absence. Amelia looked tremulously in her aunt's direction but saw, with a sinking heart, that already she was bidding her daughter good night.

The marquess sank into the space beside Connie and stretched his arms above his head. Amelia bit her lip, praying that he wouldn't say anything to embarrass her in front of her cousin.

'Tell me, my lady, can you play the harpsichord?' he asked her once the three of them were alone.

Amelia reluctantly raised her eyes and followed his gaze over to the window where one stood. 'Well, actually I can –' she managed, almost choking on the words.

'Excellent. I should like to hear you play, wouldn't you, Connie?'

Her cousin nodded excitedly and clasped her hands together. 'Oh please do, Amelia. It has been a long time since music has graced this room.'

Amelia hesitated but, seeing the expectancy on her face, she shrugged and rose out of her chair. 'Very well, but I warn you that I haven't played for some time.'

She moved towards the instrument and took a seat on a softly padded bench in front of it. A sheet of music lay open on the top and Amelia was tempted to try to play this, but eventually she opted to play a piece from memory, deciding that this was the safest bet.

She launched into a robust rendition of Bach's Italian Concerto. A few bars into it she glanced towards the settee to see if her audience liked what she was playing and immediately froze, her fingers striking discord on the smooth, ivory keys.

The marquess was leaning over Connie, his lips tracing the curve of her neck. He then moved a hand to her bodice, drew out one of her breasts, and raised its rosy tip to his mouth. Amelia heard Connie moan as he grasped the hem of her gown and, lifting her skirts up over her knees, propelled his hand under them. Connie parted her legs and leant back slightly, allowing him full access to her secret place.

Amelia scrambled up from the bench and swayed towards the door, aware all the time of the growing dewiness between her legs. When she witnessed Lucas drop on to his knees before Connie and, grabbing her by the hips, pull her slick, dilated cleft towards him, Amelia fell back against the wall. Next she saw him bury his face in Connie's groin, his nose nudging at her while his ebullient tongue darted in and out between her turgid, flushed lips.

A gasp escaped Amelia as she watched him leave that enticing cavity and lick his way up to Connie's erect clitoris. He took it between his teeth and nibbled it gently, before completely enclosing it with his lips when Connie cried out and clamped her thighs around his neck.

Amelia pushed herself away from the wall and staggered towards the sofa to get a better view of them and, collapsing against it, began to rub her pudenda up and down the carved edge of one of its arms. She closed her eyes and suddenly it wasn't Connie who was receiving Lucas's attention, but herself. She imagined his proficient tongue flicking in and out of her yearning orifice, sampling the sweetness of her inner membranes, his mouth sucking, teasing her bud.

Her movements gradually increased in line with her excitement and she leant forward over the back of the settee, pressing her straining breasts into the pliant upholstery, while she frantically worked her hips back and forth. Then she sensed Lucas's eyes on her, but she knew it would be as impossible for her to stop by that stage as it would to cease breathing. When she climaxed, her entire being was wracked by a force so strong it wrenched the breath from her in short, sharp grunts. She pushed herself against the couch, milking the orgasm for every last, ecstatic contraction she could get, before crumpling backwards into an exhausted heap on the floor.

It was only when Amelia heard movement from the settee behind her that she realised the compromising position she had allowed her lust to put her in and she hurriedly scrambled to her feet. The marquess jumped up and confronted her with hands on hips. Amelia's eyes briefly rested on the swell at his groin before she turned and rushed for the door. Lucas grabbed her by the neck, twisted her round and propelled her backwards until she was pinned against the wall. Placing a finger under her chin, he raised her face to his.

'So, you thought to escape me again? Did you honestly expect to get away so easily this time?' he teased, his eyes falling on her heaving chest. 'You cannot imagine the anger that possesses me when I think of what you did –' Amelia tried to push him away but with a swift movement he caught her wrists in one hand and raised them above her head '– nor the desire which fills me when I think of how I shall punish you.'

'Let me go, my lord. I am not your property,' she said as calmly as she could, despite the excitement which was steadily seeping back into her.

Lucas rubbed his hips against hers, his hardness nudging at her through her skirts. 'Do not doubt my intent, Lady Amelia,' he whispered, his tepid breath caressing her ear. 'I could have you right now, if I so wished.'

21

Amelia raised her chin defiantly, his arrogance touching a raw nerve within her. 'Then do it my lord, if you dare. Better me than Connie. Why, in just the short time I've been in residence here I have seen the extent of your contaminating influence upon her. Tonight only confirmed my worst fears.' Amelia glanced towards the settee and noticed that her cousin was leaning over the arm watching their every movement.

Lucas suddenly laughed, his grip on her wrists never faltering. 'Why this sudden probity? You weren't so virtuous a few moments ago.'

'Because Connie has everything to lose – her reputation, for instance.'

'And what of you?' He lightly followed the line of her neck with a finger and then dragged it down to the crease between her breasts. 'Have you truly nothing to lose? That I find difficult to believe.' Amelia swallowed hard and prayed that his finger's exploration would end there, unsure as she was of her ability to resist him for much longer.

'It is true. All that I have is my father's name –'

'And your maidenhead, no doubt.'

Amelia met his eyes and, reading the amusement in them, looked away quickly. 'I know not what you mean, my lord.'

'I am certain that you do. You are obviously well versed in satisfying your own desires, but I doubt that you know what it is to be completely possessed by a man. Am I correct?' When she didn't answer, but kept her eyes cast down, Lucas clasped her face and forced her to look at him. 'Am I?' he demanded, his raised voice echoing round the drawing room.

Amelia bit her lip as she stared into his eyes. How she longed to evade him, to show him that she wasn't about to give in to his will, but already she felt the words forming in her throat.

'You are right. I have not known the full extent of a man's touch – unlike my cousin,' she said, quietly admitting defeat.

The marquess smiled triumphantly and stepped back to adjust his cravat. 'Then I shall enjoy instructing you, as I did Connie, in the art of pleasing a gentleman. But in the meantime I suggest you retire to your lonely bed. You look tired, my lady, and I can assure you that you will need all your strength for the days and nights which are to come.'

Chapter Three

When she awoke the next morning, exhausted after a night of tossing and turning, the last thing Amelia wanted was to spend breakfast with her aunt and uncle. So she chose a walk in the garden instead, hoping that the freshness of the morning air might go some way towards vanquishing the weariness which had enveloped her since rising.

Strolling along the path, oblivious to the burgeoning beauty of the flowerbeds on either side of her, Amelia struggled to come up with an answer to the precarious position in which she now found herself.

It seemed incredible to her that just 24 hours ago, all she had had to worry about was whether or not she would be accepted by her new family. Now, not only did she have the shocking truth of her cousin's liaison with the marquess to contend with, but his intentions towards her as well.

A shiver coursed through Amelia, making her stop in her tracks as she remembered how easily he had cornered her, forcing her to submit to his questioning.

Amelia straightened up and, pulling her cloak tighter around her shoulders, continued walking. Lucas had already ruined the first night she'd spent in her new home and she was determined not to allow his memory to disturb this private time too.

Sighting a bench strategically placed against one of the finely clipped privet hedges, Amelia sank on to its cool marble seat, her thoughts turning to Connie.

Though they'd only just met, she had no trouble understanding why she'd welcomed the marquess's advances. Connie was probably so flattered by the attention he paid her, she didn't recognise the selfishness of Lucas's actions. It was possible that she didn't even comprehend the import of her actions and, knowing this, Amelia decided that it was her duty to try to make her young cousin see sense before it was too late.

As for her own predicament, there was little she could do to solve it when the marquess was such a frequent visitor to Boughby Manor. All she could hope was that she could indeed make Connie see the error of her ways and reject Lucas's advances. Perhaps then he wouldn't have a reason to call so often.

Her spirits slightly uplifted by this possibility, Amelia rose from the bench and continued her journey around the garden, this time able to take in its many splendours.

Pausing where the garden backed on to a dense forest, Amelia leaned on the stile there and took a deep breath, absorbing the scents of damp earth and pine needles. She detected movement beyond the fence and, narrowing her eyes, made out a blackbird rooting about in the undergrowth, while a squirrel, startled by her proximity, scrambled up a nearby tree trunk.

Amelia chuckled and stretched, relaxation entering her consciousness for the first time that day. She licked her lips and, hearing her stomach rumble, decided that perhaps she'd been a bit too hasty in skipping breakfast.

She started to make her way back to the house only to stop when she heard footsteps behind her. Amelia turned back just in time to witness the marquess hop over the stile and stride towards her, handing the shotgun he carried to his manservant. Fear raced through her and, stumbling, she lurched again in the direction of the house.

'Why, Lady Amelia,' Lucas breathed, drawing level with her and taking her arm. He pulled her round to face him. 'I am most surprised to find you abroad at this hour. I should have thought you would be catching up on your sleep after our conversation of last night.'

She shuddered at his innuendo. 'I shall do as I wish, my lord. Not even you can tell me what to do!' Amelia intended to leave him then, but his grip on her increased, his other hand coming to rest on her shoulder.

Amelia swallowed hard and, running her eyes over him, marvelled at how he managed to look so elegant despite being attired in plain hunting clothes. Gone was the fashionable silk she'd seen the evening before, and in its place was a coarse flannel frockcoat and breeches which emphasised his slimness of waist.

Finding her gaze lingering on the subtle swell at his groin, she quickly looked away, her heart pounding in her throat.

'What is it that you want of me, my lord?' she asked in irritation, eventually meeting his quizzical gaze. 'Am I to suffer yet another verbal assault by yourself?'

He laughed, waiting until his servant had passed by out of earshot, before speaking again. 'I should have thought it was abundantly clear what I want of you, or do you need me to remind you?' Without warning he pulled her against him.

Amelia immediately began to struggle, the sensation of his lean, hard body pressing into hers sending pleasant signals to her brain. Despite these, she put her hands against his chest and tried to push herself away, only to find that his grip tightened until she was imprisoned in the circle of his arms.

'How dare you?' she demanded, an almost painful pounding rising in her groin. 'I insist that you unhand me this instant!'

The marquess smiled but didn't move an inch. 'Do you think I'd let you go so easily, now that we're alone?'

26

He shook his head. 'How can I allow such an opportunity to pass without at least a kiss from those ruby lips of yours?' Amelia tried to pull away again, panic crescendoing in the pit of her stomach as she felt the all too familiar seepage of moisture from her already pouting sex.

Lucas moved his hands to the back of her head and began to exert pressure on it, pulling her face closer to his. Amelia knew that this was a battle she was swiftly losing and closed her eyes in resignation, waiting for the first tantalising brush of his lips.

Giving her no further opportunity to protest, Lucas covered her mouth with his own, his tongue pushing its way between her rigid lips and exploring the moist contours of her mouth.

Amelia shifted uneasily within Lucas's grasp, his relentless onslaught striking an unwanted chord within her. She knew she should fight his advance, show him how unaffected she was by it, but deep down inside she knew she couldn't. Instead she found herself pressing closer and opening her mouth to him, rubbing her aching pudenda against his loins.

The marquess responded by pushing his tongue deeper into her mouth, covering its interior with sharp, darting movements, while his hands moved between them, pushing aside her cloak in order to reach her breasts.

Amelia let out a silent gasp when his fingers touched her burning flesh, this action finally breaking the spell his proximity had cast over her. She dragged her mouth away from his and glared up at him, breathing heavily as she quickly regained her composure.

'Why, if not for the inconvenience of the open air, I'd have you right now!' he hoarsely declared, suddenly letting her go.

Amelia fell away from him, reaching out to a nearby hedge for support. 'You fiend! How dare you treat me in such a manner? If you think that I shall become like Connie, a willing partner to your lust, you are sadly mistaken my lord, for that is something I will never allow,' Amelia spat, as she struggled to pull her cloak back round her shoulders.

To add to her discomfort, Lucas only smirked at her words. 'You didn't seem very unwilling a moment or two ago. I think you should examine your true feelings before you rebuff my advances. You seem to be a little confused, my dear.'

'Do I? Well let me –'

'No woman has ever refused me once she has known my caress. I doubt that you will be different once you comprehend what I am offering.' With a speed which caught her off guard, Lucas suddenly grabbed her wrist and forced her hand down to where a rigid erection strained at the coarse material of his breeches. 'Feel it my lady, feel that which will soon be the master of you.' He thrust his hips towards her, laughing. 'Does the thought of it excite you as it does me?'

With a cry, Amelia wrenched her hand away. 'Do not fool yourself, my lord. I would rather lie with the devil himself than you!' She did not wait for him to answer, but turned on her heel and walked as fast as she could back towards Boughby Manor. By the time she reached it, entering the building through the french windows, she was shaking uncontrollably and wondering just how much more of the marquess's harrying she could take before her defences crumbled completely.

Once she'd managed to calm down a bit and look at things more rationally, Amelia realised that before she even considered tackling Connie about her relationship with the marquess, she should sort out her own problem with him.

It was this new idea which eventually forced Amelia to visit her aunt, despite not really knowing how she was going to convey this most delicate of matters to the older woman nor, for that matter, how Lady Boughby was going to receive her news.

'What is it that you want, Lady Amelia? As you can

28

see, I'm rather busy this afternoon. His lordship is taking me calling.' Amelia entered Lady Boughby's bedroom and, dodging the three maids who were busily dressing her, took a seat on the edge of the bed. She observed them hurriedly sewing the bodice of her aunt's gown into place while she tried to work up the courage to talk to the woman.

'Well, what is it girl? I haven't got all day.' Lady Boughby turned and glared at Amelia before allowing one of the servants to dust her face and neck with powder.

'Well, I, er, find it rather difficult to speak candidly in such company, my lady.'

'Is it important? Can't it wait till later?'

Amelia got to her feet and moved to her aunt's side. There were tears in her eyes as she spoke. 'No, my lady, it cannot. I, I am simply beside myself with worry and I shudder to think what may happen if what I have to say is delayed a moment longer.' Margaret Boughby looked up at Amelia and, sighing, waved the servants away.

'Very well, if it is that important, his lordship will just have to wait. Come.' She rose and held out her hand. 'Let us go into my dressing room where it's more private.'

Taking the older woman's hand, Amelia allowed her to guide her next door where they both sat on a small chaise longue.

'Now, what is it that's troubling you so? I know that it must be hard to adjust to our way of life here, but surely that's not it.'

Amelia shook her head, glancing at her aunt, and was rather surprised by the concerned look creasing her brow. 'I, I don't know where to begin, my lady. You have been so kind in allowing me to stay as one of your own that I am loath to repay such kindness by causing trouble, but I feel I must.'

Margaret squeezed her hand. 'What on earth is there that could make you feel this way?'

'The marquess –'

Margaret stiffened immediately. 'How has he upset you?'

Amelia chose her next words carefully, having already decided that it was best not to divulge what she had discovered about her cousin, but rather to stick firmly to the details of her own situation.

'I am terrified, aunt, terrified for my honour because his lordship has made it clear that he intends to, to make me his mistress!' There, it was out and, though her heart was pounding furiously in her breast, Amelia felt better for her admission.

'I see.' Margaret suddenly took Amelia's face in her hands and peered deep into her eyes. 'Now, I want you to tell me the truth, Amelia. Has he touched you in any way, made you do things which you knew were wrong?'

Amelia coloured as she remembered their last meeting. 'He, he kissed me but I managed to get away. Oh aunt, I'm so afraid of what he will do next. He always seems to know when I will be alone. Please say that you will protect me from him.' Amelia threw her arms around Lady Boughby's shoulders and, with tears spilling down her cheeks, pressed her face into the woman's bosom. 'I should hate to bring scandal to your family.'

'You've done the right thing, child. I am well aware of how insistent the marquess can be when he sets his sights on something. But now that you've told me, there is nothing more for you to worry about. I shall make a point of making sure that he is kept firmly away from you. You have my word on it.'

Despite the French windows being open for the first time that year, Amelia found the atmosphere in the morning room quite oppressive. She put down her needlepoint and, picking up her fan, glanced across the room to where Connie was engaged in a game of cards with her father and the Marquess of Beechwood. How easy they all look in each other's company, she thought. If only I could be like them.

Lucas looked up, meeting her eyes. Amelia glanced

30

away quickly, wondering what he made of these new circumstances. In the week since she'd gone to her aunt, she'd only been allowed contact with him on one other occasion, a social gathering such as this. She had hoped that their enforced separation might have dampened his ardour as far as she was concerned but, judging by the intensity of the look she'd just received from him, she very much doubted it. Amelia opened her fan and stared at the grandfather clock across the room.

'I wonder, uncle, if I should perhaps check on her ladyship to see if her headache has improved.'

Lord Boughby threw his cards down in disgust and got up from the table. 'No need to trouble yourself, my dear. I shall go.'

'But your game. Don't you want to finish it?' Amelia cried, suddenly seeing the danger building in this situation.

'I'm afraid I've lost my patience with it. I'm sure Connie and Lucas will understand.' He bowed and then took his leave of them all.

Before the door had completely shut behind him, Amelia had pushed herself out of her seat and was heading in the same direction. The marquess got there before her.

'Going somewhere, my dear?' he asked with the sweetest of smiles. 'You look rather pale. Are you unwell?'

'You know why I'm like this. Now will you let me pass. If Lady Boughby –'

'Ah, but she's not here, is she? It's just the three of us now. I wonder how we will amuse ourselves.'

Amelia gasped when she felt his arm circling her waist and guiding her back into the room. She looked pleadingly at Connie as he pushed her back down on to the sofa.

'Leave her be, Lucas. Can't you see she's terrified?' Connie put her hand on his shoulder and tried to turn him round to face her. He simply shrugged her touch away, concentrating his attention on Amelia.

'And well she should be after what she's done. Did you honestly think that seeking Margaret's aid would protect you from me?'

Amelia stared up at him, shaking. 'I will do anything to save myself from your distasteful touch.'

'Distasteful?' Lucas purred. 'Is this so distasteful?' Without warning he bent and, lifting her skirts, plunged his hand between her legs. Amelia cried out and tried to squirm away from him but a hand on her shoulder kept her firmly pinned to the seat. She felt his fingers creeping between her thighs, prising apart her swollen lips, invading her soft, slick valley, searching out the damning evidence of her secret yearning for him. She groaned as a honeyed shiver raced through her the moment a finger pressed at the taut entrance to her sex and she unconsciously arched her back, offering her secret place to the probing digit.

As suddenly as he had assaulted her, the marquess let her go, jumping up and triumphantly displaying his gleaming finger. 'There, I knew it. Does it look like my touch is so distasteful to your cousin?' He turned and presented it to Connie. 'She wants me sure enough, but her damn pride will not let her admit it. Well, perhaps I shall just have to convince her myself!'

Before he had a chance to return to Amelia, Connie caught his hand and raised the moist finger to her lips. 'Hmm, as sweet as nectar,' she whispered, lingering over it, running her tongue across its spongy tip. 'You really make me jealous when you act like this, Lucas. Anyone would think you didn't fancy me any more.' She fluttered her eyelashes at him while moving close enough to press her bosom against his chest. Grinning, he took her by the shoulders and stared deep into her eyes.

'You know that is not so. Once Amelia has learned to accept that which she already suspects about herself, I shall enjoy taking you both at the same time. One will know the pleasure of my tongue in her quim, while the other will experience my cock up her pretty little arse. I wonder which one you will be, my sweet.'

32

Connie giggled and, taking his hands, drew him away from the couch towards the recently vacated card table. 'I want you to prove to me that you still want me, that Amelia is only a diversion.' She hitched up her skirts and propped herself on the edge of the table, unashamedly displaying her glistening sex for all to see. 'Do it to me now, here, so she is forced to watch you take your pleasure with me.'

Lucas needed no other encouragement and, parting her thighs, pressed between them, his hands moving to the drawstrings of his breeches.

'It shall be my honour, Lady Constance. Perhaps our little friend will finally realise that which she has to look forward to once she ceases this idiotic behaviour of hers.'

Amelia swallowed hard, her eyes lingering on the marquess's lean, white bottom as his breeches fell into a heap around his ankles. He leant forward and, clutching Connie around the waist, pulled her against him, grinding his hips into the space between her legs at the same time, a contented sigh escaping his lips.

Amelia shuddered when he started to move, the muscled orbs of his buttocks contracting with every thrust he made into Connie. Scrambling up on to her knees, Amelia spread her own legs wide, allowing the love juices pooling in her sex to drip down, further lubricating her turgid lips as she too began to rock back and forth.

Connie groaned and, wrapping her legs around the slimness of Lucas's hips, hooked her ankles together and began to exert her own pressure on his pumping hindquarters, drawing him further into the circle of her legs.

Amelia leant forward over the arm of the settee, hoping to gain a better view of what they were doing, and caught sight of Connie's determined face peering over Lucas's shoulder, her hands tearing at the satin bag enclosing his hair at the base of his neck. She was clearly trying to tell her something, but what? Amelia repeatedly followed her gaze over to the door and in an instant it dawned on her what her cousin was trying to say.

It took the greatest of efforts for Amelia to find the strength to break from the enticing vision of the couple, but break Amelia knew she must if she was to avoid being caught in Lucas's trap.

She levered herself up from the settee and, as quietly as she could, her legs buckling slightly when she tried to stand, she staggered for the door. Pulling it open, she turned back, her eyes inexplicably glued to the sight of Lucas's ruddy penis as he slowly withdrew it from Connie before plunging it back into her with a grunt of delight.

Amelia swallowed hard and licked her lips, a sudden throbbing capturing her groin. The urge to stay and watch this sensual scene was even stronger now. However, despite this longing to remain and seek her own satisfaction with her fingers, she managed to drag her gaze away from them and lurch out into the relative safety of the hall.

Chapter Four

'You were very lucky that mama told me about this plan of hers to keep you out of the reach of Lucas. If she hadn't, who knows what may have happened.' Connie sighed and, turning away from the bookcase, frowned at her cousin. 'I cannot for the life of me understand why you have taken this drastic step and involved her anyway, but no matter. As I've already demonstrated, you can count on me to go along with mama's wishes.'

'You will? I thought –'

'You thought that because I'm Lucas's mistress I will naturally agree with everything he does?' She shook her head. 'You should know by now that I have my own mind in matters such as these. As far as I'm concerned, what he doesn't know won't hurt him!'

'You sound as if you couldn't care less about him.'

Connie laughed and took Amelia's hands, sinking on to the settee beside her. 'I want him sure enough but it simply doesn't pay to be too possessive with him. You see, Lucas isn't the type of man who can be satisfied by just one woman. I've known it for a long time. So long as he still sees me, it doesn't really matter to me who else he beds.'

'I wonder if that's how he'd see it if you took another

lover.' Amelia rubbed her forehead in confusion. 'I just can't see why you are doing this, taking such a risk. Don't you realise that you could lose everything if your parents ever found out. Oh I wish you'd stop this disastrous relationship.'

'Stop being so melodramatic. They haven't found out yet. Lucas is far too clever to allow that.'

'Well, how long has this liaison of yours been going on?'

'Three or four months, that's all. I've always had an eye for Lucas, even as a child, but it's only recently that he's reciprocated my feelings.'

'But you're only seventeen. Haven't you ever wondered why a man like him would be interested in you?'

'I am well aware of why he's "interested". Look, I don't know why you're so bothered about it. It's not as if he stole my maidenhead or anything. That went so long ago, I can scarcely remember the event.'

'What?' Amelia's eyes widened at her cousin's admission.

'Don't look so surprised, Amelia. You didn't think I was going to wait around for father to find me a husband before I had some fun, did you? Believe me, even you would appreciate the benefit of having a lover once the boredom of this place descends upon you.'

Her cousin's easy words hit a raw nerve inside Amelia and, for once, she found herself speaking without her usual control.

'What? Is that what you honestly expected me to do? Encourage the marquess's advances simply for want of something better to do? I wouldn't dream of insulting my father's memory in such a way.'

'Well, it certainly didn't stop you pursuing that stable-hand before you came here.'

Amelia gasped. 'That was different. You wouldn't tell anyone about that, would you?' Connie smiled knowingly, giving Amelia the answer she feared the most. 'You've told him, haven't you? Sweet Jesus, what am I going to do now?'

36

'I had to, Amelia. Lucas wanted to know the extent of your experience. But don't worry, your wider reputation is still intact.'

'Yes, but for how long? What happens if he decides to impart this knowledge to my aunt, use it as some sort of bargaining tool with her?'

'He wouldn't because there's nothing to tell, is there? You did tell me the truth about what you and Tom got up to, didn't you?'

'Of course I did. What do you take me for, some sort of whore?' Amelia slapped her hand over her mouth as soon as she realised what she'd said.

Connie straightened up, her expression remaining placid.

'Connie I –'

Connie raised her hand. 'There is no need to apologise. I know that to your unversed eyes my life here must seem terribly decadent, but I can assure you that it is nothing of the sort. Oh, if only you had waited and not involved mama, I'm sure we could have sorted all this out by ourselves!'

'You know why I couldn't have waited.'

'Yes, yes, let's not start that again. All we can hope now is that Lucas respects mama's authority. If you had seen how angry he was when he discovered that you'd left just now.'

'What?' Amelia caught her breath. 'I don't understand. Surely I will be safe under Lady Boughby's wing?'

'I'm not so sure. Lucas has always thrived on adversity. I think the more obstacles he has to overcome to achieve his pleasure, the better for him. That's why, if you had simply given in and allowed his advances, he would have quickly grown tired of you and moved on to other pastures. Now that you've subverted his plans, who knows what he might do.'

'I don't care –' Amelia forced a smile, trying to seem unconcerned, while deep down inside she was shaking like a leaf '– so long as I can remain my own person, free of his overbearing nature.'

37

'So you keep saying.' Connie went to the window. 'Now, would you care for my advice on your new gowns?' Amelia raised her eyebrows. 'It looks as though the dressmaker has just arrived for your second fitting.'

Amelia was dreaming. Her room was bathed in an amber glow and, detecting movement at the far end, she pushed herself up to sitting and focused her vision on the spot where Connie perched on the edge of a chair.

Arching her back until her shoulder blades dug into the back rest, her pert, peachy nipples tenting the diaphanous fabric covering her chest, Connie slipped her hands down between her uncovered thighs to the golden triangle of hair at her groin.

Amelia's mouth went dry as she watched her fingers momentarily disappear into the delicate crease of flesh there only to resurface, glistening with the product of her own desire. Connie then began to circle her already excited clitoris, teasing it out of its protective fleshy hood, pinching and kneading it in time with her suddenly rocking hips.

Amelia raised herself up on to her hands and knees, giving herself a clearer view of what her cousin was doing, her own groin beginning to throb in unison with Connie's movements. She moved her fingers to the hem of her nightgown and pulled it over her head, then covered the soft mounds of her breasts with the palms of her hands, squeezing and palpating them until their tips grew hard.

She looked across the room to where Connie had been only a few moments ago, but was disappointed to find that the chair was empty. As if in compensation for this, Amelia inexplicably felt the presence of someone else, a stranger, sitting behind her, the firmness of his thighs pressing into her bottom. She fell backwards into his arms, his large hands easily encircling her tiny waist.

Connie reappeared then, her slim nakedness highlighted by a wide beam of sunshine in one corner of the room. She was not alone however, but accompanied by a tall, familiar blond-haired man.

Amelia caught her breath as she ran her eyes over him, taking in the highly muscled chest, narrow waist and powerful thighs covered by the tightest of breeches. She raised her eyes up to his face and gasped. It was Tom!

She watched, fascination rather than jealousy enveloping her, as he lifted the back of Connie's golden mane and planted a kiss at the base of her neck before twisting her around and pulling her into his arms. His hands went immediately to her bare buttocks, kneading, spreading them, pressing his fingers into that sensitive fold, while Connie wrapped her arms around his neck and buried her face in the bronzed nest of hair covering his chest.

The hands circling Amelia's waist began slowly to inch their way forward and down over her hips, causing her to shiver and straighten up when they eventually reached the edge of her pubis.

Amelia covered the stranger's hands with her own and, guiding them into her wet valley, delighted in the sensation of his fingers easily slipping between her swollen lips and finding the tight little entrance to her excited sex. One entered her immediately, teasing, nudging, testing her slick, yearning crack for size, before another joined it, pushing into her with sharp, darting movements until both were buried in her spongy orifice.

Clenching her pelvic muscles around these questing digits, Amelia glanced up, her straining breath coming between clenched teeth, and looked once again in the direction of her cousin.

Connie was down on her knees before Tom now, her fingers furiously tearing at the drawstrings on his breeches. When at last she succeeded in undoing them, his erection burst free of its restraints and jutted towards her. It was just as Amelia remembered, long and thick, its tight foreskin drawn back to reveal the mottled, plum-coloured glans.

Amelia couldn't help licking her lips as she noticed the small bead of moisture which appeared on its tip just before Connie took it into her mouth. Amelia bore down hard on the probing fingers exploring her own sex while observing Connie run her tongue up and down Tom's shaft, tasting the essential maleness of him, and her hands seeking out the stubbly texture of his balls.

Throwing her head back, Amelia twisted it to one side, inviting the stranger's kiss. His lips immediately covered hers, while one of his hands moved upwards to pinch and pluck at one of her hardened nipples. Amelia groaned as the greatest sense of pleasure she had ever known rose in her groin and crouched in the pit of her stomach, waiting for the burst of orgasm to release it.

In her excitement, she leant even further back, delighting in the feel of the tip of the stranger's rigid cock brushing against the small of her back. Amelia pushed against the stranger, forcing him down on to the mattress. Then she swivelled round, a contented smile stretching her lips, only to gasp as she met the knowing eyes of Lucas. With a triumphant laugh, he reached up to drag her down on to him . . .

Amelia jolted awake with a sharp intake of air, her hand buried in the dark recesses of her groin. Despite the obvious connection with the marquess, she knew she couldn't stop now and furiously rubbed her clitoris until climax overtook her.

The moment was ecstatic, shuddering release surged through her, filling every pore with the glow of satisfaction, Amelia knew that she'd done the right thing in seeking out Lady Boughby's protection. Despite what Connie had said to the contrary, she realised that she had to be protected as much from herself as from the marquess.

'Damn that meddling wife of yours, John. Not only has she taken it upon herself to thwart me at every turn. It seems that she has even employed my very own mistress to work against me!' Lucas downed the last of his brandy in one loud gulp.

'With your reputation, can you really blame her? She is only doing her duty as far as Amelia is concerned,' laughed Lord Boughby. 'I cannot see why you are so obsessed with her, anyway. Amelia is no different from any other female. I'm sure you can find another diversion in the village, if you really need one that is.' He shook his head. 'Sometimes the extent of your appetite astounds me, it really does, Lucas. I should have thought that Connie would be enough for you.'

'She is truly an amazing creature but she doesn't quite have the character to fully satisfy me. I am yet to find a woman who has, though, I must admit that I find her delightful cousin, with her spirited ways, stimulating to say the least.'

'Oh I see, a challenge, is she? Well you'll have to come up with something exceptional to get Margaret to relinquish her hold over Amelia, that I know for sure.'

'Can't you help sway her a little? Get her to stop this ridiculous closeting of the girl? You know she wouldn't listen to anything I had to say. As it stands, it's a wonder that she allows me through the front door with the enmity she feels towards me.'

'She allows you, my dear boy, because you're my friend. She knows how far we go back, how I value your opinion.'

Lucas smiled. 'Would she be so tolerant if she knew of my association with her daughter, I wonder?'

Lord Boughby caught his breath. 'She must never know of it. I shudder to think what she would do if she found out. I doubt if she would appreciate the reasons behind my allowing you to pursue her. Unfortunately, my wife doesn't share my view that a certain amount of experience is to be valued in a wife. And in Connie's case, especially helpful when she marries next spring.'

'Anyone I know?' Lucas asked with only a fleeting interest.

'Not as yet, but when I let it be known that my

daughter is up for grabs sporting a handsome dowry, I'm certain that a good many suitors will come a-calling. It's a shame it couldn't be you though. I should have liked you as a son-in-law.' He suddenly stared at Lucas, his eyes lighting up. 'That's it. I have it! Why not marry Amelia? It would certainly answer your problem of producing an heir as well as this current penchant you have for her. You'd have to travel far to find a woman more suited to wedded life. She is possessed of a not inconsiderable beauty and comes from a noble family, though regrettably penniless. I would even be willing to settle a modest sum on her just to get her off my hands. You see, I find it most tiresome having three females in the household.'

Lucas rubbed his chin thoughtfully. Although the idea of marriage had always been anathema to him, preferring as he did the life of a libertine, at that moment he could think of no better way of making Amelia submit to him. It was easy for him to imagine the shock on her face when she learned of his proposal.

'I do believe you are right, John,' he said, clapping his hands together. 'By God, you are right, but what of Connie? You said she is not to marry until next year.'

'Afraid that your little student will wither without your lessons? Fear not, I can assure you that the moment your engagement is announced, she will be seeking out a likely successor to your touch.' He yawned and rose. 'I'll draw up a suitably worded document as soon as possible.'

'You really think that Margaret will allow me to marry Lady Amelia?'

Lord Boughby smiled. 'Have no fear. Even she couldn't possibly fail to notice the advantages of such a match for her niece.'

Amelia glanced across the glasshouse, her vision briefly caught by a gardener tending to one of the many varieties of dahlia Lady Boughby kept, before moving on out of sight. It was so cosy in the hothouse at that time of day that she wished she could simply spend the rest of her life there, basking in the glorious warmth without a care in the world.

She shifted her gaze to her chaperone, Lady Boughby's maid, and smiled when she observed the steady rise and fall of the seated woman's chest and heard the faint groans which seeped from her lips. It would be a shame to wake the woman now, simply for the sake of idle chatter. Amelia straightened up, pressing her spine into the hardness of the cast iron bench before resuming her watercolour.

She was so engrossed in her work, she scarcely heard the approach of someone else a good half an hour later. Only when he spoke did she whip her head up in surprise – and shock.

'Ah, painting. An admirable talent in a wife.' The Marquess of Beechwood eyed the slumbering woman with interest before sliding into the space beside Amelia. She stiffened immediately, spilling the small jar of water she'd been balancing on her knee.

'See what you've made me do!' she exclaimed, not comprehending what he'd just said, her mind suddenly occupied with trying to think of how she was going to get away from him this time. 'You seem to spend an exhorbitant amount of time at my uncle's residence my lord. Why can't you simply leave us all alone?'

With shaking hands, she bent to pick up the empty container, the pounding of her heart filling her ears. She desperately wanted to show him that she was confident enough under her aunt's wing not to be frightened by his appearance, but already memories of what had nearly happened in the morning room were flooding back into her consciousness. Only this time, there was no Connie to distract him – just the occasional snort from Lady Boughby's maid.

'Here, allow me.' He scooped the empty jar off the floor and carelessly tossed it into her lap. 'I visit often because I have more than a passing interest in two of its occupants.'

'Oh look what you've done!' she scolded, hurriedly trying to wipe a spot of paint off her skirt.

'No matter, I shall buy you a hundred such gowns when we are wed.'

'What?' she gasped, her eyes finally meeting his in alarm. 'What did you say? If this is another game –'

'It's no game, my lady. I have this very morning agreed the particulars of our marriage contract with your uncle. All that remains is your aunt's signature.' Lucas stretched, his arm curling round her shoulders. 'Yes, my dear. You have finally achieved that which you've been craving all this time. Your prudish ways have forced my hand, my lady – we are to wed.'

'Marry you!' Amelia choked, dragging herself off the bench, her painting set crashing to the ground. She looked angrily towards the maid who continued to sleep without disturbance. 'The thought couldn't be further from my mind. If I wanted to marry you, why would I seek my aunt's protection?'

Lucas shrugged but remained seated. 'Who knows? That is a question I've been asking myself ever since you did it, but no matter. That's in the past. We've got our future together to look forward to now.' He reached up and, catching hold of her hand, pulled her down on to his lap. 'How about a kiss for the prospective bridegroom?'

'How dare you!' Amelia wrenched herself away from his grasp and, picking up her skirts, ran past the slumbering maid in the direction of the door. When she reached it, her breathing hampered by the close atmosphere in the glasshouse as well as her stays, she found to her horror that it was locked.

Hearing Lucas's steady footfall nearing her, Amelia bit her lip and turned around, deciding that she had no alternative but to face whatever he had planned for her.

'What, kidnap is it now, my lord?' she asked in her calmest of voices when he eventually caught up with her. 'Unable to achieve your lewd aims by deception, have you now turned your hand to violent means?'

44

'You forget that I am a gentleman, my dear.' He rested one hand against the glass beside her head, while the other toyed with the ribbons on her stomacher.

'If I have, it is because you have scarcely acted like one these past weeks.'

Lucas puckered up his mouth in mock dismay. 'Such a condemnation! How on earth am I to redeem myself in your opinion?' He suddenly hooked two fingers inside her bodice and jerked her against him. 'Shall I prove once and for all how much you want me, Amelia? That underneath all these protestations of yours, there lies a heart yearning to be plundered?'

She began to pound her fists against his chest and twist her hips in an effort to free herself of his clutches.

Lucas smiled and, ignoring her feeble attempts at resistance, lowered his head to her bosom, his moist lips travelling over the soft orbs of her breasts.

Amelia gasped as his touch sent ripples of pleasure racing throughout her. She tried desperately to keep her mind on defending herself against his attack, but already she could sense the moisture growing between her legs, coating her tight passage in readiness – but for what? She shivered at her thoughts and raised her head defiantly.

'I beg of you, my lord. Let me go. I, I am not your property, even if this talk of marriage is true.'

'You midjudge me, my dear,' Lucas whispered, slipping his hand inside her bodice and gently cupping one of her breasts. 'I have the utmost respect for you. It is just that I know you are not being true to yourself when you continue to deny your desire for me. I suspect that you already know no other man can thrill you like I do, no other man can bring out the woman in you the way I can.' He squeezed her breast until the nipple hardened. 'Why, instead of all this defiance, I think you should be thanking your lucky stars that you have managed to find a man capable of satisfying you.' He shrugged. 'I simply think it's about time you faced the reality of you wanting me, that's all.'

45

Amelia shook her head, while at the same time experiencing a shiver of delight when she sensed him freeing her breast of its restraints and raising its knotty tip to his lips. She was near to giving in to temptation and found herself leaning closer to him, while her arm moved up to rest on his shoulder.

'Oh, Lucas,' she breathed, her lips only an inch from the top of his head, 'how I –'

'What is going on here?'

Lucas immediately stiffened and released Amelia as Lady Boughby's maid pushed past him and took her charge into her arms. 'Are you all right, your ladyship? Has the marquess offended you in any way? Shall I get her ladyship?'

'No.' Amelia coloured, her breathing inexplicably laboured while she quickly restored her modesty. 'No, say nothing of this. I think it is best if I talk to her in my own way, don't you?'

'Of course, my lady. Anything you say.' The maid began to lead her out of the glasshouse.

Amelia glanced over her shoulder and swallowed hard as she caught Lucas' arrogant expression, his knowing eyes reminding her just how close she'd come to proving him right.

Chapter Five

'And you think that by assaulting Amelia with the news that she is to marry you, when you haven't even gained my consent as her aunt, will, in some obscure way, sway my decision in your favour?' Margaret sniffed and stared up at him from the writing desk.

'So, the little chit has informed you of our meeting this afternoon. I see that her ability to keep her own counsel is as suspect as her pretended modesty. But no matter.' He shrugged and let out a loud sigh. 'I suppose she has told you some farcical tale of how I attempted to ravish her.'

'She told me exactly what went on in my glasshouse this morning and all I can say is that, from what I know of you, it doesn't surprise me.'

'Oh come come, Margaret, I was simply expressing my excited anticipation of our wedding vows. Wouldn't any delighted fiancé do the same?'

'Do not insult my intelligence, Lucas. I am not my husband. He has always been given to these flights of fancy. Do not imagine for one moment that I believe in this sudden urge of yours for domesticity, nor forgive your crassness, for that matter. There must be some ulterior motive behind this urge of yours to change your state. Has my foolish husband offered you a large dowry, or are you really so desperate to have Amelia that you are willing to give up your prized bachelorhood?'

'I simply need an heir and I want Amelia. What other way is there of satisfying both these problems? I might be persuaded to change my mind if you were to loose your hold on her . . .'

'What? And allow you to ruin her life!' Margaret threw down the marriage contract and got to her feet. 'I don't care what you want or what you don't want. I shall not give my blessing to any match of yours, and that's my last word on the subject.' She glared at him. 'Now, if you will excuse me, I have more important matters to attend to.' She moved towards the door.

Lucas followed her and, taking her arm, turned her round to face him. 'It's a shame then, that you will have no other marriage to bless.'

Margaret's annoyed gaze fell on his restraining hand. 'What do you mean? Of course I will, Connie is to wed next year –'

'If there's no match for me, there certainly will be no match for Connie. I promise you that.'

'You have no power in that area. Even John wouldn't listen to you on that score. He is well aware of the benefit of a good marriage for our only child. It's bad enough that his title will eventually go to some distant relative, without him being denied the honour of doing his best for Constance.'

'Wouldn't he? You obviously haven't consulted him lately. Why don't we go and ask him now? I'm sure he'll be only too happy to confirm my role in this most delicate of matters.'

'What are you saying?' A sudden fear gripped Margaret's heart. She knew only too well how devious Lucas could be to get his own way, but surely he wouldn't stoop so low as that?

'What I am saying, my dear lady, is that if you do not allow me to marry Amelia, I will rubbish your precious daughter's name in society so that no respectable man will have her.'

Margaret clenched her fists as she desperately tried to retain her self-control, knowing that to lose her temper would only play into his hands. 'Connie? Oh my God, Lucas, you haven't, have you?'

'A fine little cunny if ever I had one!' he quipped, laughing.

Margaret lost her battle with herself then and wrenched her arm away, slapping him across the cheek. 'You blackguard. How could you? She's just a child, just seventeen!'

The marquess rubbed his stinging cheek thoughtfully. 'You have quite a power in that delicate hand of yours, my lady. Now, will you give your blessing or no? I should hate to see Connie end up an old maid simply for want of a suitable husband.'

'I suppose John knows all about this?' She sighed. 'It doesn't surprise me. He never did afford virginity its true worth, but it seems that you do, for Amelia is indeed a virgin. I suppose that is part of the attraction?'

'As well as her fiery spirit. Yes or no?'

'Where Connie's reputation is concerned, there can only be one answer,' she said quietly, her heart sinking in defeat.

Lucas suddenly clapped his hands together. 'Excellent, I shall enjoy reminding Lady Amelia of what the future holds for her.'

'Now that I cannot allow.' Margaret returned to the writing desk, picked up the marriage contract and signed it. 'It is bad enough that I have been forced to give away my only niece to a rake like you. I will not stand by and watch you torture her as well.'

'Surely you do not intend to deny me her company like before? I believe I have a right to see Amelia, now that we're officially betrothed.'

'I agree, you do. However, that is not to say that you should be allowed full contact with her, no matter how much you crave it.' Margaret shoved the contract into his awaiting hands. 'Who is to say that you would keep to your word and marry the poor girl if you were

49

allowed your way with her. No, Lucas, I want your solemn promise, for what it's worth, that Amelia will be allowed to keep her dignity until she weds you.'

'Dignity? What can you mean?' he asked with a sparkle in his eye.

'You know exactly what I mean. I don't need to spell it out.'

'Don't you?' Lucas slipped his arm around her waist and leant against her. 'Oh go on, just for me,' he whispered, pressing his lips to her neck.

'Enough!' Despite the rush of warmth his proximity caused in her groin, Margaret tore herself away from his grasp and struggled to the door. 'Just promise me that Amelia will at least be allowed the honour of keeping her maidenhead until after the ceremony,' she said, without turning back.

The marquess thought a moment and then a smile radiated across his face. 'I think I shall be able to keep to that, my lady. After all, what fun is a wedding night without a quivering virgin?'

'Now that you have her hand in marriage, must you continue to torment her so, Lucas?' Connie enquired, putting her book back on the shelf.

The marquess lounged in a high-backed chair beside the fireplace, one well-toned thigh slung over the arm. He examined his empty wine glass and frowned. 'I need another drink, Connie.' Tutting, she took it from him and went over to the windowsill where a half-empty wine bottle stood.

'I cannot see that it makes any difference. Whether we are to wed or not, there's something about her high and mighty manner which really excites me.'

'I expect there is, but that doesn't make it right,' Connie scolded, returning with a full glass.

Lucas gulped down its contents with one swallow and then carefully placed the empty glass on the floor beside his chair. 'Nor does your behaviour of the other day. Why, if you hadn't distracted me, this entire marriage business might not have had to be. If you had left well alone, I would have taken Amelia and had done with it. Perhaps got her out of my system once and for all, but no, you had to step in on her behalf –'

'I didn't hear you complaining too much at the time,' Connie replied sarcastically, staring down at him, her hands grasping her slim waist. 'I received the impression that you rather enjoyed the experience of doing it in front of her.'

Lucas shrugged. 'Perhaps, but the fact still remains that this is all your fault. I mean, I can hardly believe it myself that I have agreed to it. Why, as far as marriage goes, I'm as much an innocent as Amelia is!'

'I suspect the experience will be to your benefit, despite your protests. It is just a shame that in doing this you have set mother even more against you. I never did understand her enmity towards you, you know Lucas. Why does she hate you so?'

'Tell me, how has she taken your role in all this?' the marquess asked, rapidly changing the subject. 'I know that she was quite shocked to learn of our "association". I hope that she hasn't punished you too severely.'

Connie shrugged, pushing a loose strand of hair back into place. 'She was angry enough, but there is little one can do with Father involved. I suppose I shall just have to put up with her awkward silences for a time.'

Lucas chuckled. 'Then you are indeed lucky for, if she had had her way, no doubt she would have liked to have seen me killed in a duel over your honour. I'm almost sorry to have disappointed her on that score.'

Connie sank into his lap, wrapping her arms around his shoulders while her eyes travelled over his tousled appearance. His red-brown hair was carelessly swept back off his forehead and fell in swirls about his shoulders, while his crisp white shirt lay open to the waist revealing the dense bed of hair covering his broad chest.

'I suppose you don't want me now that you have a fiancée?'

'Don't be silly, Connie. Your mother's made me promise to allow Amelia her dignity until after the ceremony and I, like the honourable man that I am, agreed.'

'Really?' She raised her eyebrows. 'Well at least we'll have a bit more time together.' Connie lowered her lips to his, taking the bottom one between her teeth and playfully tugging on it. 'But it still doesn't make the fact that you are leaving me any easier to bear. Once you are gone, I am sure I'll go mad!'

Lucas caught the back of her head and, winding his fingers in her golden hair, pulled her head back, revealing her slim neck. 'I cannot believe that I need to remind you of what I intend once I have conquered Amelia's will? I think we'll make an intriguing little group, don't you?' He pressed his lips to the base of her throat and then trailed them down towards her abundant bosom. 'Until then, I'm certain that you'll have no trouble finding a suitable replacement for my company.'

'I suppose you are right,' Connie mumbled, arching her back when she felt a hand slide inside her corset and scoop up one of her breasts. Pressing closer as he raised its rigid tip to his mouth, she slid her hand down to the waistband of his breeches. She slipped it inside, delighting in the bristly feel of his loins, before closing her fingers around the bulbous head of his cock.

Lucas sucked in his breath and, releasing her breast, sank back against the cushions, his hands flying to the ties of his breeches. 'Make me come with your hand, Connie. You know how much I enjoy that.'

Easing his manhood out of its bed of silk, she took its full length into her hands, marvelling at its unique beauty: the veins entwining it like indigo vines, its foreskin stretched back to display the slick, damson glans. How she longed to take him into her mouth and satisfy him with the expertise of her tongue. However, she knew that he would not be pleased if she refused his request, so instead she began doing those things which she knew would make him come faster than anything else.

She cradled his testicles in her hands, massaging them gently at first, then squeezing them harder until she heard him groan, felt him shift uneasily under her. Moving one of her hands to the base of his pulsating shaft, she began to drag her thumbnail up the length of it, circling, squeezing, tweaking it to the point where she was certain that it hurt him.

'Yes yes, that's it, don't stop,' he breathed, thrusting his groin towards her, his hand finding her breast again and cruelly grabbing it, pulling it back up to his mouth. Connie caught her breath and pressed closer to him, rolling his erection between her hands like a piece of dough while furiously clenching and unclenching her slick quim.

Sensing his approaching orgasm from the way he was beginning to writhe under her, Connie hurriedly wrenched up her skirts and, turning on to her side, took him between the flesh of her thighs. She pressed her thighs together, imprisoning his cock in the moistness of her secret valley, until she could stand it no longer and, reaching between her legs, guided his member into her yearning orifice.

Before he could protest she had kneaded him with her internal muscles. With a cry, he climaxed, letting go of her breast, and flopped back against the chair, shaking. With his fast-decreasing hardness still embedded within her, she then pressed her crotch to his and furiously rubbed her own excited pleasure-point against the roughness of his pubis until she also came, her back arching as ecstatic shudders took over her body.

'You're a crafty one,' Lucas observed when she eventually climbed off him and began to straighten her skirts.

Connie shrugged. 'I'm afraid I'm like you, my lord.'

He raised his eyebrows. 'How so?'

'It's simple. I like to take my pleasure as and when I can find it.'

'What can I say, my dear?' Margaret drew Amelia down beside her on the couch and handed her a cup of tea. 'I fear that I have failed you.'

53

Amelia stared resolutely ahead of her, aware that her aunt hung her head low, waiting for the inevitable condemnation. For a moment or two, she had no intention of disappointing the older woman. After all, Lady Boughby needn't have agreed to the match. However, there was something about her aunt's demeanour which told her this sorrow was the result of more than just guilt.

'Aunt –' Amelia touched her arm, trying to reassure her. 'I am exceedingly grateful for the generosity you have already afforded me by taking me in, but marriage to the marquess? Must I accept such a loathsome proposal?'

'I'm afraid you must. There is no other alternative. Lord Boughby and I are in agreement. We both think that this is the best thing which could happen to you. Perhaps you don't see the advantages now, but once you become Lady Beechwood I guarantee that you will.'

'Oh will I?' Amelia asked bitterly taking a sip of her tea. 'I hardly think so. I just can't understand this sudden change of heart. Why, not too long ago, you were happy to afford me protection from his lordship's advances. Now, it seems, you are happy to encourage them.'

'This is different.'

'How? Because his lewdness can now be put in the context of marriage?' Amelia knew she was fighting a losing battle but she had to put her side across if only to soothe her own, smarting pride.

'I am sure you will think differently once you – get used to married life. It is not as if you loathe the sight of the marquess, is it?'

'No,' Amelia conceded, looking away. 'I do find him attractive. It's just his manner which offends me.'

'Well, you might find that marriage mellows him, who knows? Anyway, just think of what you'll have obtained. You could not even have dreamt of achieving another title and the wealth to go along with it, in your current position.'

'I know, but I would have been happy to have

54

remained here, even taken up a more domestic role within the household, to pay you back for your generosity –'

'Nonsense,' Margaret said, flashing a smile in Amelia's direction. 'There has never been a question of you working here. You are my brother's child after all, and it is my duty to provide for you in spite of the unhappy circumstances of your birth.'

'I realise that, Aunt, but I still can't understand why you have gone to so much trouble over me when Father left the family in such a distressing way. You know, he never did tell me everything about that business – only the vaguest of facts. But it seems that his memory means a lot to you, even now . . .' Margaret slowly nodded with a bitter twist to her mouth. 'Then why didn't you support him when he needed it most of all?'

'I don't think that this is the appropriate time to go into all that, my dear.'

'I think it is. I'm not a child any more, Aunt. I certainly don't need to be protected from the truth. Please afford me this one concession before I have to leave your estates and take up with the marquess. Don't you think that I deserve to know what really went on back then?'

'Yes, I suppose you are owed an explanation, especially now, when you are about to embark on a new life of your own.' Margaret shrugged and swallowed hard before continuing. 'It was a great scandal at the time. You see, being the only son of a duke, your father's future was mapped out for him long before he reached adulthood. When he turned seventeen, your father was officially betrothed to the Countess of Chaldwell, a girl no more than ten years old. Of course, the actual ceremony wasn't to take place until the girl turned seventeen herself. When Mark took up with my governess just five years later, our parents saw the danger in the situation, but were happy to allow it to continue so that Mark could gain the necessary experience – that is, until the unthinkable happened and she fell with child.'

'With me,' Amelia mumbled, a slight blush brushing her cheeks.

'That is correct. Well, this couldn't be allowed to continue and risk jeopardising the union between the Chaldwells and us, so the girl was sent away – with enough money to see her well provided for, I might add. But Mark couldn't leave it at that. He said he loved her and couldn't live without her and when the old duke said he had to choose between staying and marrying the countess or leaving with only the titles and income he'd inherited at 21, well, we both know what decision he took.'

'You sound so bitter, Aunt. Why? It wasn't you who was wronged.'

'Oh but I was in a way, don't you see? Because of your father's actions, the Herbart name died with my father and as a family we were disgraced before society.'

'And yet you still took me in, offered me the luxury of your home. I don't understand why you should feel that you had to look after me.'

Margaret sighed and put down her cup. 'It seems that I'm going to have to tell you everything, but you must promise not to breathe a word of this to anyone, not even Connie. It would surely break her heart if she knew of it.'

Amelia frowned, wondering what on earth this shattering revelation was going to be. She sat up and nodded. 'Of course, Aunt. I would never knowingly betray your trust.'

'Very well then. At first, when I saw what effect Mark's decision had on father – he was a broken man after that, he really was, Amelia – I just could find no forgiveness in my heart for my brother. But then, when I too was forced to marry someone for whom I had no feelings whatsoever – oh yes, at the beginning, Lord Boughby was the last person I wanted to wed – I began to comprehend why your father took the stand he did. It suddenly became clear to me why he risked disownment to be with the one he truly loved. Over time, my anger towards him began to ease and, when I heard of his illness last year, I wrote to him, urging him to make use of our surgeon, but, of course, he would accept nothing from me.'

'You did?' Amelia asked in surprise. 'Father never mentioned it. According to him, he never heard from his family again after he left.'

'Well, perhaps he just said that to you for convenience, but I can tell you now that I wrote to him at every opportunity. Gradually we gained each other's confidence again and it was through our correspondence that I realised which one of us had made the right decision.'

'Oh, Aunt, I'm so sorry I –'

'There's no need to be. Although I've never loved John, I'm afraid my heart was crushed long before I met him and I've never had any reason to complain. He's always provided well for me and I believe he really loves Connie. That, at least, is a compensation.' Margaret blinked and looked away, tears welling in her eyes.

'You loved someone else? Did he die? Is that why you could not marry him?'

'Enough of this interrogation, child! Why, I swear you take after your father. He was always asking questions.' She sniffed and returned her gaze to Amelia. 'Now, about your marriage. I am being sincere when I say that I had no choice but to agree to this match. I want the best for Connie – and, well, I just want you to understand that the marquess gave me no room for manoeuvre –'

'I understand well enough, ma'am,' Amelia whispered, taking her hand and squeezing it. 'There's no need to say another word. I know just how persuasive he can be.'

Amelia pulled on an embroidered shawl and went to the window. As she watched the sun setting in the distance, she thought how, like the daylight, her chances of leading the type of life she wanted were diminishing by the second. Of course she'd expected her life under her aunt's care to be vastly different from the unrestricted one she'd had at home, but she hadn't counted on it being decided without her even being consulted.

Well, now it had and there was no way around it. Short of running away and risking being disowned by her new family, she was just going to have to face the consequences of her position and marry Lucas.

Shrugging, Amelia decided that perhaps a turn round the grounds before it grew too dark might be the tonic she needed to help take her mind off everything, and she stepped into the hall, only to meet Lucas at the top of the stairs. Amelia gasped and jumped back, seeking again the comfort of her room, but he was too quick for her and caught hold of her wrist.

'How fortunate to meet you now, my dear, so soon after our last meeting.' He smiled, pulling her slowly towards him. 'I should not have otherwise had time to see you this evening as my "visits" to Connie usually last till daybreak.'

Stunned, Amelia followed his gaze down the hall to her cousin's door. 'You swine! Your engagement only just announced and already you are flaunting your liaison with her in front of me? Have you no shame?'

'Why, Lady Amelia, not jealous are you?' He moved closer until she could feel the heat of his body on her bare chest.

'Certainly not!' She struggled to pull her arm free but he only tightened his grip, slipping his other arm around her waist. 'It's just that now our forthcoming marriage is public knowledge, I thought you would at least have the common decency to treat me with the deference one expects from a fiancé.'

Lucas grasped her chin and raised her face to his. 'Oh do you? Why then your ineffectual resistance in the glass-house? I should be delighted to afford you the attention you feel you deserve, but how can I, when the moment I make a move, you run to that officious aunt of yours and seek her protection? No, my dear, you simply cannot bring yourself to admit that, deep down inside, you crave that which I give Connie on a regular basis.' He smiled sweetly, licking his lips. 'If, however, in the unlikely event that you are prepared to swallow your pride and give in to your desires, you are always welcome to join us. I'm sure she wouldn't mind another participant.'

'Release me this instant!' Amelia breathed, biting her lip. 'Is it not bad enough that I am being forced into an unwanted match with you? Must you add insult to injury by carrying on in such manner? Have you no respect at all for me? I still cannot understand my aunt's thinking when she agreed to our union. All I can say is that you must have thought up something awful to make her give in to your demands like this.'

'She had no power to do otherwise. She, at least, is blessed with a certain amount of commonsense. Now, if you are wise, you will simply accept the situation yourself and stop this unnecessary resistance.'

'Never!' Amelia jerked her face from his fingers and looked away. 'You may make me marry you, may even force your attentions on me, but you will never ever make me obey you. I am determined to fight you all the way, despite what Connie says about you tiring of me and leaving me alone if I were to submit to you.'

Lucas raised his eyebrows and moved his hand to the base of her neck, his fingers circling the delicate skin there. 'Oh? And what else has my precious little mistress been saying about me? I hope that she has told you what you have to look forward to once we are wed?' He lowered his head until his lips were level with her ear and then whispered, 'Has she informed you of the methods I intend to employ in order to break your spirit? How I shall delight in the day when, so longing for my company, you will beg me to copulate with you?'

A thrill of excitement shot through Amelia's groin at his words, forcing her to return her gaze to his. 'How dare you?' she choked, her voice suddenly stuck in her throat as she felt his hands slide down her back to rest on her bottom. Despite the thickness of her skirt, she sensed his hands clutching, squeezing her buttocks, encouraging the wetness already pooling in her quim to drip down between her legs.

Amelia shifted uneasily and tried to look away again, but she found herself mesmerised by the intensity of his gaze as he began to raise the back of her skirts. Cool air rushed in, causing goosepimples to form on the soft skin above the line of her garters.

'Please stop,' she managed eventually, the strength leaving her knees, making her slump against him.

'Stop?' he teased. 'I gather that is not what you said to your father's stableboy.'

Amelia caught her breath, instantly straightening up. 'Tom? That's none of your business.' Lucas suddenly ceased his exploration of her nether regions, releasing her skirts, and brought his hands up to rest on her shoulders.

'Oh, but I believe it is. You see, before we marry, I should like to know the extent of your experience. You said when you first came here that you hadn't known the fullness of a man's passion. Is this true?'

'I don't have to put up with this intimate interrogation!' Amelia stormed, regaining her composure and tapping her foot on the floor.

'Perhaps not but, as your prospective husband, I request it. Now, I have been led to believe that your virginity is still intact. Is or isn't this true?'

Amelia found herself looking again into those chocolate pools of his, despite the overwhelming embarrassment which filled her at his questioning. 'If I said no would it mean that you wouldn't want to marry me?' she asked, a glimmer of hope igniting in her.

Lucas shook his head, his gaze lingering on her heaving bosom. 'Sorry to have to disappoint your feeble hopes, my dear, but I simply want to know what I'm getting, that's all. Now, are you going to tell me or am I going to have to find out for myself?'

Amelia hesitated. She didn't know what to do. The last thing she wanted was to afford him any satisfaction, and yet, if she told him the truth, wouldn't she do just that?

'Well?' he demanded, his fingers digging into her shoulders.

Amelia swallowed her pride and, raising her chin, told him what he wanted to know. 'What I said before still stands my lord, but let me say that it would not have been so, had I had my way in the matter. I wanted to give myself to him but for some reason Tom wouldn't indulge my desire. I suppose, unlike you, he was a gentleman and was thinking of my honour!'

To her dismay, Lucas burst into laughter, releasing her. 'How noble of him! Well it's his loss and my gain, for I shall enjoy deflowering you. You may count upon it, my dear, that once we are wed I will not tarry in claiming your cunny for my own.'

Amelia backed away from him, shaking, her hands gratefully coming into contact with the handle of her bedroom door. 'Is there no limit to your baseness?' she cried, kicking the door open with her heel. 'I suggest that you save your lewd suggestions for your lady down the hall!'

Once back in the safety of her room, Amelia threw herself on to her bed, burying her face in the pillow. Above the sound of her own sobbing she could hear Connie's laughter next door, quickly followed by the darker tones of the marquess.

'Damn you, Lucas!' she groaned, pushing herself up and hurriedly covering her ears with her hands. 'How can you do this to me?'

Amelia sat motionless for a few seconds, and then, getting to her feet, went purposefully to her dressing table, determined to take her walk after all. As she covered her tear-stained complexion with a dusting of powder, she quickly came to the conclusion that the only way she was going to cope with the cruel hand fate had dealt her was to play Lucas at his own game.

Well, if the thought of having a virgin pleases him, she thought, rising and returning to the door, I'll just have to make sure he doesn't get one.

Chapter Six

Amelia ignored the familiar allure of the gardens, choosing instead to traverse the unknown territory at the back of Boughby Manor. Lifting her skirts, she scurried across the gravel courtyard leading to the stables, only slowing to a normal walking pace when her feet met with the pliant texture of grass again. A wall of trees immediately behind the house cast dark shadows across the lawn, enabling her to move unnoticed past the lower-floor windows towards the part of the house which held the servants' quarters.

Amelia heard the buzz of conversation followed by the clatter of plates as she neared one such window and, peering in, saw that it was the kitchen. A scullery maid was washing up while the other servants sat around a large pine table laughing and joking.

Amelia supposed that this was the best part of the day for them, when, having completed the majority of their chores, they were able to spend a few hours relaxing with each other. She wondered briefly what kind of person would actually want to spend their life serving others, but then realised that these people probably didn't have much choice in the matter. They, like her, were probably forced into such an existence by circumstances beyond their control. Still, she thought with a shrug, they seem much happier than me.

She turned away from the window, to be confronted by the swaying form of one of the footmen. Her hand went immediately to her throat in shock as she took in his dishevelled appearance: his lack of frockcoat, his shirt hanging open at the neck and, finally, his crisp white wig resting lopsidedly on his head.

'Spying on us, were you, my lady?' he slurred, raising a bottle to his lips. 'Seeing how the other half live are you?'

Amelia straightened herself up, determined not to be intimidated by his drunkenness. 'I, I was merely going for a walk – David, isn't it?'

'Aye, that's my name.'

'Well, David, let me pass now. It's time I was returning.'

David leered, one of his hands resting against the wall near her head while the other raised the bottle once more to his mouth. 'What, leave without even giving me a kiss?'

Amelia was about to tell him to leave her alone when she remembered her previous determination to lose her maidenhead and wondered if this might not be the ideal opportunity in which to achieve her aim. It was obvious that David was hardly likely to remember anything of the event itself and it wasn't as if anyone from Boughby Manor had noticed her departure.

'Well,' she began, summoning all the strength she could, 'I was hoping to give you a little more than that.' She fluttered her eyelashes the way she'd seen Connie do when in Lucas's company.

His eyes lit up and he pressed closer, alcohol fumes battering her senses. 'You were? That's just dandy!' He staggered backwards and, throwing the bottle aside, began to struggle with the buttons on his waistcoat.

Amelia closed her eyes and, swallowing hard, pressed herself back against the wall, spreading her legs as she did so in anticipation of his lust. When what seemed like

63

minutes passed and she'd sensed nothing more than the cool evening air washing over her, Amelia opened her eyes. She looked about her but could see no sign of David – that is, until she heard a deep-throated belch emanate from the space in front of her.

Looking down, she saw that he was curled up into a ball at her feet. She prodded him with the toe of her shoe, hoping to waken him from his drunken slumber, but the only response she received was yet another belch.

Amelia sighed and, stepping over him, headed back towards the front of the house, tears of disappointment welling in her eyes. The way things were going it looked as if she was never going to get the opportunity to prove her determination to the marquess.

Connie turned away from the window and faced her father angrily. 'Now that my only chance of having some fun is about to be taken away, what are you going to do about it?'

Lord Boughby shrugged and examined his nails absentmindedly. 'I cannot see what it has to do with me. Besides, I thought you would have found someone else by now. You are slipping, my dear.'

Connie stiffened and met his mocking stare. 'You know exactly what it has to do with you. I have yet to understand what prompted you to allow Lucas Amelia's hand in the first place.' She sank into the chair opposite, shaking her head. 'You obviously didn't think of her when you agreed to the match. Have you any idea what marriage to him will mean for her? Don't you care that you may have ruined her life?'

Lord Boughby burst into laughter. 'Don't you think you're being a bit melodramatic? In her position, marriage to the marquess was the best she could hope for, better even. I only had her interests at heart.'

Connie raised her eyebrows. 'Oh yes? And what then of mine? Doesn't it concern you that in marrying Amelia off, you will be taking away the only confidante I ever had? I very much doubt that our relationship will ever be so close again. As for Lucas, do you honestly believe that I will be able to find another man capable of satisfying me like he does, around here? Or have you ideas of marrying me off as well?'

'As a matter of fact –'

'That's it!' Connie exploded, jumping to her feet. She didn't care any more how impudent she sounded. She just wanted her father to realise the frustration his actions had caused her. 'I've heard enough.' She rounded his chair and leant over the back in order to whisper in his ear. 'When you leave for London on another of your "business" trips, I want to be in the carriage with you.'

Lord Boughby caught his breath. 'What do you mean by that?'

'I know why you are so eager for these monthly visits. Pretty is she?'

'Enough! I will not be spoken to in such a manner –'

Connie smiled broadly, tugging playfully on the lace at his throat. 'She must please you greatly for I swear I have never seen you return in a foul mood.'

'I don't know what you are talking about –' Lord Boughby stammered, scrambling to his feet.

'Don't you? I'll go and ask Mama if she can enlighten me then.' Connie straightened up and walked to the door. She slowed her steps as she heard her father's hurried ones behind her. He caught her arm and twisted her around to face him.

'It's something she must never know of.'

'Like my relationship with the marquess I suppose? No, Father. I refuse to deceive her again. I hope she can take another shock so soon.'

Lord Boughby took her face in his hands and looked deep into her eyes. 'Dearest daughter, I implore you. Don't do this to me. I allowed you pleasure with Lucas, so let me have mine. Your mother –'

'How magnanimous of you!' Connie cried, pulling away from him. 'No, Father. I shall not be browbeaten like Amelia into giving up my only chance of happiness. I do not intend to spend the entire summer locked up in this mausoleum with only the ineffectual fumblings of the footmen for entertainment! Now, if you were able to make Mama see the sense of letting me enjoy a few weeks of the season with Aunt Clarissa in Covent Garden, I might just forget to tell her about your own diversion in town.'

'Impossible!' John paced the room rubbing his chin. 'Do you think that she would allow you to stay there, knowing as she does my sister's reputation for things – sensual?'

'Oh I'm sure you'll find a way of altering her opinion for, if you don't, Mama will soon find that she has a guilt-stricken daughter on her hands. One only too eager to confess how she found out the shocking truth of her father's infidelity.' Connie strode to the door and, opening it, paused and glanced back at him. 'As soon as Amelia is wed and installed as the new Marchioness of Beechwood, I shall expect to hear of your unexpected decision to allow me to come with you to town on your next journey.' She giggled and blew her father a kiss. 'How I shall look forward to enjoying those delights only London can offer!'

Amelia heard the soft rasp of the bedroom door and twisted around in time to see Connie enter the room carrying a green velvet pouch in her hands. She dropped it on the bed and then took her cousin by the shoulders.

'Why aren't you downstairs enjoying a last toast with Mama and Father? They want to wish you luck for tomorrow.'

Amelia shrugged away her grasp. 'You know why – because I don't feel I have anything to celebrate.'

'You're about to marry a marquess and you've nothing to celebrate! Are you insane?'

Amelia whipped round, her chemise swishing about her ankles. 'You seem to enjoy Lucas's company far better than I so why don't you marry him? Why are you so chirpy anyway? I thought you'd be as miserable as sin considering that my marriage will take him away from you.'

Connie tapped her nose and moved over to the bed where she flopped unceremoniously on to her stomach. 'I've sorted that little problem out. The question is, what are we going to do about you?'

Amelia shrugged and climbed on to the mattress beside her. 'What more can I do? I sought your mother's protection from Lucas but even that has failed. I suppose it's about time that I faced the facts – I've got no choice but to marry him. Oh, how I wish I'd had a chance to get my own back on him!'

'What are you talking about?' Connie gathered her cousin up in her arms and, brushing an errant strand of hair off Amelia's forehead, dropped a soft kiss on the pale skin there. 'Why, you are shaking! After what you've told me about what you and Tom got up to before you came here, I hardly believe this entire episode is simply a consequence of you worrying about sharing Lucas's bed for the first time. Come on, Amelia. Tell me what's really troubling you. Remember, it may be a very long time before we see each other again.'

Amelia blinked and, rubbing her eyes, nodded. 'Although I cannot deny that there is a part of me which is thrilled by Lucas, I have to admit that the thought of what he actually intends frightens me a bit. Call it fear of the unknown if you like, although it can't be that bad because you obviously enjoy it.' She smiled at Connie and sighed. 'But you are right, that's not what's really troubling me. I am afraid that, once I become his wife, I will cease to have my own will. My father's illness taught me how important freedom is to my wellbeing and I am certain that, once we are wed, I will no longer be allowed to think for myself.'

Connie suddenly took Amelia's face in her hands and covered her mouth with her own. Amelia's eyes widened in surprise when she felt her cousin's tongue push fervently at the crack between her lips and then, forcing them apart, begin to caress the sensitive underside of her top lip. She moaned softly as a familiar glow filled the area between her legs and, without thinking twice, she pressed her hips towards Connie.

Connie smiled and slowly lifted Amelia's chemise, sliding it up over her thighs until it bunched at her hips, revealing the dusky triangle of her pudenda. Amelia held on to her chemise while Connie reached behind her and picked up the velvet pouch.

'Just because you have no choice in marrying Lucas,' she whispered, loosening the bag's drawstring and pulling out an ivory object, 'it does not mean you have to accept the marriage wholeheartedly. There are ways in which a woman can exert her will without her husband ever knowing. Some women find solace in another's arms, while others seek out exciting, new experiences. And if you are determined enough, I am confident that you too will find a way of subjugating Lucas. Knowing the marquess as I do, I fear that your concerns about his dominance are not unfounded, so I want you to promise me that if you ever feel melancholia overtaking you like this in the future, you will bear these suggestions in mind.'

Amelia nodded slowly, her eyes glued to the highly polished dildo Connie held in her right hand. Six inches in length, it sported a thick shaft and perfectly carved knob. 'I promise. Oh, Connie, how I shall miss you! Even though we have known each other but a short time, it feels as if we have been friends for years. Why, already I feel my spirits lifting. Perhaps marrying the marquess won't be such a trial after all – if what you say is true. Who knows what I may get up to when his back is turned!'

Connie grinned and, rolling the dildo between her hands to warm it, moved closer to Amelia until their faces were mere inches apart. 'What indeed! Now, do you want me to help allay your fears about your wedding night?'

Amelia looked deep into her cousin's gentian eyes

and, seeing the glow of desire in them, swallowed hard. 'Do whatever you feel is necessary to prevent the marquess having the honour of taking my maidenhead.'

'What?' Connie caught her breath. 'Surely you don't mean that, Amelia? I only intended to help you relax a little, perhaps show you a way of pleasing yourself in secret. It would anger Lucas greatly to know that I had captured your cherry before him. Who knows what he would do?'

Amelia raised her head defiantly. 'I am well aware of that, but I care not. I have been thinking about this for a long time and was actually hoping to rid myself of my virginity – although not quite like this!' Amelia grinned. 'I think it will be a perfect way of proving to Lucas right from the start that I'm not about to give in to his every whim without a fight, don't you?'

'Well, if you are certain –'

'I've never been more so.'

'Very well, I just hope that you or I do not live to regret this.'

Needing no further encouragement, Connie reached behind Amelia and rolled the dildo over the plump mounds of her bottom before drawing it down into the crease of her buttocks where she deliberately ran it back and forth, twisting it this way and that within the muscled crevice.

Burning with a sudden fever, Amelia dragged her chemise over her head and tossed it to one side, the cool evening air feeling wonderful against her moist skin. She found her breasts and started to squeeze them, delighting in how easily her nipples reacted to her touch, as Connie drew the dildo through her legs.

Amelia's breath started to come in short gasps as Connie parted her distended, lubricious labia with the dildo, circling the entrance to Amelia's sex with the sleekly curved tip, thoroughly coating it with love juice. With a sudden impatience, she covered Connie's hands with her own, and guided the ivory penis into her yearning hole.

Amelia stiffened as it surged upwards into her virgin orifice. Connie remained motionless for a few seconds, enabling her cousin to regain her nerve, and then drew the dildo out of her until only the knob remained inside.

'Please . . .' Amelia hissed and dropped down to squat on the mattress, taking hold of the dildo herself. As Connie sank backwards on to the bed in front of her and pulled up her own skirts, Amelia pushed the dildo's full length back inside. She bit her lip and squeezed down hard on the pleasure object, enjoying the sensation of the cold bone as it filled every inch of her.

Connie's fingers went to her own clitoris, kneading and squeezing it until it pushed itself free of its hood and quivered in answer to her ministrations.

Amelia began to withdraw and thrust the dildo into herself, her movements matching every stroke of Connie's pumping hips. She started to grunt, her blood pressure rising in line with her excitement. Perspiration stung her eyes as she flicked her hair out of them and pushed down on to the mattress beside her cousin, grinding her pudenda into its springy surface, forcing her vagina to accept the full length of the phallus. She fell forward on to her hands when the first throes of orgasm overcame her, her back arching as her womb contracted wildly and expelled the dildo in one swift, fluid movement.

Amelia heard Connie's cry of satisfaction as she too reached culmination and collapsed into silence beside her.

Some minutes later, when she began to feel cold, Amelia raised herself and reached for her discarded chemise. A sudden pressure on her arm stopped her in her tracks.

'I think a bath is required before we join Mama and Father downstairs, don't you?'

'A fine evening for it, m'lord.'

Lucas dismounted from his horse and, handing the reins to a groom, took the girl by the arm and marched her round the back of the stables, out of sight of the house.

'How dare you trouble me at this hour and at a friend's residence?' he demanded, pushing Fran roughly up against the wall.

'Why, my lord, not angry are you?' She smiled up at him, fluttering her eyelashes while her hands sought his neck.

Lucas grabbed her wrists and thrust them aside. 'None of your games, girl. I haven't the time. Now, what do you want?'

Fran sniffed and straightened up. 'I got a message for you from your friend.'

'Friend? Oh, you mean that ruffian at the inn? What does he want?'

Fran pushed a grubby hand into her cleavage and retrieved a small, folded piece of paper. Lucas snatched it from her and read it hurriedly.

'Ha! He is sadly mistaken if he thinks he can exact payment with threats.' He threw the note down and ground it into the dirt with the toe of his riding boot. 'Who did he get to write that anyway? I cannot believe that someone of his dubious character would be literate enough to produce something as legible as that.'

'I did actually,' Fran stated proudly.

Lucas raised his eyebrows. 'And there I was thinking you were good at one thing alone. You surprise me. Now, what is all this really about? It's not as if I owe him a fortune – fifty guineas wasn't it? Surely he's not that desperate for it.'

'It's a fortune to the likes of Paul, your lordship. We don't all live in a palace like you. He's got a family to feed and everything.'

'How very touching! He should have thought of that before he engaged me in a game of faro.' The marquess, having had enough, turned to leave only to pause when he felt pressure on his arm.

'If he doesn't get it soon –'

'What will he do?' Lucas extricated himself and raised

her hand to his lips. 'Inform the local magistrate? I don't think so. Where are you staying anyway? Perhaps I will reacquaint myself with your company after all,' he said, running his eyes over her. 'Is it within walking distance?'

Fran retrieved her hand, grinning. 'You certainly don't act like a prospective bridegroom, m'lord.'

'Oh? You are aware of my impending marriage?' he asked, obviously shocked.

'Of course and so is Paul. In fact, the whole village is talking about it. It is said that your bride has an uncommon beauty, as well as spirit. I wonder how she will fare in your hands, m'lord.'

Anger ignited in the pit of his stomach at the thought of strangers knowing his business, invading his privacy. 'The same as you do if you do not desist with this idle chatter and tell me what this man, Paul, is about.'

'Your marriage, m'lord. He intends to disrupt the ceremony if you don't pay up.'

'How?' Lucas burst into laughter. 'By shooting the vicar? Surely you aren't serious?'

'I am. He didn't go into specifics but he said him and a few mates would make their case known if you don't make some sort of undertaking by then. Knowing him, he'll do it too.'

'I see.' Lucas rubbed his chin. It was all too easy for him to imagine how this could be achieved and, though not one usually to give in to threats, the last thing he wanted was to be made to look the fool on his wedding day. 'Well, you can tell this Paul that he will receive his money after I am wed, not before. I'm too tied up here at the moment to get to my bank. Ask him to contact me on my estates then.'

'I'm not sure he'll go for that –'

Lucas grabbed the front of her bodice and pulled her against him. 'I'm certain you'll find a way of convincing him. Just tell him I'll see him after I'm wed, not a moment before. I give him my word. I am, after all, a gentleman.'

Fran smiled, nuzzling closer to him. 'Not too much of a gentleman, I hope.'

Chapter Seven

*A*melia left the security of her bedroom and took what she knew would be her last journey down the Boughby's magnificent staircase before leaving for her new life at Beechwood House. She tried to take a deep breath but her new waist-cinching stays wouldn't allow anything more than the shallowest of inhalations. She sank down on to the hard wooden bench and, fanning her undulating bosom, caught sight of herself in the mirror across the hall. A shudder coursed through her as she took in her appearance.

Her once blue-black hair was now an ashen grey, having been liberally covered with powder, while her usual creamy complexion sported stark, white tones, punctuated only by a heart-shaped patch above a pair of wide, carmine lips. Amelia's eyes travelled lower and she noticed with a sense of shame how her new corset made her breasts bulge indecently over the top of her bodice, their coral tips almost visible above the line of the garment.

So this was how her new husband wanted her to look – like a whore. She sighed, remembering how Lucas had entered her room one afternoon and turned out every one of the gowns she'd had made for her trousseau, as well as those Lady Boughby had bought for her, and ordered for all of them to be altered to this new, more revealing style. As if that wasn't enough, he then went on to instruct her maid on how her face should be made up.

Amelia could only guess what her aunt and uncle must have thought when she had entered the church today dressed according to instructions but, judging by their shocked expressions they, like her, had thought the attire unsuitable for a bride.

Amelia fingered the diamond ring on the third finger of her left hand and shivered, knowing it was only a matter of time before she would finally be made to face that which she most feared: her desire for Lucas. She knew this would be the hardest battle of all for her to win, especially when she remembered the intense feelings he had inspired in her when he had taken his place beside her at the altar, resplendent in the finest suit of shot silk she had ever seen. And what about the look he'd given her as soon as the priest had declared them man and wife? Amelia could have sworn that, but for the presence of the guests and clergy, he would have taken her there and then.

She snapped shut her fan at the approach of her husband.

'Feeling overheated, madam?' The marquess strode towards her carrying a feather-trimmed tricorne hat under his arm. 'Well, do not think that you can feign illness when we arrive at Beechwood House. Your duty will be to the guests which await us, as well as to me.'

Amelia caught the meaning behind his words and gasped. 'I, I meant no such thing, my lord. I am simply overwhelmed by this momentous day.' She allowed him to help her to her feet, finding the sensation of his firm hand encircling her arm strangely exhilarating.

'Come,' he breathed, guiding her towards the door. 'We must not keep the driver waiting.'

'But what of my aunt and uncle? Am I not even allowed to say goodbye to them?' she demanded, stopping in her tracks and staring incredulously at him.

The marquess shrugged while tugging her towards the door. 'I thought it best not to linger over farewells. I do hate them so.'

Amelia thought to argue but, seeing his determination, sighed and went with him out to the carriage.

Amelia watched out of the window as they bumped along the uneven road. Seeing the undulating pastureland which stretched for miles in either direction, she couldn't help but marvel at just how beautiful the countryside was during this time of year. She breathed the cool July air which rushed in through the open window, making out the distinctive scents of the wild parsley and meadowsweet which flanked the road as they passed from the Boughby estates.

Amelia reluctantly turned away from this pastoral scene, fervently hoping that these natural pleasures wouldn't be denied her in her new existence as Lady Beechwood, and cast her gaze in the marquess's direction. She noticed with a tightening of her throat how his strong, almost Roman profile was silhouetted against the sunlight which flooded into the carriage.

Sensing her attention, the marquess met her eyes and smiled. 'Why do you look so bemused, my dear? Is it because you have finally realised your good fortune?'

Amelia snorted. 'What? Oh, do not flatter yourself, my lord. You know as well as I do that I had no say in the matter. Why, if the decision had been left up to me, I wouldn't have married you for a thousand pounds!' She whispered the last sentence under her breath but he still heard it.

'What was that?' the marquess demanded, grabbing her wrist and pulling her towards him. 'I had hoped that by now you would have seen the futility of your antagonism towards me. However, it seems you still have a lot to learn.'

Amelia tried to twist herself free of his grip but it only tightened, his fingers digging into her flesh.

'Let me go! You cannot treat me like this.'

Lucas's lips stretched into a grin. 'I can treat you

however I see fit. I own you now. You are my chattel and therefore mine to do with as I please.' He caught her other arm and, with an unexpectedly swift movement, drew her towards him. Amelia fell forward on to her knees in front of him. Lucas settled back in the seat and gazed down at her, his tongue flickering over the surface of his lips. His hand went immediately to the ties of his silk breeches.

Amelia watched in horror as he slowly undid them and his erect penis burst free of its restraints, pointing emphatically towards her. Flushed pink and interlaced with blue veins, it leant slightly to the right, its foreskin drawn back to reveal the distended, purple glans.

'You will now demonstrate the skills you aquired with that stablehand, my lady.'

Amelia slowly shook her head and backed away as she considered what he intended, knowing that if she did as he wished she would surely be lost. 'Never!' she gasped. 'How dare you speak to me in such a manner?'

'I dare because I believe it is about time you learnt what obedience means.' Taking hold of her hair, the marquess pulled her face between his legs. He pushed his prick towards her, its tip pressing at her pinched mouth. 'Do it now before I am forced to make you, wife!'

Amelia refused to comply at first, still in possession of her will, her mind desperately seeking a way out of this situation but, when he wound her hair tightly around his fist, she cried out, allowing the access he required. He drove his full length into her moist cavity, giving her no opportunity to breath, let alone protest further.

Moving his free hand to her cleavage he cupped one of her breasts, his fingers teasing the tip until the nipple hardened against his palm. Amelia forgot herself then and, with a moan, began to run her tongue up and down his shaft, enjoying the musky taste of him. She moved her hands to his balls, their skin firming, tingling under her caress, while her tongue slipped under his cock skin and teased at his glans the way Tom had taught her.

The marquess pushed himself deeper into her throat

then. 'Do it faster, madam,' he growled between clenched teeth, his breathing reduced to hoarse rasps. 'Pleasure me until I spend in your mouth.'

Amelia's nails scratched at his thighs as she started to suck him more strongly and quickly, sensing liquid beginning to coat her already dilated labia. She squeezed her sex, longing for her own release, while still keeping up the rhythmic stimulation of his penis.

Lucas surged towards her with one last thrust, his cock throbbing with orgasm. His semen shot into her mouth, wrapping her tongue in a hot, saline blanket, choking her with its potency.

With a cry, Amelia fell away from him spluttering, her fingers urgently seeking the hem of her gown and her own culmination. Lucas reached down and grabbed her wrists, ruthlessly dragging them away from the floor and holding them high above her head.

'Oh no, my sweet. You will not achieve satisfaction that way.'

'What?' Amelia blinked up at him, her breathing still laboured, her desire unfulfilled. 'You cannot possibly be so cruel. Must you continue to torture me in this way?'

Lucas laughed, his triumphant tone battering her senses.

'If you think that I have finished with you, you are much mistaken, my dear. You will have to learn that your pleasure rests solely in my hands. It is I, as your husband and master, who chooses whether you have it or not, and at this moment I prefer to watch you suffer for your lust.'

Struggling for breath while fighting the overwhelming sense of defeat which seeped into her consciousness, Amelia jerked her wrists away from him and sobbing, climbed back into her seat.

'So, this is what marriage to you is going to be like?' she asked, forcing herself to meet his eyes, despite her tears. 'Am I to become a prisoner of my own desires?'

Lucas shrugged. 'That is entirely up to you. It depends on how willing you are to play the game.'

'You mean do everything you ask without question?

Give in to your tyranny?' Amelia raised her head defiantly. 'Never. You may own my body, may even deny me fruition, but you will never have my will, my lord. Of that I am certain. I will fight you every inch of the way to prove that point.' She stared at him, waiting for the inevitable anger to flare within him, and was surprised to see amusement light up his eyes instead.

'Splendid,' he announced, clapping his hands together. 'Just as I hoped. I shall enjoy teaching you just how futile your attempts at disobeying me are. But be warned: this is just the start of your lessons. I promise that those which follow may not be so pleasant – for you at least.'

Amelia started when the door opened and Mary, her new maid, swept into the room, a swathe of crimson silk in her arms. Amelia sat up and, wiping her sore eyes, watched Mary as she laid the gown over the back of a nearby chair. Two other servants followed the maid and quickly filled the hip bath at the foot of the bed with steaming water before leaving the two of them alone.

When they'd eventually arrived at Beechwood House, Amelia was relieved to find that, after the indignity of the carriage journey, Lucas hadn't forced her to endure the rigours of meeting his friends as well, but had allowed her some time alone. She knew, however, that this was no courtesy on his part but, rather, a way of extending her suffering by allowing her space to worry about what was to come.

Lucas had actually said very little about what was to take place that night but, knowing his penchant for proving over and over again his mastery of her, she guessed her humiliation played a great part of it. Now, with only an hour to go before she was to join him downstairs, Amelia felt fear creep once again into her consciousness.

She rose and allowed Mary to help her into the bath. As she sank into its soothing, perfumed depths, Amelia tried to relax, clearing her mind of all disturbing thoughts. She concentrated on Mary's experienced touch as she rubbed and caressed her skin with a soft flannel, running it over her feet and then up her legs to her thighs. It was only when she didn't stop there but moved the flannel up to rest at the boundary of her pudenda, that Amelia opened her eyes and looked questioningly at the maid.

'It's all right, m'lady. M'lord's instructions were to awaken your desires in readiness for later.'

Amelia swallowed hard as Mary pushed the flannel deeper between her legs, her padded finger plunging between her burning lips and pressing at the entrance to her sex.

Amelia arched her back, offering the tight nub of her clitoris to the maid's probing finger. Mary easily surrounded the bud with the flannel and pinched it between thumb and forefinger, while Amelia began to thrust her hips in time with the maid's flexing digits. She caught her breath as shiver after shiver radiated through her, her movements causing the water to undulate and splash over the sides of the bath as she sought that welcome release.

Amelia ground her buttocks against the bath and hooked her ankles over the sides in order to prepare for the rush of pleasure she could sense building within her.

Mary suddenly ceased her ministrations and, almost roughly, caught her mistress under the arms and pulled her from the water. Amelia fell forward on to her hands and knees, panting, her body shaking with disappointment. She glanced up at the maid, her hand poised over her dark mound ready to finish the job but, seeing the girl's determined glance, the towel wound tightly into a thin strip between her hands, Amelia knew it would be pointless trying to bring herself to climax and fell back on to her haunches, defeated once again.

Mary had followed her instructions well. She had brought her to the brink of orgasm, increasing the yearning in her belly until it had become a veritable knot of pain centred over her pubis and then left her there, demonstrating once more that the only way to satisfaction for her was through the marquess.

Slowly and with resignation, Amelia got to her feet and allowed Mary to dry and dress her, despite the agonising ache in her groin. She was rather surprised when the maid informed her that she was to wear no chemise or corset under her dress that evening. She was even more disconcerted when, being laced up, she found that the neckline plunged so low it arced under her unfettered breasts, while the whole front panel of the skirt was missing, creating a triangular gap between the swell of her panniers.

When Mary had completed her handiwork, Amelia stepped in front of the mirror and gasped as she looked at her new image. Her breasts hung pertly over the edge of her stomacher, their erect tips defined by scarlet rouge. The space between her legs stood uncovered for all to see, her raven-haired mound barely concealing the flushed, turgid lips of her sex above the line of her legs, which were lightly covered by the sheerest of stockings held up by satin garters.

Amelia swallowed hard and turned to Mary, who was busily arranging her hair into a tight bun at the back of her head. 'Surely he doesn't intend for me to go downstairs and parade myself in front of our guests attired thus?' she croaked. 'Who does he think he is?'

'You have nothing to fear, m'lady,' Mary said as she picked up a box from the floor. 'His lordship's friends are not like those you are likely to have met before. They share his taste for the unusual and could not possibly fail to appreciate your beauty.' Her compliment did nothing to quell the dread sweeping over Amelia when she contemplated doing that which was required of her as his wife. 'Anyway, you should feel honoured. Not all of us were shown such regard.'

'My God.' Amelia turned around and faced the maid. 'He's had you too?'

Mary chuckled and, lifting a tightly curled wig from

80

the box, carefully placed it on Amelia's head. 'He's had us all in his time, m'lady. It's part and parcel of the job.'

'Well, I'm not in his employ so I won't do it!' she cried suddenly, clenching her fists in front of her and sinking back down on to the stool in front of the mirror.

'His lordship ain't going to like this,' Mary breathed harshly behind her.

'I don't care if he doesn't. I will not be treated in this insulting fashion.'

As she heard the maid's hurried footsteps disappearing down the stairs, Amelia buried her face in her hands and started to cry, not caring if it ruined her make-up.

Though she was well aware of Lucas's determination to punish her for what she'd done to him over the previous weeks at her aunt's residence, she had never imagined he would sink this low. What a fool she had been to imagine that a man like him would be satisfied with consummating the marriage in the privacy of their bedchamber! It was obvious to her now that he intended her inauguration into the delights of sex to be a public affair, a realisation which sent a spasm of panic, as well as excitement, racing through her.

'Tsk tsk, what's this I hear? Can it be true that my new bride is reluctant to share our happy union with our guests?' Amelia struggled to her feet and faced Lucas, her body swaying as she tried to keep her balance in her new, high-heeled shoes.

He stood in the doorway, his russet hair falling free on to the shoulders of a damask housecoat.

Amelia blushed as she felt his appraising gaze focus on her exposed sex. 'That is correct, my lord. You seem to forget that I am your wife and not some doxy you have just plucked from the street.'

'Have I? How remiss of me. I do apologise. But it's hardly surprising, considering that you aren't exactly acting like a lady.' He walked towards her, his robe fluttering about his ankles as he moved.

Amelia stiffened when she saw the unmistakable swell of his manhood under the fabric at his groin. 'I will not parade myself dressed like this –' she began, only to stop short when he wrapped his arms around her, surrounding her with the heavy folds of his housecoat.

'I wonder why you shake, madam?' he whispered, grasping her shoulders and propelling her towards the door. 'Is it because you know that you run the danger of incurring my anger if you continue to refuse my command, or is it because you are alive with anticipation of that which is to come?' Amelia stopped in her tracks and attempted to pull away from him. His grip never faltered but kept her firmly at his side.

'Do you really need to ask after I have been forced to wear this scandalous attire? Why, I confess you treat me with no respect at all!'

Lucas shrugged. 'You will only gain my respect when you have earnt it, not before, and certainly not by acting in this childish fashion.' He unexpectedly burst out laughing. 'Oh, my dear Amelia, you have so much to learn about life – about me. I shall enjoy teaching you about us both, but for now, will you join me downstairs or do I have to demonstrate once again who is master in our marriage?'

Amelia considered refusing but, seeing the resolute set to his jaw, she decided that it would be best not to. Instead, she wiped her eyes and, raising herself up to her full height, allowed him to escort her from the room.

The moment they stepped across the threshold of the Great Hall, Amelia sensed a hush descend in the room as twenty pairs of eyes appraised her semi-naked body.

A blush sweeping across her cheeks, Amelia hurriedly tried to cover her nudity with her arms while she took in the grandeur of the lofty gilded ceiling, the magnificent plaster friezes which decorated the powder-blue walls and, finally, lit by a hundred candles, the raised stage at the far end of the room.

'My friends, my I present my wife, Amelia, the Marchioness of Beechwood?' Lucas boomed beside her, making her jump.

The crowd surged forward then, fashionable ladies

and gentlemen jockeying for position around her, their hands probing, searching out her nakedness. Amelia shied away from their foreign touch, trying to twist to one side in order to shield herself against her husband's chest as they pressed closer. He simply grabbed her arms and, pushing them flat against her sides, turned her back round to face his friends. Amelia was powerless to do anything other than stand there while he allowed them to ogle and feel her body.

One man, naked to the waist under an aquamarine frockcoat, leant towards her and ran a finger around the dimpled surface of one of her artificially tinted aerolae before bending to place the lightest of kisses on its hardened tip. Amelia shuddered, not so much from the shock of this uninvited caress, but from the dark ripple of pleasure it caused in her groin. She bit her lip and closed her eyes, marvelling at how she was able to feel anything other than loathing at such an intimate gesture.

Lucas tugged her away from his friends and towards a settee positioned a couple of feet from the stage. She gratefully accepted a large bronze goblet from him when they sat down, hoping that what it contained might help to dampen the sense of terror currently boiling in her belly.

Once everyone was seated, the marquess snapped his fingers and two young men and a woman stepped from the shadows and mounted the stage. The men were attired in lawn shirts tucked into baggy breeches secured by a wide band of red silk about the waist, their dark hair flowing down their backs. The woman, sporting the same dark features, wore a white scooped-neck blouse and full, multicoloured skirt which fell to brush her bare feet. Amelia noticed that she wore a heavy silver bracelet round one ankle which jingled as she climbed the steps.

The men positioned themselves at either end of the stage, one crouching with a small drum firmly held between his legs, the other placing a violin under his chin. The woman stepped forward and, after casting the marquess a look so full of lust Amelia wondered if he'd had her as well as her maid, she signalled for the music to start.

When its throbbing cadence filled the hushed room a few seconds later, the woman began to move, raising her arms high above her head, swaying from side to side in time with its pulsating beat. As the tempo increased, she gradually lowered her arms, her hands slipping inside the neckline of her blouse to squeeze and massage her breasts.

After their dusky tips had stiffened to press into the thin material, she sank down on to her knees and crawled to the very edge of the stage. Looking directly at Amelia, she opened her mouth and ran her tongue slowly over her ruby lips, lubricating them with saliva, while at the same time dragging the blouse out of the tight waistband of her skirt.

Amelia caught her breath as she watched the woman lift the blouse over her head and casually throw it behind her on to the stage, the burnished, olive skin of her breasts catching the subtle light as they flopped free of their covering.

Bending over, the woman brushed the floor with her erect nipples, before suddenly rolling on to her back. She then drew her hips up, her hands resting on either side of them, supporting her split, spreadeagled legs, this provocative posture presenting Amelia with a full view of the woman's gaping sex.

Amelia swallowed hard as she focused on the woman's flushed labia, their slippery outlines parted like the petals of a rose, revealing the enticing, pink interior of her cunny.

Amelia leant forward to get a better view, her own sex-lips suddenly feeling heavy and moist, and noticed out of the corner of her eye that the marquess had shifted position too. She switched her attention to him and watched, transfixed, as he produced a small purse and, after emptying six or seven gold coins into the palm of his hand, started to toss them in the direction of the woman's parted legs, much to the delight of the others in the room.

The first two coins missed their target, but the third connected, sliding easily into the moist cleft and disappearing from sight. Amelia sank back against the settee, perspiration peppering her skin, while her fingers itched to explore her own womanhood, despite the presence of the others.

As if reading her thoughts, Lucas leant towards her and, placing a hand on her bare thigh, began slowly to caress it, his fingers leaving a trail of goosepimples as they inched closer to her groin. Amelia knew that she should shy away from his touch, prove that he had no contol over her, but already her defences were crumbling at the glorious sensation his fingers were creating on the delicate flesh there.

She inched closer to him and, placing her head on his shoulder, lifted her thigh so that it rested against his lap, affording him access to her secret place. The marquess twisted his head in her direction and, covering her lips with his own, finally found her bristly mound with his fingers. Amelia opened her mouth and allowed his tongue to enter and skirt its interior with sharp darting motions as she sensed his fingers parting her damp folds, pushing at the entrance to her sex.

When her mouth closed on his foraging tongue, Lucas disengaged his lips from hers and, chuckling, indicated for her to look again at the stage.

Amelia raised her head and trained her attention on the scene directly in front of her. What she saw caused a shiver to race through her, making her bear down hard on his probing fingers.

The man who had been playing the violin now knelt behind the woman, his hands resting on her buttocks while he lowered his face to her slick valley. Amelia watched transfixed, her breath suddenly coming in harsh rasps, as the man buried his face in her lubricious folds for a few seconds and then, with an unexpected shriek of delight, dragged his head away from her pudenda to display triumphantly the shining gold coin which was lodged between his teeth.

The marquess's questing digits pressed deeper into Amelia then, his thumb finding the hard node of her clitoris. With a sharp intake of air, she returned her attention to her husband and, without thinking, raised her pelvis towards him, an inexplicable longing rising in the pit of her stomach.

As stealthily as he had penetrated her, he withdrew his hand and scooped her up into his arms. Easily lifting her slight frame, he carried her up the steps and on to the stage where a chaise longue now stood in the centre.

When he swung her round and gently deposited her on its pliant upholstery, Amelia caught sight of the dimly lit room and noticed that a few of the couples had already found their own diversions, while a good many others were still watching their every move.

A blush of self-consciousness swept over her as she felt the marquess undoing the belt which held her panniers in place. These dispensed with, he took off her wig and placed it on the floor before busying himself with divesting her of her gown.

Amelia now understood the reason behind her not wearing any undergarments; they would only get in the way of – what? She shuddered at the thought of what was to come and, looking up, was presented with the startling image of Lucas kneeling over her completely naked.

Her mouth went dry as her eyes took in the potent image of his cock thrusting towards her from its bed of dense chestnut curls, the candlelight playing on its mottled surface, highlighting the jewelled bead of moisture which decorated its tip.

Amelia began to fidget under Lucas, trying to cover her nudity with her own hands, suddenly wishing that she hadn't gone along with this so easily. She felt the cool rush of air on her skin as he pushed her unlaced gown over her shoulders and stared down at her, appraising her body with satisfied eyes.

Amelia tried to draw up her knees in an effort to retain some decency, but he simply grabbed her ankles and, tugging them towards him, crawled on to her, his cockhead prodding the smooth surface of her belly.

'This is no time for timidity, madam,' he breathed as he scooped up her breasts in his hands and raised one to his lips, his tongue immediately going to work on the nipple.

A moan escaped Amelia as he closed his mouth around the nipple and ran its hardness between his teeth before releasing it and trailing kisses back down her abdomen to the edge of her pudenda.

'Please,' she gasped, close to climax, 'not here ... somewhere private –' Her words were cut off when she felt him lifting her hips, his fingers digging into the pliant flesh of her buttocks.

Lucas fell back on to his haunches and pulled her towards him until the soles of her feet brushed his shoulders. Raising her quivering sex to his mouth, his tongue began to circle her soft, damp lips in slow, teasing motions until Amelia's moan prompted him to move his mouth up to her rigid pleasure-bud.

Amelia tensed as she felt his lips surround it, his tongue pushing back its protective hood of flesh, while he greedily sucked on it. Sweet ripples of ecstasy radiated out from her clitoris and travelled upwards to release the knot of frustration left in the pit of her stomach by Mary's ministrations. His actions created a yearning in her unlike anything her own attempts at satisfaction had produced.

She twisted uncontrollably, her breath coming in short, harsh grunts as orgasm burst deep within her, sending glorious streamers of sensation rocketing throughout her being, making her shake wildly within his grasp.

The marquess lifted his head triumphantly and stared down at her, his grinning face shining in the lamplight. His eyes focused on the irregular rise and fall of her chest.

'Do you wish for me to take you now, my lady?' he

whispered as he lowered her hips down on to the cushions and crawled forward to hover over her once more. 'Shall I make you come again?' he murmured, easing his rampant penis into the space between her parted legs. 'Shall we delight our guests? Is that what you want?'

Amelia met his burning eyes as she felt his knob pressing at the entrance to her vagina and, in that moment, she experienced the same want which had filled her when they'd first met at the inn. It blocked out the last vestiges of defiance left in her, filling her only with a desire to experience again that all-consuming rush of feeling which had possessed her only moments before.

'Yes, Lucas,' she panted, clutching his shoulders. 'Take me now. I want nothing else but to feel you inside me.'

The marquess set his jaw and, with no further hesitation, drove his full length into her yearning orifice. Amelia gasped and dug her fingers into the sweaty flesh of his back as his cock filled every inch of her, her membranes stretching to accommodate its prodigious size.

With the sound of the excited cheers of the guests ringing in her ears, she abandoned all modesty and wrapped her legs around his hips in anticipation of his thrusts.

However, Lucas didn't move, but remained stock-still within her, his laboured breathing the only proof of his excitement.

'You scheming chit,' he eventually growled and, ruthlessly withdrawing his manhood from her, grabbed her by the waist and flipped her over on to her stomach. 'So you thought to dupe me with your pretended innocence, did you?' he demanded, grabbing her hair and pulling her head back.

'I, I don't know what you mean,' she cried, sensing his weight shift to the back of her legs.

'The hell you don't!' Lucas slipped his arm under her and raised her buttocks towards him. His finger found her slippery hole and probed deep inside her. 'Tell me who captured your maidenhead and by God I'll run him through for this outrage. Was it that stablehand after all? Tell me!'

Amelia bit her lip, knowing that she only had herself to blame for this ugly scene. Connie had warned her that this might happen. 'It is true that I have never known a man, you are the first –'

The marquess laughed bitterly, his grip on her hair tightening to a point where Amelia thought her neck might snap under the pressure he exerted on it.

'You expect me to believe that? Did you honestly think that I wouldn't notice? You may fool your aunt but not me, my girl. I'm not some bumpkin used only to a few night-time gropings, you know. I can tell when a wench has been had before. Now, are you going to tell me who it was or do I have to break that pretty neck of yours?'

'All right!' Amelia cried, trying to twist round to look at him. 'It was my way of getting back at you. Connie visited me yesterday and I told her to –' She broke off unable to finish the damning confession.

The marquess suddenly let go of her. Amelia fell forward, violently coughing, reaching for her throat.

'So, you thought you could deny me my pleasure?' he growled. She felt him push his hand between her legs and scoop up some of her love juice. 'It seems that you still haven't realised that my desire is everything. Well, my girl, it's about time you learned just what that means!' He laughed between clenched teeth, pushing a moistened finger into the rigid circle of her anus. 'I was promised a virgin and a virgin I shall have by God!' He swiftly withdrew the finger and replaced it with the surging flesh of his cock. 'I'll wager not even Connie has had this little jewel with that ivory dildo of hers!'

Amelia groaned as she felt her buttocks contract to accommodate his shaft while a potent pressure began to build in the small of her back. Well lubricated, his penis easily moved within her tight passage as he thrust harder and harder into her, forcing her to take the full length of his prick as he fucked her mercilessly, the strength of his movements pushing her deeper and deeper into the cushions. Lucas reached under her and, cruelly clasping her breasts, squeezed them in time with his frantic movements. 'Well, my little vixen, you have a lot to learn if you think I'll forget this quickly,' he croaked between strokes, his tepid breath fanning her back.

Despite the violence of his actions, Amelia arched her back against him as the ferocity of his thrusts exerted the most exquisite pressure on her already excited clitoris, causing the burning rush of excitement to race through her once more. Heat rose from her body, creating a sticky layer between them while she shivered at the sensation of his teeth grazing her neck, his fingernails scarring her breasts, his manhood claiming her forbidden orifice as its own.

Orgasm swiftly surged again within her as a consequence of her husband's roughness, a driving pleasure-pain which possessed her completely, blocking out all her concerns, save that of obtaining such a wonderful release.

Amelia came with a low cry into the upholstery, her vagina contracting at the same time as her arse closed around Lucas's plundering cock. He answered her climax by stepping up his pace, ramming himself deeper into her, pushing her further along the length of the settee until, with a sharp gasp, he too reached completion, his penis shuddering, flooding her secret channel with his seed.

Amelia stirred and, sensing the first fingers of a chill creeping across her shoulders, sat up and pulled on the loose folds of her gown. She blinked and glanced around the room, the bright sunlight which flooded in through the open windows stinging her grainy eyes.

The Great Hall lay in disarray before her, empty wine bottles and upturned chairs littering the room like so much rubbish. She detected movement close by and trained her eyes on a sleeping couple, their entwined limbs hanging over the edge of a sofa. Amelia shivered and looked quickly away, this potent image of fulfilment making the memory of the previous night flood back into her consciousness.

She remembered how Lucas had picked her up, when she was still shaking from the effects of that first time, and carried her throughout the room, one hand lifting and parting her buttocks, parading her recently opened passage among his friends, encouraging them to touch, to probe that damp channel, as if it were a sacred object to be revered.

Amelia swallowed hard, knowing that this had been just the start of a night filled with dark couplings. No surface had been spared: the floor, the sideboard, even someone's lap; nothing had been out of bounds to Lucas in his wild pursuit of continuing satisfaction. And though she had struggled a few times, tried to reason with him when her spirit refused to give way to his, Amelia knew that despite these protests, she had enjoyed his touch, delighted in the feel of him straining deep inside her, his hands roving over her body, arousing sensations within her she'd never imagined were possible.

Amelia coloured and chided herself for being so weak, as she realised that, even now, in the cold light of day, she longed again for his embrace. She looked at the space beside her and, seeing that it was empty, frowned and rose to her feet, her body stiff from last night's labours. She descended the stage and walked down the centre of the room, her bare feet skirting the highly polished floorboards as she made her way to the door.

'Going somewhere?' A voice from the corner caught her unawares, making her stop in her tracks and slowly twist in its direction.

The marquess leant against the wall, a woman's head bobbing between his outstretched thighs. He looked down at the redhead for a few moments and then violently pushed her away. 'Time you started work, girl. My wife will soon be requiring her breakfast!' He waited until the maid left before jumping up and, pulling on his dressing gown, padding towards Amelia.

She couldn't conceal her shock at her husband's blatant behaviour and her mouth fell open while she watched him unconcernedly lean against the wall beside her as if he'd done nothing more than conduct a conversation with the maid.

'You look surprised, my dear.' He reached out to catch her face but Amelia managed to recover her composure and shy away from his hand.

'Don't touch me!' she hissed, alive with a sudden, inexplicable anger. 'Our marriage only a day old and already you are – entertaining yourself with another woman.' She shook her head. 'Do you think so little of me, your wife?'

Lucas laughed and caught her by the shoulders, forcing her to meet his gaze. 'You should know by now that my desire is immense – too much, surely, for even your eager mouth.'

Amelia blushed, recalling how he had made her publicly fellate him in front of his friends only a few hours before.

'So, this is how you intend to punish me for what I allowed Connie to do? Parade your mistresses before me?'

The marquess shook his head. 'Oh no, my sweet. I haven't yet decided how to repay you on that score.' He moved his hands underneath her gown to rest on her buttocks. 'She was just a diversion and will remain so until I tire of you which, incidentally, I do not expect to happen for a very long time, for I must admit that you please me greatly, far more than I'd originally envisaged. You have a unique talent for fornicating, my dear, even though it was enhanced by a philtre last night.'

'What?' Amelia's eyes widened. 'You mean you drugged me without my knowledge? How dare you?' Amelia tried to wrench herself away but he only inched closer, his erection insinuating itself between her legs. She shifted uneasily, sensing her already slick lips parting in readiness to accept him, in spite of her outrage. 'Is there no end to the liberties you take with me?'

His grip on her buttocks gradually increased, forcing her thighs to close around his pulsating penis. Amelia caught her breath, feeling its warmth, its hardness pressing into the sensitive skin there.

'Still at it, eh? I must commend your enthusiasm and your stamina, my dear boy!'

The marquess cursed and released Amelia; she slid down his legs into a heap on the floor.

'Damn you, Carterall. You have the worst timing!' he barked, turning to confront the source of this interruption.

Amelia struggled to her feet and, clutching the folds of her dress around her shivering, damp body, glanced at the intruder. Her heart skipped a beat when she recognised him as the one who had paid particular attention to her breasts the previous evening.

Not quite as tall as her husband and stockier in build, he carried the mark of the fop, his sandy blond hair being caught in a beribboned queue at the base of his neck, while his powdered, oval face sported a patch on its left cheek. She also noted, with a certain amount of relief, that this time he was fully dressed in a salmon-pink suit.

'Good morning to you, Lady Beechwood,' he said, swooping into an exaggerated bow. 'Since Lucas seems to be displaying his usual boorishness, allow me to introduce myself. I am Lord Carterall, but you may call me Rafe, if you like.'

Amelia allowed him her hand but immediately snatched it away when she felt his tongue brush the tips of her fingers. 'I, I shall retire now – have a bath,' she said as calmly as she could while walking to the door, aware all the time of Rafe's eyes watching her every movement. Lucas got there before her, blocking her way with his towering frame.

'You will not leave until I say so. I have been too

lenient with you, allowed your charms to cloud my judgement, but no more.'

Amelia stared up at him, wondering if his friend's presence was the cause of this sudden outburst of authority.

'So what am I to do? Catch my death down here while you dither over whether or not I can go to my room? I think not!' She tried to push past him but he caught her arms and, forcing them behind her back, propelled her back into the room to stand in front of Lord Carterall.

'You see what I mean about her? She just cannot be left to her own devices. Will you keep an eye on her when I go away for a few days next week?'

Amelia bit her lip as she watched Rafe approach, circling around her like a peacock. A cool shaft of air stung her rump as he lifted her skirt and examined her, and then, returning to face her, closed his hand over her pudenda, his fingers creeping into the ebony hair there, probing between her slick lips.

Amelia shuddered and looked towards her husband with a futile hope that he would put an end to this indignity but, seeing the expression of pleasure on his face, she surmised that he was enjoying watching her suffer this man's attention.

Despite the throbbing Rafe's touch created in her groin, she managed to take a deep breath and address him. 'Sir, is this how you introduce yourself to every lady?' She raised her head and looked straight into his startling blue eyes. She saw laughter in them.

'Only the fortunate ones, madam,' he chuckled and, withdrawing his hand, pressed two fingers to his lips, obviously savouring the honeyed taste of her secret juices.

'I should be delighted to look after your charming wife, Lucas.' The marquess let go of Amelia's arms and, placing a hand on the other man's shoulder, led him towards a door in the far corner.

Amelia turned to leave, only to stop dead when she

heard Rafe speak again. 'You can rest assured that I will not allow her an inch when you are away. Why, once I'm through with her, I promise you that she will never question your authority again.'

Chapter Eight

*A*melia unfolded the letter and read it again, hardly believing what it contained. The thought of Connie being allowed to travel to London in order to experience the season there, while she was stuck at Beechwood House, a virtual prisoner of her husband, was almost too much for her to bear. How she longed to be with her cousin, free to do whatever she pleased, instead of being at the beck and call of Lucas and his extraordinary desires.

Amelia threw down the parchment and picked up her fan, and, in doing so, realised that she was shaking. This hardly surprised her. After only a week of marriage to the marquess, her nerves were already near to breaking.

In that short time he had proved over and over again his mastery of her. That she wanted him, craved his touch, was without question – their wedding night had demonstrated that beyond measure – but, despite this, Lucas still insisted on imposing his will on her at every opportunity. It was as if he wasn't happy merely possessing her body. He craved that which she fought so hard to retain – her self-respect.

Amelia shuddered as she remembered when he'd taken her to the very same inn where they'd first met and forced her to stimulate him with her hand in full view of every drinker in the establishment. How, after dinner one evening, he had brought her to the verge of orgasm with his libertine's skill and then had Lord Carterall restrain her in her seat while he openly copulated with a maidservant on the table in front of her.

She knew that in doing these things he hoped to wear her resistance down, make her admit, once and for all, that only he knew how to satisfy her; that he was both her sexual and mental master.

Amelia swallowed hard, knowing that the way she felt now it would only be a matter of time before she gave him exactly what he wanted, full and utter submission. This was a thought which sent a chill racing into the very centre of her soul.

With a sigh, she rose and went downstairs. She found her husband conversing happily with Lord Carterall. Probably discussing their next method of humiliation, she numbly thought as she accepted a glass of wine from Lucas before taking a seat on the sofa.

'You look rather pale, my dear,' he said with a smile, staring down at her. 'I wonder if it is because I am about to leave you? Could you be pining for me before I have even left?'

Amelia nearly choked on her drink. 'Do not flatter yourself, my lord. Any time spent away from you can only be a bonus for me!'

'I see that she still retains some of her spirit,' Rafe commented with a chuckle. 'Far better for my purposes to have her thus. I find complete obedience rather tiresome, don't you?' He looked to the marquess who nodded and, catching hold of Amelia's wrist, dragged her up into his arms, making her spill her drink in the process.

'Of course. I wouldn't want her completely devoid of spirit. That would be most boring.'

Amelia ineffectually pushed against his chest and kicked out with her feet as his mouth descended on to hers, his tongue imposing itself between her lips. Her struggles gradually decreased as she felt the all-too-familiar fire raging in her loins, and she opened her mouth to him, urging his tongue deep into her throat.

When he eventually raised his head, her breathing was laboured, her hardened nipples pressing painfully into her stomacher as she struggled to fill her lungs.

'I commend her to your care, Carterall,' Lucas said, pushing her into his friend's arms. 'My coach awaits so I must away, but rest assured that I already hunger to return to see what changes you have effected in this little vixen.' Without another word he strode from the room, leaving the two of them alone.

Neither Amelia nor Rafe moved until the sound of a carriage driving away outside drifted into the room and broke the silence. She wrenched herself from his grasp and went to stand behind the settee, her hands resting on its back.

'I wish to dine alone tonight,' Amelia said, her trembling tone barely disguising the fear brewing in her belly.

Rafe shrugged. 'As you wish, my lady, but I promise you it won't make any difference to the plans I have for you. I should have thought you would prefer to get to know me better before I put them into action.'

'I know you well enough, sir. You have already demonstrated your scant regard for my feelings, this past week. I need no further proof of your debauchery. Like my husband, you seem proficient enough in it.' She headed for the door, her heart thundering in her chest.

'Very well, if you refuse to offer me courtesy, namely, in dining with me, then I shall do the same with you.' Rafe rang the bell-pull. 'You obviously need harsher treatment than I first suspected.' He shrugged. 'All the better for me.'

The footmen appeared at the door and, ignoring Amelia, went straight to Lord Carterall. She stared at them incredulously, hardly believing they could be so discourteous towards their mistress.

'You know what to do. His lordship has spoken to you?'

The liveried men nodded and turned towards Amelia, their arms outstretched.

'What is the meaning of this?' she cried, shying away from their grasp until she was pinned against the wall and unable to stop them taking her by the shoulders.

'I shall tell you what it means, my lady. You will be locked in your room until I have supped and then you will be brought to the library to await my pleasure.' Rafe lurched to the door and, wrenching it open, indicated for the footmen to follow with their charge.

Though kicking and twisting ferociously, Amelia found herself forcibly propelled across the hall and into the library. A gasp flew from her lips when she eventually ceased her struggles and took in its contents.

One of the four bookcases which rose from the floor all the way up to the ceiling had been emptied of every tome and stocked instead with what looked to Amelia like instruments of torture.

Leather harnesses, straps and cat-o'-nine-tails of all shapes and sizes were neatly placed on each shelf in order of size and, presumably, effectiveness. Amelia couldn't help blinking and swallowing hard when her gaze fell on a fearsome-looking whip, its tapering, plaited tail spanning the entire length of one of the shelves.

'Surely you don't mean to . . .' Amelia trailed off, her mouth suddenly dry as she observed Rafe lovingly finger one of the wrist restraints which had been crudely nailed into the wall beside the bookcase.

'I do, and I will, madam. Tonight I shall have you begging for release and satisfaction.' Sensing her interest, he picked up the whip and lightly flicked it on to her chest, allowing the knotted end to slide down and rest in the crease between her breasts. Amelia shuddered, the sudden coolness of the leather against her burning flesh causing a ripple of excitement to race straight into her groin.

'And then, if you are a good girl, I may take pity on you and allow you culmination. Would you like that, my dear?' He suddenly looped the whip around her neck and drew her closer to him until she could feel his tepid breath on her cheek. 'Would you like me to make you come?' he sweetly whispered.

Amelia began to fight against the footmen again, twisting her shoulders back and forth, trying to break free of their grasp, but the men easily held her firm between them, forcing her to accept Rafe's attention without question.

'You wouldn't dare. Lucas –' she hissed, meeting his leer with a scowl of her own. Rafe smiled and slowly withdrew the whip from her neck, its snake-like movement making Amelia catch her breath.

'You seem to forget, my dear, that all this is in accordance with his wishes. When he returns he expects to find an obedient wife, one who knows her place.'

'And you think that this is how to achieve it? Never! You may beat me within an inch of my life, but my spirit you'll never have.'

'That remains to be seen but, for now, you will enjoy a brief stay in your room while I sup – unless of course you have changed your mind about joining me?'

Amelia shook her head violently.

He shrugged. 'Very well then. Your maid will visit you later with some suitable apparel for this night's activity. In the meantime, I suggest you prepare yourself for what is to follow, for I promise you it will be like nothing you have ever experienced before.' He raised her hand to his lips and then left her to the company of the footmen and her rising terror.

Amelia paced the bedroom, wringing her hands in front of her as she struggled to think of a way out of this mortifying situation.

She crossed to the window and shivered as a tepid breeze, heavy with the sweet scent of roses, wafted into the room. Leaning on the sill, she closed her eyes, the soft rustling of the ivy just below the ledge soothing to her battered senses.

The ivy.

Amelia quickly opened her eyes and craned her head over the sill to stare down at the thickly gnarled climber which clung to the wall. Was it possible? Could she really do it?

She shrugged and pushed herself up. She would just have to find out. After all, what did she have to lose? There certainly wasn't anything at Beechwood House worth staying for, save a beating, and Connie was bound to have arrived in Covent Garden by now.

Amelia moved to the dressing table and, after ridding herself of the only reminder of her marriage, her diamond ring, she picked up Connie's letter and hurriedly undid the belt which secured her panniers. Stepping out of them, she returned to the window and clambered up on to the sill. Casting one last, rueful glance around her bedroom, she twisted on to her stomach and began to climb down.

The descent wasn't as hair-raising as she'd imagined it would be, but the blood was pumping in her ears all the same and her legs were shaking by the time she landed at the bottom. However, she didn't let this deter her and, clutching her skirts about her knees, ran round the back of the building in search of the stables.

Passing the glowing rectangle which denoted the dining room window, she briefly trained her gaze inside. The sight of Lord Carterall savouring a balloon of brandy, one silk-covered leg propped up on the table, was enough to dispel her curiosity and send her scrambling on her way again.

The stables were situated at one end of a gravel courtyard at the rear of Beechwood House, and far enough away from the main building for Amelia to feel a certain amount of safety as she crept towards them. Nearing one of the stable windows, she noticed with alarm the flickering of a lantern emanating from within. She hadn't counted on the grooms being up at this hour and paused to rethink the situation.

It didn't take her long to realise that she had no other

alternative but to go in and confront them, hoping above hope that they too hadn't had instructions from her husband.

She took a deep breath and crossed the threshold, her feet immediately connecting with the slippery covering of straw which littered the dirt floor. She skidded in her high heels and fell back against the wall, the smell of leather and horses filling her nostrils.

'Are you all right, my lady?' a voice said beside her, swiftly followed by the image of a cheeky face peering at her from out of the gloom.

Amelia blinked, blinded by the glare from the lantern the groom held up.

'Yes, thank you,' she replied, quickly regaining her composure. 'I want you to saddle me a horse, one with a lot of running in it.'

'Going somewhere, are you?' The groom eyed her curiously, his gaze resting on her unfettered skirts.

Amelia started at his impertinence. 'That's correct. Now, if you will excuse me, I shall wait outside.' She turned to leave, only to stop dead when she felt his hand on her arm.

'I'm afraid I can't do that. His lordship gave strict orders –'

'Damn his orders!' Amelia exploded, frustration welling up inside her. 'I command you to saddle me a horse – now!' She narrowed her eyes and took a good look at the groom then. He was not as tall as Lucas, nor as powerfully built, yet there was something about him which brought lust flooding into her groin. Was it the way his shirt hung open to reveal the burnished surface of perfectly rounded chest muscles? Or was it how his tight flannel breeches barely concealed the unmistakable line of an erection arcing over his stomach?

'Will you do as I wish,' she whispered, digging her nails into the palms of her hands, trying her hardest to ignore the delicious spasms which travelled up her spine as she addressed him.

The groom smiled, a smile full of knowledge, as if he

sensed the reaction he'd caused in her. 'They say that her ladyship's passions can't be easily satisfied, not even by her own husband.'

Amelia raised her chin, her eyes on his. 'I do not think that is any of your business.'

'I think it is, my lady. You see, if you want me to saddle a horse –'

Amelia gasped, the flush of embarrassment filling her. 'Are you suggesting what I think you are?'

'I am. Jim and the others have gone to the tavern this night, so we are alone, save for the horses. You want a horse, I want you. The answer is simple. Lie with me and you can have your pick of the stable.'

Amelia thought a moment, her heart somersaulting at the thought of what he was suggesting. It wasn't so much that she didn't want him – her body had made that perfectly clear to her already – but would she have the courage to go along with her desire? What if one of his friends came back early and disturbed them, or Lord Carterall, for that matter? She wasn't sure of her ability to talk her way out of such a dangerous situation if that were to happen.

'I don't know – someone might hear us,' she muttered, but she didn't flinch when she sensed his arm encircling her waist, pulling her against him, their hips meeting in delightful collision. She remained stock-still, savouring the excitement steadily building in the pit of her stomach. 'If Lord Carterall comes looking for me and finds us together . . .'

He shrugged. 'That's a chance I'm willing to take if you are.'

Amelia thought for a moment and, remembering the beating she already faced, nodded, deciding that she had nothing to lose by indulging her passion for him. Without warning, she grabbed the back of his head and pulled his mouth to hers for the briefest of kisses. Their foreheads touched, his untied hair caressing the smoothness of her cheek.

Amelia pressed her body closer to his, running her lips

103

down his neck, the natural scent of perspiration and newly cut hay which rose from his moist skin tantalising her nostrils, reminding her of long-lost encounters with Tom.

'What is your name?' she asked hoarsely, raising a leg and curving it around his hip, offering her thigh to him. He trailed his fingers over its smoothness, beyond the line of her garter, to finally rest in the dewy crease of her groin.

'It's Seth, my lady.'

'Very well, Seth,' she breathed, pulling his shirt out of his breeches and sliding her hands up over the swell of his chest. 'I agree to your terms. I shall keep to my side of the bargain –' she sought his mouth again, catching his bottom lip between her teeth and gently nibbling on it '– if you promise to keep to yours.'

Seth pushed his fingers between her distended, slick folds and, dragging them up to her clitoris, rigorously pinched and twisted it until the tiny node hardened to press against its protective hood of flesh. Amelia gasped and pulled her mouth away from his, shuddering when he moved his lips down to skirt the mounds of her breasts bulging above the line of her stomacher.

Suddenly wanting to reciprocate the courtesy he was affording her, Amelia pushed her hand inside the waist-band of his breeches and, taking a deep breath, closed it around the excited flesh of his cock. She ran her fingers up and down its length, enjoying the sensation of its pulsating strength as she pushed back his foreskin and ran the tip of her little finger in small circles over the surface of his moist glans.

This was so different from what she had experienced with her husband. There was no dominance, no sub-mission commanded, only a mutual need which had to be satisfied. A fact which caused the heady rise of orgasm to build within her, even at this early stage.

Seth placed the lantern on a nearby ledge and, with-drawing his hand from her groin, began to undo his breeches. Amelia noticed how his softly tanned face was twisted in concentration as he struggled with the ties, and, laughing, she roughly slapped his hands away and deftly undid the ties herself.

His manhood reared up between them, its flushed nob glistening in the dull light. Amelia caught the viscid bead of moisture which appeared on its tip with her finger and raised it to her mouth, sampling the salty taste of him. She put her lips together and smiled. 'Very nice.'

She reached down and, clasping his balls, drew his penis towards her until its length rested between her legs. She pushed forward, drawing him between her wet, expectant lips, squeezing him gently with her loins.

Seth leant towards her, one hand resting against the wall above her head, while the other lifted her chin.

'You certainly are an eager one, my lady,' he panted, brushing her cheek with his mouth. He dropped a hand to her breasts and scooped one up out of its restraints, raising its rigid tip to his lips.

Amelia shivered, ribbons of pleasure radiating out from where his tongue flicked and teased its way over the sensitive nipple and, arching her back, pressed her palms against the cold stone wall.

'I want you, Seth,' she rasped, swallowing hard. 'I want you inside me – now.'

He raised his head, a smile radiating across his features. 'Is that so? Then I shan't disappoint you.'

With one swift movement, he pushed his hands behind her and, grabbing her buttocks, rammed his hips against her. As his thick cock surged upwards into her, parting her satiny inner membranes, Amelia spread her legs wide and, bending them slightly, bore down on him, the top of her thighs grazing the bristly reaches of his groin.

When Seth began to move, the force of his thrusts pushing her bodily up the wall, Amelia caught his shoulders, her nails digging into his flesh. He pulled back from her until only the tip of his cock remained embedded within her tight passage before plunging it back in with a low growl of satisfaction.

Amelia's mouth fell open as, with every movement he made, his cock drove higher and higher into her vagina, pressing at the very mouth of her womb, creating a sensuous pressure which crescendoed behind her pubic bone. She clenched her internal muscles as he withdrew, kneading, massaging his prick, keeping him as long as she could in her well-oiled recess before allowing him leave to draw back for another stroke.

'Yes! More! More!' she cried in time with his powerful movements, her hands embedding themselves in the tangle of hair at the base of his neck as she felt the exquisite crescendo of orgasm spiralling into the pit of her belly. She threw herself against him, wrapping her ankles around his, swivelling her hips against his, surrounding, submerging his manhood with her quivering orifice.

Seth came at the same time as Amelia, a cry escaping his lips as he fell forward against her, the sound of his straining breath filling her ears.

Once her own breathing had returned to normal, Amelia dabbed her moist chest with a handkerchief and, after straightening her skirts, moved away to the door, her legs trembling as much as they had before their secret coupling. She bit her lip as she turned back to the groom, embarrassment returning to envelope her when she observed him stuffing his flaccid cock back into his breeches and hurriedly doing them up.

'I shall wait outside for the horse.' She forced a smile. 'Please don't keep me waiting any longer than necessary. I must leave before I am missed.'

Lucas took off his hat and cautiously entered the seedy ale-house. He narrowed his eyes and, peering through the smoky air which filled the chamber, looked about for a familiar face before making his way to the counter.

Squeezing past a particularly buxom wench balancing on the knee of a middle-aged man, Lucas couldn't help smiling to himself. It had been in such a place as this where he had received his first taste of sex at the tender age of twelve. How far he'd progressed since then!

He eventually made it to the bar and managed to order a drink from the harassed bartender, only to feel a pressure on his arm when he attempted to take a sip of it.

'I'd drink that in the next room, if I were you,' a voice intoned to his right.

Lucas turned in its direction and looked straight into the determined eyes of Paul James, the man to whom he owed the fifty guineas. 'Is it possible that you are addressing me?' he asked, his gaze falling on the small knife Paul was brandishing.

'That's right, your lordship. I think we'll have more privacy there. Me and Lennard will see to that.'

A giant of a man stepped forward presenting Lucas with a broad, almost toothless smile.

'I'll come when I've finished my drink,' the marquess calmly replied, determined to show them that he was unmoved by their brutish display.

'You'll come now –'

'Hush, Paul,' Fran suddenly interrupted, throwing her arms around him. 'You ain't dealing with your usual bar-room roughs now, so you can put that knife away for a start!' She turned to Lucas and smiled.

'He meant no harm, my lord, honest. He just ain't used to your type of company, that's all. Come on, why don't we go somewhere less noisy, somewhere we can discuss this little disagreement without all these onlookers?'

Lucas considered refusing her but decided the sooner he sorted this out, the sooner he could get back to more salubrious surroundings. He shrugged and, downing the rest of the ale, followed her out of the main chamber and into a smaller one with space for only a table and four chairs.

'Your rough and tumble attitude does nothing for your case, gentlemen!' he announced, promptly opening the only window and taking a seat on its sill.

'We're not violent men, your lordship, but we didn't think you'd come any other way.'

Lucas shrugged. 'I'm here, aren't I, but I must say I find all this rather tiresome.'

'Do you, my lord?' Paul enquired aggressively. 'So do I. You owe me a lot of money and I want it now!' He shook his fist in Lucas's face but Lucas merely pushed it aside and got to his feet.

'I haven't come here to be threatened.'

'Oh haven't you? Then pay up now and that'll be an end to it.'

'Impossible. Do you honestly think I'd be foolish enough to visit a place like this with that sort of money on me?'

'Well, when can you pay?'

'Whenever I can get to my bank.'

'That ain't good enough.'

Lucas shrugged and headed for the door, only to be stopped in his tracks by Lennard standing in the doorway, his thick hands resting purposefully on his hips.

'It will have to be. As I stated, I don't carry that amount of cash on me. You'll just have to wait until the next time I visit town.'

Paul stared at Lucas for what seemed an interminable time, frustration apparent in his face. 'I don't know how much longer I can wait for my money.'

Lucas sighed, suddenly deducing that the only way he was going to get out of this distasteful situation was to tell them what they wanted to hear, even if he had no intention of keeping his word.

'All right.' He raised his hands in mock resignation. 'As soon as I can, I will make a point of visiting my bank and have a draft drawn up in your name. Fran can even come with me if she wants and deliver it to you personally. Does that satisfy you?'

Paul thought a moment and then slowly nodded, indicating for Lennard to move aside.

'I'll trust you on this one because you're a gentleman

but cross me again and I'll come looking for you for sure, mark my words.'

'Of course.' Lucas briefly smiled and, grabbing Fran's wrist, tugged her into the hall with him.

Neither said a word until they were free of the cloying atmosphere of the ale-house and the marquess was hurriedly untying his horse.

'I've never been to London before,' Fran remarked, letting him lift her up on to the horse. 'How long will it take us to reach it?'

In one fluid movement, Lucas swung his lean body into the saddle in front of her and, taking the reins, urged the animal forward on to the path which went round the back of the inn.

'I have no idea. We aren't going to London.'

'What? I thought –'

'That was just to get your importunate friends off my back. Do you really think I would give in so easily? No, my dear. London couldn't be further from my thoughts. I had hoped that we could spend a few days together at my lodgings before I take you back to Beechwood House and introduce you to my wife.'

'You really are a devil, aren't you?'

'Well,' Lucas laughed, 'why should I give in to such petty threats? I think we should have some fun first, don't you?' He glanced at one particularly well-lit window at the back of the tavern. When he spotted the figure silhouetted there, plainly watching their departure, he raised his hat to the observer.

'Of course, I am counting on it,' Fran whispered, snuggling closer to him.

'Excellent,' Lucas smiled, his eyes remaining fixed on the window. 'I should hate this outing to have been a complete waste of time.'

Chapter Nine

'I expect, niece, that you are anxious to sample the delights only Covent Garden can offer.' Clarissa Stevens reclined on a small settee, her slim figure barely concealed under the loose folds of a taffeta robe.

'Yes, Aunt, I am. I just wish my cousin Amelia could sample them with me.' Connie remembered the letter she had sent four days ago and wondered what Amelia would think of her escapade.

'I am certain that you will make other acquaintances whilst you are here, my dear. Tonight, for example, Sir Mandeville Draper will be visiting me and he has promised to bring someone along who I am certain will amuse you.'

'Really?' Connie involuntarily squeezed her sex as she thought of what that would mean. 'I do hope so, it has been a long time since –' She broke off, suddenly unsure of whether or not she should tell her aunt everything.

Clarissa laughed and, swinging her legs off the settee to the floor, patted the space beside her.

'No need to be coy with me. I know why you have come here; it is the same reason I bought this house. After Reginald died I found that my life was lacking a certain excitement, so I decided to settle in Covent

Garden. I can honestly say that it has been the correct decision for me.'

'And this Sir Mandeville, is he, he –'

'My lover?' She chuckled. 'One of many I'm happy to say. I am no one man's domain. Why, it's one of the reasons I chose not to burden myself with the rigours of marriage again, though I had many offers at the time.' She poured two glasses of wine from a carafe on a nearby table and gave one to Connie. 'So, what of you, niece? I presume you had a lover at Boughby House and now he is gone away.'

Connie briefly related what had happened to make her seek out her aunt's company.

'Beechwood, you say? He must have been a good lover for you to take such drastic action as coming to London. I'll wager you felt jealous when he married your friend.'

Connie shook her head emphatically. 'Jealousy couldn't have been further from my mind. My only concern was, and is, for Amelia's welfare. I know what Lucas is like. If she were to take one step out of place – well let's just say that he would not be pleased and, believe me, I know just how many forms his anger can take.'

'I'm sure your friend can look after herself.' Clarissa touched Connie's face. 'Now, I want you to forget about her for this night at least. I have something very special planned for you which I know you'll enjoy.'

At that moment a footman, attired in green livery, entered the room to announce the arrival of Clarissa's guests. She jumped to her feet and hurried towards a door on the other side of the room, her hands instantly moving to her golden hair.

'You'll have to entertain them while I dress, Connie dear. I do declare I've quite forgotten the time!'

Connie shrugged and followed the footman downstairs and into a small ante-room just off the hall. Two gentlemen rose at her entrance and stepped forward to introduce themselves.

Sir Mandeville was a tall, slim man in his early forties

111

and impeccably dressed in a suit of scarlet brocade, but it was his younger companion who Connie was really interested in. Small in comparison with Sir Mandeville, he sported ink-black hair which fell in tight curls halfway down his back, the ends plaited with indigo ribbons. His shoulders, though not broad in the traditional sense, gave the impression of strength under the folds of a grey velvet frockcoat, while a white lace shirt was tucked into a pair of skintight buckskin breeches.

Connie noticed that he also had the darkest of eyes, fringed with black lashes, but even these features paled into insignificance when she allowed her eyes to rove. His skin, the colour of toffee and as smooth as the finest silk, enchanted her, filling her with the longing to run her hands all over him, to sample for herself every inch of his body.

Connie found that she was shaking when he eventually took her hand and pressed his sensuous lips against the back of it. She could understand now why her aunt had said this man would amuse her. Why, even this most innocent of touches was enough to cause liquid to build in her already pouting labia.

'Lady Connie, I presume?' Sir Mandeville asked. She nodded dumbly, her eyes fixed to the mahogany ones of the man in front of her. 'I can see that you are taken with my charge, child,' he chuckled, taking her arm and drawing her away to a couch. 'His name is Nathaniel Johnson, a friend from the colonies.'

Connie reluctantly dragged her gaze back to Sir Mandeville and smiled. 'I have never –'

'Most gentle people haven't, my dear. He's the son of an English plantation owner and, shall we say, an enforced worker from Africa. As you can imagine, the moment I saw him, I knew he wasn't meant for servitude, so I convinced him to accompany me back to the motherland, as it were, so that he too may sample its pleasures.

'And he's in your employ now?' Connie blinked and returned her eyes to Nathaniel, who now had his back to her, studying one of the miniatures on a nearby table. She noted with a tightening of her throat, the gentle swell of his calves, highlighted by whiter-than-white silk stockings.

'Not exactly. It amuses me greatly to see how he reacts to the many varied delights here and the formality of our society in comparison to the liberal life he led in the colonies.'

'And has he met many people?'

'Yes, I have, my lady,' Nathaniel drawled, strolling over to them and sinking into an armchair, 'but none as pretty as you.' His voice was surprisingly deep and was accented by an unusual, deep twang.

Connie looked sharply at him and, seeing him smile, shifted uneasily in her seat. There was a self-assurance about Nathaniel which reminded her of Lucas. It was apparent to her that he was a man at ease with himself, one who knew exactly what he wanted from life.

'You are exceedingly forward, Mr Johnson.' She returned his friendly glance, fluttering her eyelashes as she spoke.

'You'll have to forgive him, Lady Connie. He hasn't yet adjusted to our polite ways.'

'It's all right, I find it – refreshing to find someone willing to speak their mind.'

'See, what did I say, Niece?' Everyone turned to witness Clarissa sweep into the room, draped in an orange gown. She moved to stand beside the settee. 'Shall we leave these two youngsters alone to get – acquainted?' She raised her eyebrows and stared at Sir Mandeville.

'Oh yes, of course.' He scrambled to his feet and then hurriedly performed a bow, before following her to the door.

'Feel free to partake of the wine. Oh, and, Connie – I've heard Mr Johnson is an exceedingly find acrobat. I'm certain that, if you ask him, he'll be only too pleased to demonstrate his many talents!' Clarissa giggled and, grabbing Sir Mandeville's sleeve, pulled him into the hall with her.

Nathaniel slipped into the seat beside Connie, his arm inching round her shoulders. Feeling the warmth of his breath on her cheek, she looked towards him, a tremor wracking her body as she peered into his walnut eyes. He was older than she first thought, perhaps 24 or 25, but no less stimulating.

'So – Nathaniel – is it true what my aunt says, that you are an acrobat?'

He laughed, his pearly teeth glinting in the candle-light. 'You could say that, my lady. As she said, I might be persuaded to give a performance, but only if I'm assured of an appreciative audience.'

Connie smiled and moved her hand to the buttons of his shirt, her fingers taking hold of the lace.

'Have no fear there, Nathaniel. I can tell that, no matter what you do, it will please me.' Using both hands now, she undid the remaining buttons and pushed the shirt away from his chest to reveal the firmness of muscle under a dense covering of thick, black hair.

A shudder ran through Connie when her fingers eventually made contact with his warm skin and she brushed them over his chest, sensing every feature of its satiny surface. She ran them under his arms, delighting in the subtle wetness there before easing them down to rest on either side of his abdomen. As she moved them lower, her fingers made contact with metal running over the curve of his hips and she gasped. A thick silver chain resembling a shining serpent coiled around his narrow waist before plunging down under the tightness of his breeches. She met his amused glance with a quizzical one of her own.

'You'll have to do better than that if you want to discover my secret,' Nathaniel whispered, cupping her face in his hands and drawing it in his direction. He lightly brushed her mouth with his own before com-pletely enclosing it within the circle of his lips.

She relaxed as his eager tongue plunged into her

supple orifice, and she slid her hands back up to rest on his shoulders. With one swift movement, Nathaniel pulled her on top of him and sank backwards on to the cushions.

Connie fell between his outstretched legs, her stomach meeting the hardness of his groin. She pulled nearer to him until her pudenda pressed enticingly against his, her throbbing, moist lips opening in readiness to receive him. She lowered her head to his chest, the scent of sandalwood which wafted from him tantalising her nostrils when she buried her face in the dark hair there. She darted her tongue out, flicking it over the raised surface of one of his nipples, while her arms pushed under his back, drawing him even closer.

It had been so long since Connie had found satisfaction with anything other than her own fingers, that just this man's proximity brought orgasm baying at the edge of her consciousness.

'I want you,' she intoned, raising her head until her lips were mere inches away from his. She puckered them up, yearning to have his mouth conquering hers again.

Nathaniel ignored her gesture and, reaching between the two of them, dug his fingers into the rigid supports of her bodice, easing out her breasts until they rested, exposed, on his chest. He cupped them, pinching their knotty tips between thumb forefinger.

Connie, unable to control the exhilaration which raced through her veins as a consequence of his ministrations, dragged herself up into a sitting position, her secret wetness coating the tautness of his stomach. She gathered up her skirts and, leaning forward, rested her chin against his shoulder.

'Frig me, Nathaniel,' she whispered, nibbling his earlobe. 'Make me come with your fingers. I can't wait any longer. I'll do anything you want afterwards. Just make me come now.'

He chuckled, his body rocking with the strain. 'You English girls certainly are the hearty ones. It would be an honour, my lady.' He slid his hands away from her

115

breasts to creep between her legs. The moment his middle finger penetrated her engorged sex, his knuckles pressing into the mound which surrounded her clitoris, Connie straightened her back and, digging her heels into the soft upholstery, bore down on his hand, urging Nathaniel to find that hidden place within her, the one she instinctively knew would drive her wild.

'Oh!' she gasped when he located it and, pressing the pad of his fingertip into the sensitive membrane there, covered its surface with small figures of eight.

Connie placed her palms on his chest and, thrusting her buttocks high into the air, squeezed her pelvic muscles in time with his finger, her pendulous breasts swaying as her movements took on a frantic rhythm. She fell back on to her haunches, screwing her bottom into Nathaniel's stomach as orgasm exploded within her, wrenching a cry from her pursed lips.

She shuddered, her excited quim still fibrillating when Nathaniel gently withdrew his hand and lay back against the cushions, his strained breath coming between clenched teeth.

She wiped the stinging perspiration out of her eyes, noticing the dull sheen which also covered his olive features, and sank against the back of the settee. She was hot and, unable to bear the smothering closeness of her gown and its undergarments a moment longer, started to unlace it.

When she'd successfully released herself from the constriction of her stays, Connie sensed his attention on her and glanced in his direction. Her heart skipped a beat when she observed him get to his feet and, tossing aside his damp shirt, undo the drawstrings of his breeches.

'Now that the appetiser is out of the way, would you like to sample the main course, my lady?' he asked with a cheeky smile.

Amelia noticed a dull light shining through the trees ahead of her and prayed that it wouldn't be another

116

disappointment. She'd been riding non-stop for the past eight hours and was badly in need of refreshment and somewhere to rest her aching limbs.

For the first few miles she'd ridden as hard as she could, pushing her horse to its limits, making certain that she was a safe distance away from Beechwood House before beginning to relax and taking on a more steady, sensible pace.

She'd had plenty of time to think things over while she passed along the dark, dank path towards London. Prominent among her concerns were her meagre finances. As it stood, she had barely enough money to cover the price of a night's lodging, let alone anything more permanent once she arrived in London. She'd realised with a sinking heart that, once there, she had no alternative but to avail herself of her cousin's charity, no matter how much her pride protested. There was no way she was going to return and face Lucas's wrath. On that score she was resolute.

Though she'd experienced much enjoyment in her short marriage, been taken to levels of sensation she'd never believed possible, the price Lucas commanded for such pleasure, namely, total and utter obedience to him, was simply too much for Amelia to pay – the scene with Rafe proving that fact beyond doubt.

Amelia dismounted and, leading the horse behind her, approached the posting inn. The sound of boisterous laughter and song which drifted out through its open windows sent a chill down her spine while she secured the horse. It wasn't difficult to imagine what type of reception she would receive among its occupants, but enter she must.

The main bar was packed with men, some reclining on benches, others simply leaning against the walls, every one, however, united in one activity, drinking. Amelia swallowed hard and, ignoring this bacchanalian scene, pushed her way to the counter where a fat, balding man stood wiping a tankard with a strip of cloth.

She felt his eyes flicker over her and rest on her bulging cleavage as she leant forward to address him.

'Have you a room, sir?' she shouted, trying to make herself heard above the noise. A man staggered past her, his fetid breath brushing her neck as he collapsed to the floor beside her.

The barkeeper smiled and, putting down the tankard, leant his arms on the counter.

'I might have, miss, but I don't think it's for the likes of, you.'

Amelia stiffened. 'I don't care what it's like. I have to get some sleep. Please may I see it?'

The man shrugged and motioned to one of the serving-girls. 'This here lady wants the room. Show her it will you, Nell?'

The woman, not much older than Amelia, her fine, blond hair loosely tucked under a cap, moved towards a nearby door and gestured for Amelia to follow, picking up a candle on the way. They passed down a narrow hallway and stopped outside one of the doors at the end.

'Are ye sure about this, miss?' Nell sniffed, fingering the fine fabric of Amelia's gown. 'We don't usually get the likes of you here.'

'I'm heading for London and I need to get some rest before continuing tomorrow. My horse –'

'Your best bet would be to take the coach, miss. It's quicker and more – comfortable. It leaves here at eight tomorrow morning.'

Amelia smiled, despite her somersaulting heart, knowing that she wouldn't be able to afford such a luxury.

Nell opened the door and stepped inside, arcing candlelight over the room's shabby contents: the tea-chest which served as a dressing table, a broken looking glass propped up on its surface alongside a chipped washbowl and jug; the rail nailed to the wall where Amelia supposed she was to hang her dress.

They were right: it certainly wasn't like anything she was used to, but then, she hadn't come for comfort.

She took the candle from the girl, moved over to the

bed which was little more than a pallet pushed against the wall, and prodded it with her foot.

'This will do fine,' she yawned, wiping her moist eyes. 'How much is it?'

'No need to worry about that now, miss. I'll get one of the lads to stable your horse or it might not be here tomorrow. You just get some rest and I'll bring you something to drink in the morning.' Nell left, only to return a moment later. 'Oh and, miss, if I were you, I'd lock the door. Our customers can get a little frisky at this time of night.'

Amelia nodded, pushing the bolt firmly home and, without even bothering to take off her dress, flopped on to the coarse, straw mattress.

Exactly two hours later she was awoken by the sound of a dull knocking followed by the drone of raised voices. At first, Amelia had no idea where the noise was coming from and, sitting up, rubbed her eyes, rather annoyed by this disturbance. But then, as her senses returned to her, she realised that the sound emanated from the other side of her door.

Dragging herself off the pallet, she trudged over and opened it, ready to politely ask whoever it was to quieten down so that she could resume her slumber undisturbed. However, what she discovered made the request die on her lips.

Nell was pinned against the opposite wall by a rough, unshaven man, one of his hands clasping her by the throat, the other tearing at her bodice. Amelia heard the sound of desperation in her voice when she asked him to stop, but he took no notice and carried on loosening her dress.

Though longing for sleep, Amelia knew that she couldn't just shut the door on the incident and Nell's apparent distress. She had to try to help the serving-girl out, even if they'd only had the briefest of meetings just a few hours before.

'How about a kiss, darling?' the man mumbled, pressing even closer to Nell.

'I think you should leave the young lady alone, don't you?' she managed in a forceful voice, despite the fact that inside she was suddenly shaking like a leaf. 'She obviously doesn't want what you are offering!'

The man angrily let go of Nell and turned towards her, his eyes widening in surprise. Taking a nearby taper off the wall, he leant closer, his eyes raking over her dishevelled appearance.

'And who might you be, then?'

Amelia straightened up as his alcohol-laced breath brushed her face. 'Oh, just a friend.'

'Well, friend,' he leered, 'how do you intend to stop me?' He licked his thick lips. 'Or are you offering yourself in exchange?'

'Do not flatter yourself,' Amelia said haughtily. 'I'm too good for the likes of you, and so is Nell here. Now, are you going to release her or not?'

'And what are you going to do if I don't?' The man made a grab for Amelia then, his free arm stealing around her waist. Amelia tried to draw away but she stumbled and fell backwards on to the hard, oak floor, pulling him with her. His heavy body landed on hers, crushing the breath out of her. She lay there paralysed, unable to do anything to prevent one of his hands burrowing under her skirts, seeking out her secret place, his wet lips brushing the delicate skin of her neck.

Amelia struggled for breath, aware of a fumbling, the sound of crockery scraping against crockery behind her, and then blessed release when the man suddenly groaned and slumped against her, his unwanted invasion of her privacy abruptly stopped in its tracks.

Suddenly regaining her strength, she frantically pushed against his weighty body and, after what seemed an eternity, finally managed to roll him off her and sit up.

Trembling, her extremities consumed by pins and needles, Amelia blinked and looked up into the relieved face of Nell, a cracked water-jug balancing precariously in her hands while she hurriedly stubbed out the fallen taper with her foot.

Chapter Ten

Nathaniel stood naked before Connie with hands on hips. She blinked and ran her eyes over his compact body, before resting her gaze on his groin. His penis, surprisingly long and full girthed, rose proudly out of its thick nest of ebony hair, its muddy, engorged tip splayed to reveal the equally dark glans. Something glinted in the soft light and, narrowing her eyes, Connie noticed with a gasp, that the chain she'd seen earlier swept down from his hips to tightly circle the base of his shaft.

'Isn't that painful?' she mouthed, running her tongue over her lips as she leant towards him.

He smiled and, chuckling, held out his hand. 'Not at all, I find it – stimulating. So will you, I hope.'

Connie let him pull her to her feet and into his arms. Her bared breasts pushed pleasantly against his chest, while his fingers worked on the ties of her petticoats. Releasing them, they dropped into a heap around her ankles.

Nathaniel stepped back and looked her over. 'Mighty fine indeed,' he exclaimed clasping his chin. Connie beamed and reached out to wrap her arms around his neck, but he shook his head and, grabbing her wrist, pulled her over to the fireplace. Pushing her back against the cold marble, he stooped and pressed his mouth to her abdomen.

Connie shivered as his lips kissed their way down, over the subtle roundness of her stomach, and then met with the honey reaches of her pudenda. She felt his tongue probing, plunging in between the thick crease of flesh surrounding her clitoris and, finding that sensitive bud, enclosing it with his mouth.

Nathanial found her buttocks, stroking them while he pulled her nearer, burying his face in her groin. She squeezed her legs together, her sex oozing wetness, painting her vaginal lips with luscious liquid, and placed her hands on the back of his head, pulling his mouth closer. He sucked her pleasure-bud free of its protective hood of flesh and drew its minute hardness between his teeth, nibbling it softly.

Suddenly dropping on to his knees, Nathanial moved his hands to the back of her thighs and, digging his fingernails lightly into the pliant flesh there, spread them, arcing her crotch upwards to meet his greedy mouth.

Waves of pleasure radiated out from between Connie's legs, wrapping her in an exhilarating blanket of excitement, as he explored her dripping lips with his tongue. She sensed another orgasm building, rising upwards from the pit of her stomach, and dragged her hands up to her breasts, her fingers pinching and kneading their erect tips in an effort to heighten her stimulation.

Nathaniel drew away from her then to crouch a couple of feet away, his braided hair partially covering his handsome countenance as he stared up at her, grinning.

'Please –' Connie began breathlessly, only for the words to die in her throat as she watched him effortlessly dip into a backward roll and come to rest on his hands and knees near the settee. Panting, he motioned for her to join him and, without thinking twice, Connie ducked down on to all fours and crawled towards him, licking her smooth lips in the process.

Nathaniel grasped her waist and, turning her around,

pushed his erect penis into the pouting crease of flesh above the tops of her thighs. Connie ground her buttocks into the hardness of his legs as he began to push his cock back and forth within the sheath of her swollen, lubricious lips, its tight tip nudging her quivering clitoris. His hands went immediately to her breasts, squeezing them in time with his movements, while he traced the line of her spine with his mouth.

Connie raised her head, hoarse sounds coming from her mouth. How she wanted to have him inside her, possessing her once and for all.

'Nathaniel,' she gasped, straining to see him over her shoulder. 'Take me now. I can't bear much more of this!'

Much to her irritation, he released her and, in doing so, pulled his prick away from her legs.

'If you want that, then you must work for it, my lady.'

Connie raised her eyebrows and swivelled around to face him. Nathaniel stood behind her, his fingers tugging at the chain which circled his penis. Before she had a chance to say anything, he raised his hands above his head, and in one fluid movement bent backwards until his palms rested flat against the floor and his back was arched high above his shoulders. His hair fell in a sable shower which brushed the carpet, which his cock, straining against its silver restraint, curved vertically upwards from his groin.

She crept towards him still on all fours. Her fingers made contact with his ankles before sweeping up over the gentle swell of his calves to the tautness of his thighs, finally resting on the rounded orbs of his buttocks. Connie pushed her body between his legs and stretched upwards, her mouth seeking the tip of his penis. Her lips surrounded it, drawing his knob into her moist orifice, her tongue delving under the tight rim of his foreskin and covering the surface of his glans with tiny, feather-like strokes. She sucked his cock deep into her mouth, sampling, tasting the spicy flavour of his masculinity, while she ran her tongue up and down his shaft.

Sensing his body stiffen with approaching orgasm, she

raised her head and got to her feet and, using his hips for leverage, clambered up to sit astride his abdomen. Nathaniel retained his position under this added weight – if anything, he arched his back further to create a more level surface for her to rest on.

Connie lifted her buttocks slightly and, clenching her teeth, sank on to his rock hard member. It slipped easily into her, parting her inner membranes, stretching, filling her until the metallic presence of the silver chain met with the slick opening of her love channel.

'Oh, sweet Jesus,' Nathaniel murmured, his hair swaying, as if caught by the faintest of breezes as she squeezed him internally. 'Rest your feet on the floor, my lady.' Connie did as she was told, the soles of her feet pressing into the softness of the carpet while she leant back and, tossing aside her golden hair, clutched his waist.

With a hoarse grunt, Nathaniel arched his back still further, until he was balancing on the very tips of his fingers and toes and, tensing his legs, began to bob up and down, his pelvis rocking back and forth between Connie's cleaving thighs.

She flung her head back, her eyes focusing on the ceiling as his surging prick pressed at the entrance of her womb time and time again, causing the most exquisite burning to ignite in her groin and pepper her already damp flesh with wave after wave of delightful heat.

Connie let go of his waist and, clutching one of her breasts, dragged it to her mouth, her tongue flicking over the nipple, while her other hand quickly found the hard nub of her clitoris, her fingers pinching it in time with Nathaniel's frantic movements.

The power in his thrusts propelled her higher and higher into the air, her bottom bouncing off his stomach with every stroke. Connie wrapped her legs around him to stop herself sliding off and bore down on his plundering cock, feeling his clammy balls pressing into the bloated flesh of her labia. She shivered. If she could have taken them into her greedy orifice as well as his cock, she would have, so great was her own crescendoing need.

Connie dug her nails into his stomach as climax ripped through her, making her body jerk against his fluttering hips, forcing a gasp through her pursed lips.

In those last, frenetic moments, Nathaniel was unable to maintain his position, and together they crashed to the floor. Without even pausing to catch his breath, he grabbed Connie's shoulders, flipped her on to her back and drove his hips against her in one, last violent movement before he too reached culmination.

Connie sensed his cock shudder inside her, propelling his burning seed high into her vagina. She stroked his silky hair and kissed his moist cheek, lapping up the salty essence of his labour as he collapsed on to her, gasping. No one, not even Lucas, had made her feel this good and she wondered briefly if it was possible for her to experience anything better than what she had just had.

Amelia lowered her cup and, after savouring the bitter-sweet taste of chocolate, smiled at the girl opposite.

Though the events of the previous night had been disturbing to say the least, Amelia had managed to get a good amount of sleep after all and was feeling refreshed for the first time in a long while.

'I can't thank you enough, for helping me out,' Nell enthused.

'From what I remember, it was you who finally put a stop to that awful man's unwanted advances. I suspect he'll have a rather large headache this morning to show for his efforts.'

'And so he deserves it to.'

'Tell me, is he, or should I say, was he your lover?'

Nell laughed, finishing her drink. 'Hell no, he was just chancing his luck, like they all do when they've had a few. I can usually handle them, but last night he got the better of me. Thank God you came along when you did.'

'Yes indeed.' Amelia shuddered as she considered

125

what it would have been like to have made love with him. 'That would certainly not be a welcome fuck.'

'Oh, ma'am, you are funny,' Nell gushed, suddenly laughing.

'Oh? How so?' Amelia asked, raising her eyebrows, not understanding her companion's sudden mirth.

'Why, to hear you speak so, anyone would think you were no better than me. Certainly not a lady!'

'Don't be ridiculous, Nell. I'm no better than you, or anyone else for that matter.'

'Whatever you say,' Nell replied, obviously not believing her. 'You still haven't told me how you come to know such words.'

'That's simple. I learnt them from my husband. He was a master of the obscene and took every opportunity to remind me of the fact.'

'And now you are running away from him?'

'Is it that obvious?'

'What do you think? We don't often get fashionable ladies in here, I can assure you. Especially unaccompanied ones who are only half dressed.'

Amelia smoothed down her unstructured skirts. 'It made it easier to ride you see –'

'There's no need to explain. You obviously have your own reasons for what you are doing, but what I don't understand is why you chose to run away when you obviously had everything. Seems such a shame.'

'That, Nell, is a very long story, but let me say that my husband cared very little for my feelings. He was arrogant enough to believe that he could simply impose his will on me and I'm afraid I wasn't about to put up with that.'

'Is that all? I certainly would have put up with it for the advantages you have.'

Amelia raised her eyebrows. 'Would you indeed? I doubt that even you could tolerate what I've had to –'

'Oh no, ma'am. Take it from me. What you are talking about is not unusual. Why, I'd wager that every married woman suffers it from time to time. Call it our lot, if you like.'

'You are married?' Amelia asked in surprise, thinking for some reason that being a servant-girl she would be single.

'Why yes, to Ted. He likes to assert himself now and again, and most of the time it's quite fun –' she winked '– if you know what I mean.'

Amelia swallowed hard, incredulous that anyone would enjoy the mental punishment Lucas had been so eager to serve her.

'But when he does get out of hand, I simply withdraw his conjugal rights for a few days and that usually softens him up a bit!'

The unexpected sound of driving rain bombarding the roof above suddenly made Amelia realise the urgency of her journey and, gulping down the last of her drink, she glanced at the clock across the room. Not yet 7.30.

She dearly wished she could afford the luxury of taking the coach for, although what she was hearing was probably only a warm summer shower, the last thing she wanted was to arrive at Connie's looking a sopping mess.

She sighed and, shaking her head, started to get up.

'Bit early for the coach, miss,' Nell said, remaining seated. 'It don't leave for another half an hour or so.'

'How much did you say the room was?' Amelia tossed the required payment for her bed and breakfast on to the table and thoughtfully fingered the remaining penny she held in her hand, knowing that it couldn't possibly be enough to book a seat.

'A shilling, ma'am.'

She flinched. 'Then you had better have my horse made ready. I'm afraid I shall have to ride the rest of the way to London.'

Nell suddenly leant across the table and took her hand. 'Look, if you really haven't got the money, there is another way in which you can secure a place.'

127

A shiver ran through Amelia and she stared sharply at the serving-girl. 'How?'

Nell grinned and jumped up. 'I'll just get Ted. I'm certain he'll be able to help you out, especially after what you did for me last night.'

Amelia watched her skirt the tables, her feet kicking up dust from the straw-covered floor as she disappeared through a door behind the counter. A couple of minutes later the bartender appeared, closely followed by Nell.

'Wifey here tells me that you want to travel on the coach,' he said, wiping his hands on the greasy cloth which hung from the waistband of his breeches.

'Yes, but I haven't the money. Perhaps I can help out here for a day or two, though I really should be leaving –'

'No need, miss. The answer's a lot simpler than that. Let me have that fine animal of yours and I'll buy you a ticket for this morning's run.'

A relieved chuckle rose in Amelia's throat at his offer and she rose to her feet. 'Why, yes. Of course you may have him. He is yours, with my pleasure. How can I thank you for your kindness, sir, or you, Nell?'

'It's no kindness on his part, miss,' Nell chirped. 'He's been on the look out for a horse for some time. You've just saved him a trip to Mainfield Market next week.'

'I don't think this is such a good idea,' Fran commented, clambering out of the carriage, the voluminous skirts of her new dress catching in the door. 'I mean, what is her ladyship going to think when she sees me?'

Lucas shrugged and, taking her arm, led her up the steps of Beechwood House. 'I care not what she thinks. She's just going to have to accept my every whim without question, which includes you, my sweet.' He paused on the threshold of the hall to chuck her under the chin, remembering as he did so, just how they had amused themselves over the past few days. He had to give it to Fran – if nothing else, she certainly knew how to keep a gentleman interested, something which he hoped his wife had learnt by now.

'Carterall, where are you, you old dog?' he bellowed, letting go of Fran and striding into the drawing room in search of his friend. He found him standing with his back to the door gazing out of the window.

'Where's Amelia? I had hoped she'd be here to greet me like an obedient wife should. I pray you weren't too harsh with her. I should hate to think that you had rendered her unusable, for I have plans –' He stopped short, his smile fading when Lord Carterall turned around and faced him, a pained look scarring his countenance. 'What is it? My God, you haven't –' Lucas rushed forward, grabbing his friend's arm, shaking him until Lord Carterall was forced to pull himself away.

'No, Lucas, nothing as tragic as that, though, I am loathe to tell you what has indeed happened. Perhaps you'd better sit down.'

'I will not, damn it! Just tell me what's happened.'

Lord Carterall sighed and shook his head. 'She's gone, Lucas. Run away.'

'How?' he demanded with controlled anger.

'The night you left her in my company, she managed to escape the confines of her room, and took a horse –'

'Enough, I've heard enough!' Lucas ran a hand through his untied hair, while moving back towards the door. 'I cannot believe you could have been so lax, my friend, but I suppose this is partly my fault for I did not warn you about my wife's resourcefulness. I should have known she'd do something like this once my back was turned.'

'Well, what are you going to do? I have deliberately not made any enquiries on your behalf for I did not think you'd want too many knowing about this embarrassment.'

'A wise move and I thank you for your discretion, but I'm afraid the only way to find out where that little chit has gone is to make a direct approach, beginning with her relatives.'

* * *

The gentle rocking of the carriage, combined with the softness of the cushion propped up behind her head, lulled Amelia into a kind of half-hearted slumber. She drifted in and out of consciousness, her eyelids briefly snapping open when the sound of conversation from the other occupants cut through her dreams.

Shifting position, she snuggled her shoulder into the cushion in an effort to gain a few more minutes' respite before they entered London proper. The first fingers of sleep crept over her, bringing waves of comforting numbness to her bruised mind, while at the same time introducing relaxation to her stiff joints.

She was suddenly transported to a distant country, a place where summer never ended and the people who worked on the land were bronzed like the highly polished statues she'd seen at Beechwood House.

She reclined on a chaise longue in the middle of a huge expanse of garden, its edges bordered by bougainvillaea, while her nostrils were filled with the tangy scents of lemon and lime which drifted across from the surrounding orchards.

She stretched, enjoying the warmth of the sun's rays on her lightly clad body, its strength causing perspiration to prick the smooth skin of her waist and trickle down into the crease between her legs.

A cool breeze, heavy with the smell of the sea, unexpectedly washed over her, causing a shiver to race down her spine and forcing her to open her eyes and stare across the garden. A figure was sauntering towards her carrying a basket of flowers.

The young man, naked to the waist, his golden chest glistening under a thin film of sweat, moved with the stealth of a panther, the subtle movement of his thighs ruching up the cloth at his groin until Amelia was able to make out the sharp outlines of his testicles.

He placed the basket at the base of the chaise longue and, drawing out a scarlet rose, trailed it over the curves of her calves and across her thighs to rest in the centre of her gauze-covered pudenda.

Amelia looked up smiling and, noticing the intensity of his amber eyes and his unblemished complexion, grabbed his wrists and pulled him down on top of her, his hardness insinuating itself between her legs. She wrapped her arms around his waist, her fingers sweeping up over the broad expanse of his shoulders. Arching her back, she pressed her wet, dilated sex into the pliant surface of the chaise longue, while entwining her legs in his.

The man lowered his head to her breasts, their coral tips supporting the filmy fabric as Amelia pushed her chest up to meet his hovering lips. He suddenly raised his head and stared down at her chuckling.

Amelia shuddered as his youthful features swiftly changed to the rugged, older ones of Lucas, his mouth twisted into a sardonic smile.

She started awake, a hand flying to her neck as she gasped for breath.

'Are you all right, miss?' a voice enquired from the seat opposite.

Amelia glanced at the elderly gentleman and, biting her lip, nodded. This was the second time Lucas had invaded her dreams. Was no area of her life free from her husband's tyrannical influence? Was this the price she would have to pay for denying her marriage vows?

Amelia shook her head and turned her attention to the less frightening prospect of London's suburbs. Whatever the case, she was determined that, if she could help it, she wasn't going to let his disturbing memory ruin what could be her only chance of happiness. As far as she was concerned, she was on her own now and the only person she should be worrying about was herself.

'I take it that you found Nathaniel satisfactory, my dear,' Clarissa asked, her hand sliding under the table to rest on Sir Mandeville's thigh.

Connie nodded and glanced out of the window. She was bitterly disappointed that he hadn't spent the night as she'd wanted, but had left, protesting another engagement across town.

'What was it about him that excited you the most, child?' Sir Mandeville stared at her, a mischievous grin playing at the corners of his mouth.

'Oh, nothing in particular, my lord,' was all she could bring herself to say. She found the thought of discussing her sexual proclivities with this man, even if he was her aunt's lover, rather disturbing.

Before he had an opportunity to question her further, the door opened and the footman entered, bearing a salver, which he offered to Clarissa. She looked at the tiny scrap of paper resting on its surface and scowled, her gaze falling on Connie.

'It seems, my dear, that you have a visitor.' She nodded in the footman's direction and waved him away. 'This should prove amusing for a few minutes at least.' She rose and ushered her guests into the adjoining drawing room.

'A visitor?' Connie questioned, sinking on to the settee beside her. 'Is it Mama?'

'Oh no, someone much more interesting.'

'Connie!' Amelia rushed into the room and, throwing her arms around her cousin, drew her to her feet. 'How I've longed for this moment!'

Startled, Connie didn't say anything for a minute, but savoured the sensation of Amelia's warm body pressing into hers. Her mind was racing as she considered the implications of this unexpected visit.

'What are you doing here?' she asked at length, realising afterwards that she must have sounded more shocked than pleased.

Amelia suddenly let go of her and stepped back, a blush flying to her cheeks. 'I'm sorry. I didn't mean to intrude. I thought you wouldn't mind if I came to stay for a while.'

Connie smiled and, noticing the disappointment in her cousin's eyes, took her hand. 'Of course I wouldn't, cousin. You've just taken me by surprise, that's all.' She turned to her aunt and the man. 'This is Aunt Clarissa and Sir Mandeville Draper.'

Amelia curtsied to them both and addressed the older woman. 'I know that it is an imposition, Mrs Stevens, but may I stay for a few days until I can find lodgings of my own. You see –'

'You are my brother's niece?' Clarissa asked, casting a disdainful glance over Amelia's dishevelled appearance. 'Well, if this is the case, you must of course stay. Connie has spoken much of you and I think it will be pleasant for her to have someone nearer her own age to converse with.'

Connie shot Amelia an excited glance and squeezed her hand. 'Think of the fun we will have discovering the delights this area has to offer. I simply cannot wait!' She started to pull Amelia towards the door.

'Just a moment, Connie dear. There is one more thing I wish to say to Lady Beechwood.'

Amelia stopped dead, jerking Connie back against her. 'You know my name?'

'As I said, my niece has told me all about you and this is one of the reasons why I feel it necessary to tell you that, although you will be residing in my household, do not imagine that it will afford you any special protection. I won't pry into the reasons behind your coming here alone – that is your business – but if your husband were ever to discover that this is where you are residing, I won't stand in the way of any petition he may make concerning your person. I do not feel that it is my place to come between man and wife. Do I make myself clear?'

Amelia nodded slowly. 'Perfectly, my lady. I thank you for accepting me into your house. I give you my word that if such a situation arises, I will not cause you any dishonour.'

Clarissa inclined her head. 'Good, we understand each other. Now, may I suggest that you bathe and I'll arrange for my dressmaker to call on you tomorrow. In the meantime, perhaps you can borrow one of Connie's dresses.'

'Of course she can,' Connie breathed, opening the door. 'It won't be the first time, will it, Amelia?'

Chapter Eleven

*T*he marquess entered the morning room unannounced and swept into a deep bow before sinking into the seat beside Lady Boughby. She swiftly opened her fan in an effort to conceal her shock at his unexpected arrival.

'I am afraid, my lord, that John is not at home but in London on one of his business trips. I have yet to discover what it is that commands so much of his attention there,' she sighed, 'but at least it affords me some peace from his tiresome company.'

'It is probably business of the female kind,' Lucas replied sarcastically. 'You shouldn't allow him such foibles my dear. It could damage his reputation as the loyal husband.'

Margaret snapped the fan closed with a flick of her hand. 'What is it that you want, my lord? Surely it's not simply to insult me.' She tried to rise but a firm grip on her arm held her where she was. She shuddered but managed to keep her composure. 'Why haven't you brought Amelia with you today, anyway? I should have thought she'd enjoy some time in company other than yours.'

The marquess leant towards her, his tepid breath painting the supple skin of her cheek. 'Why do you continue this feud after so many years have passed? Can you honestly find no forgiveness in your heart for me?'

'What? When you ruined my life?'

Lucas looked around at the ornate splendour of their surroundings and tutted. 'I certainly would not call this ruin.'

'Don't toy with me, Lucas. You know very well what I mean. When we met I was only fifteen years old and knew nothing of the world. You took advantage of that fact and, in one fell swoop, destroyed every chance I had of securing the marriage and position I deserved. Though I cannot deny that John has been an excellent husband and father, I still can't help wondering what my life would have been had you not stolen my honour.'

The marquess guffawed and shook his head. 'I hardly think that is an accurate description of our – liaison. Perhaps I may have been a victim of my own youthful thoughtlessness but, if my memory serves me correctly, you weren't exactly a passive partner in the matter. Why didn't you stop me pursuing you after that first time if my advances offended you so much?'

'Please!' Margaret wrenched her arm from his grasp and struggled to her feet. She strode to the french windows and, pushing them open, stared out across the gardens. A cool breeze caressed her flaming chest, making her shiver. 'I cannot be blamed for a moment's whim. How was I to know that even at seventeen you were a practised libertine? I was a fool to believe your lies then, and I certainly won't now.'

'You misjudge me, Margaret. I'm a changed man –'

'Oh really? If that is the case, why did you see fit to seduce Connie? Why, it was a blessing in disguise that Amelia came to live with us. At least marriage to her took you away from my home and my daughter. No, the fact still remains that you are a ruthless cad who doesn't care who he hurts in the pursuit of pleasure. Thank God Amelia saw you for what you are and ran away before it was too late.'

'What?' The marquess jumped up and, rounding the

135

settee, confronted her, his handsome features twisted into a scowl.

'How is it that you know this? Only Carterall is aware of it, unless of course, your dear niece has written to you.' He placed his hands on her shoulders, delighting in the shiver which wracked her body when he turned her round and drew her against him. 'Oh, my dear Margaret, I do believe you have let the secret slip. How unfortunate for you. There's no point in denying it any longer. Now, where is she?'

Margaret looked into the chestnut depths of his eyes and swallowed hard. Despite her contempt for him, she couldn't deny that his proximity still excited her. She ran her fingers down the firmness of his back, sensing the tightness of muscle under the light fabric of his frockcoat, and gasped, this simple action bringing back potent memories of that time long ago.

Suddenly remembering herself, she pulled away and, turning her back to him, resumed her position at the french windows. 'You are correct. I am aware of Amelia's whereabouts but, no matter what methods you employ, you will not extract that information from me. I have no desire to help you destroy yet another young woman's life.'

'Is that so?' the marquess asked, drawing so close behind her, Margaret could feel his breath teasing the hairs on the back of her neck. 'Well, let's just see how strong your resolve is, shall we?' Without hesitation, he lifted her skirts until he was able to rest the heavy silk on the swell of her panniers and her bottom was bare before him.

'Please, Lucas, have you no respect for me?' Margaret cried, reaching out to the window frame for support when she felt the cool air brushing the swell of her rump.

The marquess moved even closer and rested his chin on her shoulder, his hands seeking out the ties of her stomacher. 'Oh, doubt me not when I tell you that I have the greatest respect for you, my dear. It's just that I believe John has not been performing his husbandly duties correctly these past eighteen years.'

'And you mean to rectify that?' she demanded between clenched teeth, desperately struggling for control as she sensed his fingers slipping inside her bodice. 'I command you to unhand me this instant. You forget that I am your friend's wife and not one of your strumpets!'

Margaret stamped her foot on the floor but he took no notice. Instead, he pinched her nipples between thumb and finger until they grew hard within his grasp and then dragged her backwards against him, her exposed bottom wedged against his crotch. With his hands still embedded in her cleavage he began to rotate his hips, pressing his hardness into the pliant flesh of her buttocks while, at the same time, forcing a thigh between her legs.

Margaret bent forward, pressing her cheek against the wall when she felt his knee push upwards and ram into her dilated, wet valley. Tears formed in her eyes and she sniffed hard as she realised that, once again, he had gained the measure of her. She'd forgotten how persuasive he could be, but this aggressive reminder of his presence swiftly brought back the delicious memories of what she had once experienced with him.

Lucas ran his tongue up her neck and nibbled her earlobe while pushing his knee harder and harder against her silky folds.

'Just as I thought,' he whispered, his hands caressing her breasts in slow, circular movements. 'You want me as much now as you did then. The question is, what are you prepared to do for your pleasure?'

'Anything,' Margaret sobbed into the panelling, finally giving in to the yearning which had been brewing in the pit of her stomach ever since Lucas had touched her. 'Anything. Just do to me what you used to do. John could never do it like you . . .'

With a triumphant cry, the marquess withdrew one knee in order to undo the flap of his breeches. He moved closer to Margaret and, parting her flushed, turgid lips, rammed his prick into her dripping orifice.

Margaret stiffened as he filled every inch of her, forcing her tightness to accommodate him. She reared up and, supported by his arm which encircled her slender waist, pressed her legs against his, her buttocks compressing his balls as she bore down hard on his cock, longing for deeper penetration.

Lucas began to thrust upward, his powerful movements forcing her to lean backward against his chest while her hands clutched at his neck for support. His fingers worked their way down from her waist to the front of her skirt, dragging it up far enough to give him access to her pert pleasure-node. As he increased the tempo of his strokes, he took her clitoris between his fingers and massaged it in time with his thrusts.

Margaret gasped and, swallowing hard, closed her eyes. So practised, so precise, the marquess knew exactly what to do in order to bring her swiftly to culmination. Why, already she could feel the heady fire rising from her groin to engulf her abdomen and she started to lift herself up and down on her toes, matching his rhythm exactly. She shivered, her chin falling forward on to her chest, and prepared herself for the exquisite release that was eighteen years in coming.

Lucas stopped what he was doing and attempted to pull away.

'Oh no, don't stop now! I'm so close, so close to spending, I will surely go mad if you do not release me now!' Margaret knew she sounded desperate but she didn't care, she would have given the world there and then just to make him continue. Even when she realised what his game was, what he would ask next, she cared for nothing other than her own satisfaction, something John had never been able to give her during their marriage.

'Well?' he questioned, his breath escaping him in short, sharp bursts. 'I believe you have some information for me?'

'Damn you, Lucas! She's in Covent Garden with Connie – they are staying with John's sister, Clarissa. Now for pity's sake make me come before I lose my mind.'

'Certainly, my dear, I'm only too happy to oblige.' With a masterful laugh, the marquess tightened his grip on her and resumed plundering her quim.

Margaret flexed her pelvic muscles around his questing cock, her hips rocking faster and faster, urging orgasm to fill the empty void which had existed for so long within her. When it finally did, its explosion sending wave after wave of shudders throughout her, shaking her very soul with its potency, she slumped forward, pushing her quivering sex high against Lucas's abdomen. This action forced him to clasp her hips and push her yearning orifice back down on to his own quaking member as he too reached culmination with a loud cry of satisfaction.

'So glad to be of service, my lady,' Lucas said coolly a few minutes later as he adjusted his cravat in a nearby mirror. 'Do not hesitate to send word if you are ever in need of my company again. I shall be only too glad to indulge your desires. Good day.'

Margaret watched him go and then, after straightening her dishevelled hair, went straight to the drinks tray, an uncharacteristic bounce to her step.

'Where are we going? Mrs Stevens said I was to bathe –'

'Why, to the Hummums, of course.' Connie spoke briefly to her maid and, handing Amelia a mask, headed for the front door. Amelia didn't follow but crossed her arms in front of her chest and tapped her foot on the floor.

'I'm not going anywhere until you tell me what this "Hummums" is and why we have to wear masks to visit it.'

Connie sighed and turned back. 'Do not tell me that you have lost your sense of adventure. Has marriage to Lucas affected you that much?'

'I shall tell you all about that later, but right now I want to know what is going on.'

Connie took the mask from Amelia's fingers and offered to help her on with it. 'These are simply a precaution so that we aren't recognised as we traverse the square and, if you must know, the Hummums are the local baths. I thought it would be much more fun if we bathed there. I've heard so much about it from my maid –'

'Oh, Connie, are you sure about this? I should hate to get off on the wrong foot with Mrs Stevens so soon after arriving.'

Connie secured the ribbons on Amelia's mask and then did the same with her own. 'Nonsense. You will do no such thing. Since I have been here, she has allowed me the utmost freedom, which I am certain she will afford you too. Why, it wouldn't surprise me if she didn't frequent the baths herself! Now come on, after all that time spent travelling I expect you are longing for a wash. Julie will follow later with suitable attire for you.'

Amelia thought about protesting but she had to admit that she was beginning to feel as intrigued about the Hummums as her cousin was, and she certainly couldn't deny that she could do with a bath.

'All right. But if I don't like the look of the place, I shan't stay.'

Sultry, tepid air filled Amelia's lungs the moment they entered the public baths, forcing her to cough and catch her breath as she took in the startling scene in front of her.

Marble pillars rose from each corner of the room, supporting a high domed ceiling emblazoned with gilded cherubs and other seraphic beings. Sunlight streamed down from the stained glass windows contained there, casting a rainbow of colours through the mist which hovered above the gently undulating bathing water of the large rectangular pool which dominated the room.

Amelia approached it warily, careful not to slip on the

moist tiles underfoot, and bent to dip a finger into the water.

'It's agreeably warm,' she remarked, returning her attention to Connie. Connie didn't answer but kept her gaze fixed across the room. Amelia followed it and was stunned to see a woman step out of her chemise and sink nude into the water. She gasped and, clutching Connie's arm, jerked her around to face her. 'I never imagined that when you said these were public baths, you meant that they were communal.'

'What of it?' Connie shrugged. 'It makes no odds to me, nor to you, I should imagine. After marriage to Lucas I'm surprised that you still exhibit such inhibitions, Amelia. If you truly want to enjoy yourself in Covent Garden, you really are going to have to relax you know.'

Amelia didn't know how to answer this stinging reproach and silently followed Connie through an archway on their right. Light from hundreds of candles reflected off the tiled walls so that she had momentarily to look away till her eyes got used to it.

When she turned back, she was greeted with the sight of six tables, three of which were occupied by reclining women, their naked flesh bronzed under the glare of the candlelight. White clothed men bent over the women, their hands, slick with oil, rubbing, kneading, caressing the pliant flesh – fingers circling nipples, smoothing hips, lubricating the delicate space between the thighs.

Amelia caught her breath as an involuntary spasm enveloped her pubic area at this potent sight of manual stimulation and she squeezed her legs together, enjoying the sensation. Something glinted, drawing her attention to the groin of one of the women. She blinked and moved closer, hardly believing what she saw.

The woman was pierced, her excited, erect clitoris standing free of its hood of flesh, its tip circled by a thin, golden ring.

'I've heard that such adornment greatly enhances one's pleasure,' Connie whispered, noticing her interest.

'Does it? Then I should like such. I wonder if it's very painful?'

'You aren't serious? Only a few moments ago you were expressing concern at sharing your bath with others of our sex and now you wish to be pierced?' She shook her head. 'You certainly are a mystery, cousin.'

'Not at all. Perhaps I am a bit wary of flaunting myself in front of strangers, though it would not be the first time.' Amelia remembered her wedding night with a shudder. 'But this is something entirely different. If it increases one's satisfaction as you say, then I should like to try it, if only I had the money . . .'

'If that's all you are concerned about, then I should be happy to pay for it on your behalf.'

A shiver ran through her at Connie's words. Could it be possible? Amelia stiffened as she realised that she'd encroached upon her relative's generosity enough already. To ask this would surely be stepping beyond the bounds of politeness.

'I couldn't expect you to do that. I'm indebted to you and your aunt as it is. It would be unfair of me to take advantage of your kindness unnecessarily.'

'Nonsense. You would be doing no such thing. Besides, I should like to know if what I've heard is true for, if it is, I should like to try it myself.'

Amelia sighed and smiled. 'Very well then, you have convinced me cousin, but let us bathe first. Maybe it will give me the necessary courage!'

'About time you bloody showed up,' Paul chided, drawing Fran into his arms. 'I was about to give up on you.'

She shook her head and twisted out of his arms. 'I might as well tell you now. I ain't got the money.'

'What?' Paul frowned and tried to catch her arm but she managed to avoid his grasp, darting around the edge of the kitchen table. 'Why not? Been having too good a time to think of me, your husband?'

'Don't be silly.' Fran couldn't find the courage to meet his eyes for she knew that his accusation was true. The

142

marquess had shown her another, more sensual side of life, one which she found very easy to get used to, and one which she knew she would never experience with Paul, no matter how strong her feelings for him were.

'I may be uneducated, Fran, but I ain't stupid. I know that, if given the chance, you'd leave me for his lordship.'

'Paul . . .' She finally managed to draw up enough strength to raise her eyes to his and the pain she saw in them made her throat tighten. 'No matter what you think, I still love you. It's just that –'

'No need to explain what his lordship does for you. I see it whenever you return from visiting him. I know that I could never make you that happy.'

Fran sighed and, retracing her steps, wrapped her arms around his neck. 'You are a good man, Paul. If you hadn't rescued me from that lowly bawdy house, who knows what might have happened.' She planted a kiss on his forehead and brushed his hair out of his eyes. 'You saved me then and have always done your best to provide for me since, but we both know that as far as the bedchamber goes we are not equal. I need more than you can give and the marquess, well he –' she smiled bitterly '– anyway, you don't have to worry about him any more. He'll soon be leaving to go in search of his wife. It seems the silly bitch has flown the nest and is now residing in Covent Garden.'

'What?' Paul caught her by the shoulders. 'He ain't gone to get the money?'

Fran slowly shook her head. 'He never intended to get it. That night at the ale-house was just an act to get you off his back.'

'Right.' He let go of her then and went to the shelf above the fire.

'What you going to do, Paul? Isn't it best to leave it now? Accept that you aren't going to get the money?'

'No, it ain't.' He turned back to her, a pistol resting in his hands. 'I'm determined not to let his lordship get away with this.'

Fran touched his arm. 'Forget, it Paul. We both know

why you're doing this and I'm telling you, it ain't worth you getting hurt.'

'Hurt?' he shouted, violently pulling away from her touch. 'It ain't me who's going to get hurt. Me and Lennard are going to make sure, once and for all, that his lordship realises just who he's dealing with.'

'Perhaps I was a bit hasty in thinking I wanted to be pierced after all,' Amelia mumbled as she followed one of the white-clothed men into a cubicle. It wasn't so much the idea of being pierced which troubled her, but the fact that she had caught Connie speaking almost conspiratorially with the man beforehand. She couldn't help feeling there was something they weren't telling her about the procedure, something which would surely make her change her mind if she knew what it was.

'If you could lie on the table, miss.'

Amelia looked at the man and swallowed hard as she realised that, once she did so, there would be no going back for her.

'Don't worry.' Connie placed her hand on her cousin's shoulder. 'I'm going to be here while you have it done. In fact, it seems that I'm to play an active role in the process.'

'What?' Amelia gasped while lowering herself backwards on to the table.

'It's not as bad as it seems. If you just relax, you may even enjoy it,' the man said while raising her chemise and gently spreading her legs. The sudden burst of tepid air on Amelia's stomach made her shiver.

She closed her eyes and bit her lip in anticipation of the pain she was certain would soon follow. But, surprisingly, instead of the agony she expected, she began to feel the all-too-familiar stirring of desire as a hand slipped between her thighs. She parted them wider, welcoming the exploring fingers into her secret place.

Amelia felt secretions seep out of her as the fingers were replaced by the softness of a tongue. The inside of her thighs were the first to receive its ministrations. Soft darting movements covered the delicate skin there, leaving a thin film of saliva in its wake. Amelia began to writhe against this attention, a sudden, frantic longing surging through her groin.

The stranger spread her legs further still, the tongue edging up towards her slick vagina. In seconds, a mouth replaced the tongue and began to caress the swollen outlines of her vaginal folds: tugging, sucking at them, drawing their enlarged outlines between half-open lips, teasing excitement from her with every experienced movement.

Amelia arched her back and inched forward, enjoying the moistness of the unknown mouth on her mingling with her own wetness, the tongue licking her clitoris with long, wet movements, urging her to push her quivering orifice closer to the source of such delight.

Reaching between her legs, she grasped the questing head and pulled it against her pudenda. She squirmed as the tongue which had tantalised her externally only a few moments ago plunged deep into her this time, probing, thrusting in and out of her, searching for the orgasm which was but seconds away from bursting within her.

Amelia drew herself up in time to see the man lower what looked like a pair of pliers towards her arching groin and, at the very moment climax overtook her, causing every muscle in her body to fibrillate, she was aware of a sharp burst of pain in that most sensitive of organs. However, instead of sending her spiralling into agony, the pain mingled with the pleasure, drawing her up into a vortex of ecstasy she'd never imagined possible.

'Ah!' she cried, falling backwards on to the cold marble table, her hips pumping rhythmically in time with her racing heart. Her breath came in short gasps as her fingers tore at the lace of her chemise, seeking relief from the flush of heat which was engulfing her and pricking her skin with perspiration.

Gradually her movements decreased and her legs

dropped listlessly back on to the table. Amelia pushed her torso up and, still breathing heavily, stared down at the person who was kneeling at the base of her feet. A mixture of surprise and confusion washed over her as she gazed at the moist, smiling face of Connie.

The younger girl got to her feet and came round the table to take Amelia's hand. 'See, I told you it wouldn't be so bad, and look at it, isn't it beautiful?' Amelia tore her eyes away from her cousin's and focused them on her cherry-red clitoris. A narrow band of silver rose vertically out of its bloated, angry tip, the centre line of the ring highlighted by a hair's breadth of yellow gold. 'I've been told that it will be sore for a time,' she whispered, helping Amelia to hop off the table and hobble over to where her maid waited with an unlaced gown. 'Just imagine the fun you'll have when it heals though!'

Amelia didn't answer, her mind still numbed by the knowledge that it was Connie who had brought her to fruition, and allowed the maid to dress her in full view of the man who was busily tidying the room in readiness for the next customer.

'Connie –' she began while they donned their masks in preparation for returning to Clarissa's house across the square.

'You don't have to say anything, Amelia. I know how shocked you are. It's written all over your face.' She laughed. 'Believe it or not, I was once, but with time and experience, you too will lose your embarrassment –'

'But in front of that man? What must he have thought?'

'It was his suggestion. Why, I expect he found it rather stimulating and is relieving himself even as we speak. Don't worry about it. I was simply doing what any good friend would do, just as I did before you married.'

Amelia briefly smiled and turned away shaking. Though it was easy to use it as an excuse in front of her cousin, she knew deep in her heart that what she was

experiencing now had nothing to do with embarrassment. It was the knowledge that what Connie had done
had finally allowed her to realise the vast possibilities
open to her as far as her own satisfaction was concerned.

Chapter Twelve

*A*melia stretched and ran her fingers hesitantly over the taut skin of her stomach to the ebony line of her pudenda.

Although Connie had urged her to attend this debauch or that over the past few weeks, Amelia had refused every one of her invitations, easily recalling the intense discomfort she'd caused herself the first time she'd attempted to touch her clitoris since being pierced.

Despite her pain, restlessness had built up as a consequence of her deliberate abstinence, and it now crouched at the back of her consciousness, an irresistible reminder of her body's needs – needs which she knew had to be filled soon or she would lose her mind with frustration.

Amelia swallowed hard and continued her exploration of her secret place. She gently squeezed the bulge of her right breast with one hand as the other slipped into the soft crease of flesh surrounding her pleasure-node.

She sucked in her breath and stiffened as one of her fingernails accidentally caught the edge of the silver ring and pushed it against the already stimulated tip of her clitoris. She shuddered, twisting her body as a paroxysm of pure pleasure raced throughout her, infiltrating every fibre of her being, completely blotting out the memory of the pain.

Amelia dragged herself up into a sitting position and, gritting her teeth, took the ring between thumb and forefinger and began to rotate it back and forth within its sheath of flesh, the slightest of movements causing an intense throbbing to grow in her groin. She closed her eyes, increasing the pace of her manipulation while her mind replayed the sweet memory of the last night she and Tom had spent together.

He lay on the grass before her, his head bobbing between her outstretched thighs. Shuddering with every foray of his ebullient tongue Amelia craned forward until her lips brushed his silky mop of hair. Her hands clutched his shoulders, pulling him towards her until he hovered above her, his potent erection pressing into her abdomen.

'I want you, Tom,' she whispered, her voice sounding strangely hoarse even to her own ears. 'Don't make me wait until we marry. I want to know you now.' Tom smiled down at her and, teasing her lips with his own, gently lowered his firmly muscled torso on to hers.

Amelia shivered as she remembered the sensation of his hardness pressing at the entrance to her slick crevice before he'd cruelly dragged himself away.

Amelia moved her hand from her breast and, delighting in the goosepimples her touch left in its wake as she brushed over one of her hips, flopped backwards on to the bed in order to secure better access for her probing index finger.

Entering her own moist cavity, she began to pump the digit back and forth within its pliant walls, while at the same rotating the clitoral ring faster and faster through its sensitive enclosure.

Drawing her legs up until she was able to lock her ankles at her groin, Amelia closed her powerful internal muscles around her thrusting finger. She drew it deeper into her milky depths then allowed free rein to the orgasm building in the pit of her stomach. It rocketed throughout her, the sweet release it brought to her taut nerves making her sway back and forth on the mattress, incoherent syllables issuing from her pursed lips.

'You ought to get out more,' Clarissa chirped, sweeping into the room, 'if that is all you have to gain satisfaction.' Without giving Amelia a chance to make herself decent, she sank on to the edge of the bed and smiled at the younger woman.

Amelia coloured and hurriedly tidied her ruched-up skirts, a thin film of sweat peppering the skin above her top lip. 'I, I am ashamed that you have found me enjoying myself in such a manner. I –'

'There's no need to apologise.' Clarissa pushed a lock of hair out of Amelia's eyes. 'I quite understand. Connie explained the brave step you took at the Hummums and I applaud you for your self-control. I know I would have broken down long before now. It must have been unbearable for you, dear, to go so long without release.'

Amelia blinked and, raising her eyebrows, stared questioningly at her. 'You do? I thought –'

'That I was straightlaced?' She chuckled and patted Amelia's knee. 'Oh no, my dear, I can assure you that I am nothing of the kind, a fact which I think you will realise when you meet the guest I have invited to dinner this evening. I believe this person has the answer to your problem of accommodation, as well as a novel way of developing your burgeoning desires.'

'You think so? Well, who is it?'

Clarissa rose, laughing. 'You'll find out soon enough once you have washed and changed for dinner. Connie will be along in a moment to help you choose a suitable gown. I promise you won't be disappointed.'

Amelia was overwhelmed by anxiety when she joined Connie in the hall later on. It wasn't so much that she was worried about meeting this mysterious person but, rather, who it might be. She had been wracking her brain all evening as to why a stranger should want to help her out. The only conclusion she came to was that this 'good Samaritan' was a male friend of Clarissa's who was looking for a mistress. Amelia supposed that by introducing them, Mrs Stevens hoped to solve her need for accommodation and satisfaction in one fell swoop.

Although Clarissa obviously meant her gesture kindly, Amelia knew she could never accept such an offer, and this troubled her. The plain truth was that she didn't know how to refuse Clarissa's generosity without offending her. But refuse she must if she was to live her life the way she wanted. After the outrages she'd suffered at the hands of Lucas, she was determined she would never again submit to one man's will, be one man's property.

'That colour suits you.' Connie interrupted her thoughts, fingering the scarlet silk she wore. 'Our guest would have to be blind not to recognise the potential in your looks.'

Amelia looked up sharply, meeting her eyes.

'If my looks are so important to this guest, then my suspicions are correct.' She shivered and glanced away.

'Why, Amelia, you look positively worried,' Connie laughed. 'I can assure you that there's no need for concern. Aunt's plan is only for your benefit.'

'Is it?' Amelia snapped. 'I can see no benefit in binding myself again to a man.'

Connie took her arm and led her towards the drawing room. 'Everything will be revealed in a moment or two.'

Sensing perspiration break out above her top lip, Amelia's first impulse was to turn tail and run back to her room, but something stopped her. It was the very same sense of duty which had made her accept Lucas's proposal of marriage.

Amelia swallowed hard and forced a smile across her rigid lips. All she could do was pray that in this instance she wouldn't suffer the same sorry conclusion.

Following Connie into the drawing room, Amelia scanned the interior, searching out its occupants and was surprised to find that only Mrs Stevens and another woman were present.

'Ah, there you are. We've been wondering where you two had got to.'

'Sorry, Aunt.' Connie let go of Amelia's arm and moved towards the settee. 'Amelia had an attack of nerves. For some reason she imagined that she would be meeting a gentleman this evening!'

Amelia coloured as the two women approached her.

'What's all this?' Clarissa asked, a concerned expression creasing her brow. 'You have nothing to fear from this meeting. No one is going to make you do anything you don't want to.'

'Of course,' Amelia breathed in relief. 'I was just being silly. Please forgive me.'

'There's nothing to forgive,' said Clarissa. 'Now, allow me to introduce a very old acquaintance of mine, Mrs Featherstone.'

Amelia dropped into a curtsy before both women and then addressed the stranger. 'I believe that you can help me, ma'am.'

Running her eyes over her features, she couldn't help but feel in awe of the woman's elegance. A good inch taller than herself, Mrs Featherstone was slim of waist and sported a surprisingly firm bosom for a woman in the latter years of her life. Her greying hair was delicately powdered, while a touch of Spanish paper added a subtle glow to her cheeks.

'That is correct, child. Now come into the candlelight so that I may have a better look at you.'

Amelia obediently followed her over to one of the sconces on the far side of the room. Mrs Featherstone took Amelia by the shoulders and swept her gaze over her face and chest before bending unceremoniously to lift her skirts. Amelia stepped back, a gasp flying to her lips when she felt a sharp draught on her legs.

'Madam –' she began, sensing the woman's finger slip between her thighs.

'Hush, child.' Mrs Featherstone's warm breath brushed Amelia's cheek as she pressed her lips against her ear. 'There is no place for coyness if you want to come and live with me.'

Amelia glanced over the older woman's shoulder and

noticed to her chagrin that both Clarissa and Connie were observing them closely.

Mrs Featherstone pushed her index finger into Amelia's moist crack. 'Now I want you to squeeze as hard as you can.' After a moment's hesitation, Amelia complied, placing her palms flat against the wall as she thrust her pelvis towards the woman.

'Splendid, no need for alum treatment to firm you up.' Mrs Featherstone suddenly withdrew her hand and trailed her fingers up to where Amelia's clitoris already stood to attention, her fingers briefly clasping the silver ring protruding high above the tight crease of her pudenda. 'And this is where the pleasure lies for you, does it not, my dear?'

Amelia couldn't utter a word, her lips being clamped together in silent ecstasy.

Mrs Featherstone stepped away then and rejoined the others. Amelia followed shortly afterwards, wildly fanning her heaving bosom.

'You are just what I am looking for to complete my happy little band.'

Amelia sank on to the seat beside her. 'I am?' she mumbled, closing her fan.

'I told you that she would be, Jenny,' chirped Mrs Stevens as she accepted a glass of wine from the footman. 'She has so much potential, so many desires yet to be discovered.'

'Welcome to my home, Lady Beechwood. I trust that it fulfils all your needs.'

Amelia glanced round at her new surroundings, a gasp rising in her throat at the unexpected splendour of it all. Everything, from the smallest picture frame to the heavy sideboards which flanked the passage, spoke of quality. Ormolu mingled with the finest of woods, china and porcelain and created an impression of wealth and good taste befitting the home of a fine lady.

Amelia turned back to face her hostess, a blush playing at her cheeks.

'You look bemused, my dear. Is there something wrong?'

'No, it is just that I never imagined a, a bawdy house to be like this.'

'Is that what you think it is? A brothel?' Jenny chuckled. 'Oh no, child. You do have a lot to learn if that's your interpretation of my establishment.'

'But I thought –'

'And you are correct in your assumption. My girls have a good time here, to be sure, but not without reason or purpose.'

Amelia frowned. 'I don't understand.'

'Of course you don't. My place is unique. It seems that I am going to have to show you what I mean.' Jenny motioned for Amelia to follow her further down the hall. 'It's not a practice I approve of, mind you, but in your case I believe a demonstration is warranted.'

Amelia shivered as spasm shot through her quim at the thought of what this demonstration might amount to.

'Are you there?' Jenny called from the darkness. Amelia remembered herself then and hurried along the hall only to be reprimanded for her boisterous behaviour when she eventually caught up with Jenny a few seconds later.

'Silence is of the utmost import here, child. We must not disturb them or we'll ruin the lesson.' She tiptoed towards a door on the right and slowly opened it, revealing a small cupboard.

'If you wait in here, you will be able to view the activities which are about to begin at any moment in the next room.' She indicated the minute crack in the panelling allowing a thin band of light into the darkened space. 'Sit on one of the shelves if you like. We will be able to discuss matters better tomorrow, once you have settled in. As for now –' she grinned '– enjoy yourself. Remember, my dear. Tell no one of this. It will be our little secret.'

Nodding, Amelia positioned herself as instructed on

the shelf and trained her gaze on the crack in the panelling. Inside the room, bathed in the golden glow from the many tapers fixed to the walls, a girl of Connie's age stood with her back half turned to Amelia. Reaching up, she slowly took the pins from her sable hair, allowing it to fall like a silky blanket around her shoulders, before turning and undoing the ties on her bodice. Amelia shifted uneasily, this simple sight igniting the fire of desire in her belly. She learnt closer to the crack to get a better view, while at the same time stifling a groan as a heavy throbbing rose between her legs.

The girl allowed her intricately embroidered stomacher to fall to the ground while the remaining opalescent fabric flapped open like the pages of a book, revealing the ample swell of her bosom above the tight line of her stays. Shrugging off the bodice, she stretched her arms high above her head before sharply dropping them and swivelling round when someone else entered the room.

Amelia shivered, a rush of warm air teasing her face as the door was shut. She pressed her eye to the crack, swallowing hard when she observed two people join the girl.

A man, dressed only in a white shirt and breeches, his hands and forearms covered by tight leather gloves, took her by the shoulders and bending to briefly kiss her, manoeuvred her backwards until she tumbled on to the bed.

The other person now came into view – an older woman, perhaps 30. She reached into her bodice and produced two scarlet ribbons which she proceeded to tie about the girl's wrists.

'What are they for?' the girl asked, concern clearly marking her face.

The woman smiled and continued with her work, securing first the one and then the other wrist to the nearby bedposts.

'They are nothing for you to worry about, Susan, as you will soon see. Just part of the lesson, that's all.'

While she was speaking, the man moved to the foot of the bed and, after carefully taking off Susan's shoes, secured the girl's ankles in the same way.

Amelia was just as interested in what was about to take place as Susan, and, quietly hopping off the shelf, shuffled even closer to the crack, pressing her body against the cool wood while fixing her gaze once more on the occupants of the next room.

The woman was stroking Susan's head and the man slowly drawing up her skirts, revealing the whiteness of her thighs which contrasted sharply with the blue of her garters. Amelia shivered when he slid a gloved hand between Susan's legs, the fingers disappearing into her dark mound, his other hand continuing to push her skirts up over her panniers.

Susan instantly began to squirm, struggling against her confines as the man found her clitoris and pinching it between thumb and forefinger, enticed it to full stiffness. The girl rolled her eyes, arched her back and, with a guttural groan, thrust her hips towards him, urging him on in his intimate exploration of her.

'Oh yes,' she breathed, throwing back her head and wildly twisting it from side to side. 'Make me come now!'

The man laughed and, with one quick movement, pulled his hand free of Susan's legs. She maintained her position for a few seconds before disappointedly falling back against the mattress, her bosom heaving erratically.

Amelia, watching this scene unfold, unconsciously slid her left hand under her own skirts and, easily finding her damp cleft, rotated the slick ring between her finger-tips, gently tugging at her rigid pleasure-node now and again. She pressed her face against the panelling and squeezed her legs together, the sound of Susan moaning drawing her attention back to the room.

The woman was crouched on the bed, leaning over her. Scooping one of Susan's breasts out of its confines, she took it into her hands and raised its tip to her lips, her rosy tongue eagerly sliding over its dimpled surface, teasing the nipple to hardness.

The man knelt on the bed beside Susan, his face hovering just above her groin. Placing his hands under her buttocks, he raised her pelvis up just enough to give the required space for him to move his knees under her until her bottom rested in his lap, thus giving him easier access to her moisture-ridden pudenda.

Ruthlessly grabbing one thigh, he tilted her pelvis towards him and, finding her clitoris once more, covered its sensitive tip with the velvet strokes of his tongue. Susan clenched and unclenched her vaginal muscles against the man's foraging mouth, the rounded orbs of her buttocks jiggling with the effort, her actions gradually taking on a more frantic pace.

'Please can it be this time?' Susan cried, harsh gasps escaping through her clenched teeth.

'Not yet!' the man barked, dragging up his head and casting a meaningful glance at the woman. The woman fell back on her haunches, releasing Susan's breast before climbing off the bed. 'I haven't finished with you yet,' the man said, returning his attention to Susan who was quivering under his touch. 'You'll not gain release until I think it right. Remember, I'm the master here.'

With her eyes still glued to the scene in the other room, Amelia withdrew her hand from her groin and pressed her own pudenda against the wall. Arching her back, she began to rub her groin furiously up and down the panelling, delighting in the sensation of her silky moistness against the hardness of wood. She didn't know or particularly care why Susan was being forced to bear such agony. All she hoped was that it would continue at least long enough for her to reach culmination herself.

The man knelt over Susan, his thighs straddling her trembling legs, and undid the flap on his breeches. His cock sprang forward, its engorged tip sporting a slick, ruddy glans half hidden under the tightness of foreskin. He slowly ran his fingers along his bloated shaft, rubbing and squeezing it as he shifted his position until he knelt in between her spreadeagled legs.

'Are you ready for it now, Susan?' he teased, lowering himself on to her until his cock disappeared into the dark recesses of her groin. 'Have you learnt your lesson yet?'

'Yes!' she cried, her voice ringing out in the small room. 'I've waited long enough! Just make me come this time.'

'Very well. Here endeth the first lesson.' The man smiled at his own humour and then, drawing back his hips, roughly thrust his pulsating prick into her. Susan writhed against him, pushing her hips upward to meet his questing cock as he withdrew it until only the tip remained embedded within her, before propelling it back in with a sharp intake of breath.

Amelia turned away from this scene, her own breath coming in gasps as one of her hips collided with the sharp edge of the shelf. This simple action caused her clitoral ring to retreat back into its succulent bed of flesh and connect with its highly sensitive core, finally tipping her over the edge. She fell away from the shelf shuddering, orgasm exploding in her groin, her pelvis fibrillating wildly as she sank down on to her knees.

On hearing Susan's joyous cry, Amelia shakily dragged herself up and tidied her skirts. She couldn't help smiling to herself. At least two people in Mrs Featherstone's establishment would retire to bed that night satisfied.

Chapter Thirteen

'*I*cannot believe that Amelia is really gone. I do so hope she enjoys her new life.' Connie stretched her arms high above her head and swung her legs off the chaise longue. It was all too easy to get used to these afternoon naps, but she knew that if she was to make the most of her short stay in Covent Garden, she would have to find entertainment for the afternoons, as well as the evenings.

'I promise you that Jenny will not rest until all Amelia's needs are catered for,' remarked Clarissa, looking up from her book. 'She takes such an interest in her girls' welfare, I'd swear they were her own children!'

'It's a pity you didn't think to include me when you introduced them. Her establishment certainly sounds a lot of fun. I'm quite envious!'

'Why, Connie dear, not bored are you?'

She met her aunt's inquisitive glance, the faintest of blushes sweeping across her cheeks.

'Not exactly, it's just that since Amelia left, excitement has been a little light on the ground for me. At least you have Sir Mandeville or one of your other lovers for company. Who do I have?' Connie gasped, suddenly realizing that what she'd just said must have sounded terribly rude. 'Oh, Auntie, I'm sorry. I don't mean to seem ungrateful. It's just that I had hoped to have

159

experienced much more here than I have so far. After all, it will only be a fortnight before Father returns to take me back home again.'

Clarissa tossed the book aside and went to the nearby drinks tray. 'I quite understand, my dear. There's no need to apologize. Remember, I was young once too you know. I know how hard it can be when there seems to be no outlet for one's urges, especially for someone with your obvious appetites.'

'You do?' Connie blinked in her direction, her gaze taking in her aunt's stylish, yet carefree appearance. Her golden hair was simply caught in a satin ribbon, while her shapely curves were barely concealed under the gossamer folds of an unstructured gauze wrap.

Clarissa was the only woman she knew who refused to wear any form of female support during the day, preferring stays only in the evenings when it was absolutely necessary. And even then, Connie got the impression that if not for her rigorous social life, her aunt would go without them permanently. Though many would consider this decision to fly in the face of convention a bit eccentric, Connie couldn't help but admire her for expressing her individuality in this unique fashion. At least she had the gumption to conduct her life the way she saw fit, rather than allowing the world outside to dictate to her how she should live.

'Of course.' Clarissa handed Connie a glass of Rafatia and then leant against the wall, staring down at her. 'However, it's no excuse for drowning in the wealth of sensation available in Covent Garden.'

'Why not?'

'Because I don't think it's healthy to expect a constant outlet for your desires. You must pace yourself or things will soon begin to pall. Believe me, I've had it happen to me on several occasions.'

Connie raised her eyebrows, hardly believing that such an obviously sensual woman as Clarissa would tire of the pleasures of the flesh.

'Oh don't look so surprised, my dear. Lovemaking is

160

like a fine wine: a few choice sips here and there is tantalising to the senses, but over indulge and even the greatest vintage sours the palate. It's as simple as that. That's why I decided you should have a respite before embarking on your next escapade.'

'You've got something else planned for me?' A sudden excitement rose in Connie making her squirm against the seat. 'If he's like Nathaniel –'

'You were really taken with that boy, weren't you child?'

'You could say that. It was a shame he couldn't have stayed longer.'

'Well, Sir Mandeville obviously had other plans for him which took him away. But you needn't despair, Connie, dear, for I am sure that what I have arranged will be an equally stimulating diversion for you. Perhaps you will be able to find a replacement for your Nathaniel as a consequence of it.'

'I do hope so,' Connie breathed excitedly, her eyes glued to her aunt's face. 'What is it you've planned?'

Clarissa laughed and moved back across the room to refill her glass. 'Shh, have patience, Connie. You act no better than a child on her birthday!'

'Oh please, Aunt, do tell. I cannot bear it!'

'Oh very well,' she sighed. 'It's nothing really. It's just that I have managed to secure us both an invitation to one of the season's most prestigious events – namely, a party in honour of the Lord Chancellor.'

'Come in, child. I've been expecting you.'

Amelia hesitantly closed the door behind her and entered Mrs Featherstone's bedroom. Brightly lit by the early morning sunshine, the room was dominated by the largest bed Amelia had ever seen. Thickly carved oak posts rose to support a heavy rectangle of green velvet which canopied and curtained the bed. The mattress was decorated by an intricately quilted coverlet and perhaps fifteen or twenty gold-stitched pillows.

Beyond the bed, Amelia noticed another, half-open

door and, moving towards it, she found Mrs Featherstone enjoying a bath.

'Ma'am –' she began, her gaze falling on Jenny's naked breasts, their hardened tips poking out above the line of the water which lapped at her chest. 'I'll wait in the bedroom if you wish.'

'What for? I'm sure this isn't the first time you've seen another woman naked so you might as well stop all this false modesty.' She patted a stool beside the hip bath. 'Come and sit here. You can scrub my back if you like.'

Amelia did as she was told, taking the flannel Mrs Featherstone offered her.

'I must admit, ma'am, that I've never held a conversation like this before!' Amelia chuckled, beginning to wash her back.

'I'll wager that you will experience many things here which you never deemed possible before. For instance, what did you think of what you observed last night?'

Amelia didn't know what to say. Although what she had witnessed then had afforded her the greatest satisfaction, the thought of discussing it with this older woman brought embarrassment flooding into her. As a consequence, she fumbled for a suitable answer. 'Well – I – er – it was interesting.'

'Oh come on, girl. Out with it! I'll wager it made you devilish aroused.'

Amelia coloured and, despite the fact that Mrs Featherstone couldn't see her face, she looked away, wishing that she could be as forthright in her speaking as everyone else here seemed to be.

'I suppose so –'

'As I said when we first met, there's no room for coyness in this household, my dear. It looks as though I'm going to have to correct you, and fast, if you are to be of any use to me.'

Amelia bit her lip, a stab of fear coursing through her at the possibility that she might not be what Mrs Featherstone was looking for.

'I'm sorry, ma'am. I do so want my stay here to be

successful. It's just that – oh, I don't know!' She threw down the flannel and, struggling to her feet, went to the window. Pushing it open, she took a deep breath of the fresh morning air in an effort to help calm her frazzled nerves.

'Tell me, why did you leave your husband, Amelia?'

Amelia caught her breath and whipped round to stare at the woman. 'Ma'am? I don't understand what you mean. How do you know about that?'

'Enough of this formality. My name's Jenny.' She dragged herself out of the water, soap suds clinging to the downy covering of her pudenda, and reached for a nearby towel. 'Clarissa told me how you came to be residing with her, that's all.'

'Oh well, there's nothing much to say about it except that it was the worst experience of my life and I had to get away before I went mad.'

'Oh surely it wasn't that bad.' She padded into the bedroom, indicating for Amelia to follow her. 'Perhaps you were simply frightened by your husband's attempts at lovemaking?'

'I can assure you that it wasn't that, madam,' Amelia sniffed, slightly riled by this woman's suggestion. 'What he did to me had nothing to do with love. From the very beginning of our marriage he made it abundantly clear what role he intended me to have. It was as if my feelings didn't count at all so long as he achieved his fulfilment. He took his pleasure of my body without a thought for what I would have liked. As far as he was concerned, I was no better than one of his servants, there simply to tend to his needs.'

'And you gained no satisfaction at all during your time with him? A girl like you? I find that hard to believe.'

'I cannot deny that there were times when he allowed me a certain amount of pleasure ... but why this interrogation suddenly? I thought you wanted me to join your establishment.'

'I do indeed. I'm just trying to get to know you better.

Let me tell you a little more about my place. Perhaps then you'll be able to understand why I have to ask these questions.' She slipped on a chemise and took a seat at a dressing table beside the bed. Amelia remained standing, her arms folded defensively in front of her chest. 'What you witnessed last night was the first of several lessons Susan will have to help her build up her self-control.'

'A lesson, you say?' Amelia asked, narrowing her eyes in confusion. 'I don't follow you.'

'As I stated when you first arrived, this is no ordinary bawdy house. My young ladies come to me for one specific reason. Namely, to fill the gaps in their sexual education. This is usually in preparation for a forthcoming marriage. However, some of them are already married and come simply to brush up on their skills, expand their knowledge, as it were. This is where my specialist "teachers" come into their own, providing a sophisticated service to my more discerning clients.' Jenny pinned her hair into a tight bun before continuing.

'As you witnessed with Susan's lesson, not only do I need to be confident of the instructors I employ, I also need to feel the same way about their helpers, and that is why I believe eventually, with a little polishing, you could become just the right type of person to join my little team in such a capacity. Who knows, in helping out with the lessons, you might even learn a thing or two in the process yourself. God knows you could certainly do with some help. Why, I've never met such a vexed girl as you. What on earth did that husband of yours do to create such a reaction? Come, you must tell me, child. Besides my curiosity, I have to know the extent of your experience and whether you are a shrinking violet or whether your sexual tastes veer more towards the outrageous.'

Amelia swallowed hard, realising that Jenny's patience probably wouldn't last much longer. It looked as if she was just going to have to ignore her embarrassment for once and tell this woman everything she wanted to know, no matter how hard it was for her.

With a heavy sigh, she drew away from Jenny and then launched into a passionless description of the outrages Lucas had subjected her to before and after their marriage.

'Well, after hearing that little tale, all I can say is that I truly feel sorry for you, my dear, and I take back all I said earlier,' Jenny sympathised when Amelia had finished her narrative. 'It seems to me that, because of your husband's selfishness, you remain as ignorant of your innermost desires as the day you married. How frustrating it must be for you, but you needn't worry. I have just the thing to ease this discomfort of yours. It's a rather interesting way of releasing all that pent-up tension, while at the same time showing you another side to your nature.'

Jenny jumped up excitedly from the dressing table and rang the bell-pull. 'What do you say, Amelia? Do you want to put your past behind you and finally get on with your life?'

Amelia shrugged and then slowly nodded, not really knowing what she was agreeing to, but enjoying the thrill of it all the same.

A few seconds later a maid came scurrying into the room and dropped a deep curtsy before Mrs Featherstone. 'Prepare the green room would you, dear? I do believe that we shall presently be requiring its facilities.'

When the maid had left, Jenny took Amelia's hand and led her back into the small room. Taking a detour around the hip bath, she drew her over to the far wall where a door was partially concealed in the panelling.

'This is my personal wardrobe,' Jenny said, proudly standing back to allow Amelia a view inside the closet. 'It has taken me many years to build up this collection, which I am certain you can appreciate.'

Amelia's mouth dropped open when her eyes settled on the startling number of gowns and other fashion items that hung in there. She'd never seen such an array of silks, brocades and damasks before and, stepping closer to the rail, she reached out to touch one of the dresses.

Jenny caught her arm and, smiling, shook her head. 'I quite understand your interest my dear, but I think you'll find what you require at the far end of the closet. Here, let me help you.' She disappeared into the closet, only to return a few seconds later carrying what looked to Amelia like a few squares of leather connected by scarlet ribbons.

'What's that?' she asked, following Jenny back into the bedroom.

Jenny didn't answer until she'd laid the item out on the edge of the bed. 'That, my dear, is to aid your stimulation.'

'What?' Amelia narrowed her eyes. 'Surely you don't mean me to wear such a flimsy article? I had enough of that on my wedding night!'

'Ah, but this is different. I can assure you that this item is made for a woman's stimulation and not her humiliation. Why don't you try it and see?'

'I don't know . . .' Amelia stepped closer and touched the outfit, running her fingers over the supple leather, the sensuous feel of it sending a shiver of delight down her spine to her groin. Could she really wear something as scanty as this, even with Mrs Featherstone's reassurance?

'I presume that this has a part to play in a lesson you have planned for me? Pray, what is it?'

Jenny smiled and threw her arms round Amelia's shoulders. 'Always so inquisitive, aren't you? Must you question everything? Can't you simply accept me at my word when I say that, by wearing this, you will greatly enhance your pleasure? I promise you that nothing untoward is going to happen to you, not while I'm in charge, anyway. I have, after all, only your best interests at heart. Now –' she picked up the leather outfit '– be a good girl and allow me to help you on with this. The sooner we get this over with, the sooner you can get on and begin to enjoy yourself!'

Amelia sighed and, bowing to the older woman's greater experience, allowed her to strip her of her clothes and dress her in this tantalising new outfit.

'There, nearly finished. Why don't you take a look in the glass and tell me what you think before I tie this last ribbon?'

Amelia nodded and slowly moved in front of the full-length mirror, her hand immediately flying to her mouth when she took in this new, powerful image of herself. Gone was her gown and underthings and in their place was the stunning sight of leather interspersed with the stark whiteness of bare flesh. The squares, secured by a tight line of ribbons down the front and back, formed a figure hugging bodice which supported the ample swell of her unfettered breasts. Casting her gaze lower, Amelia caught her breath when she noticed how naked, how exposed her sex was, its black, bristly reaches inadequately covered by only an inch-wide strip of leather between her legs.

'Exhilarating, isn't it?'

Amelia shuddered when she sensed Jenny's presence behind her, tugging, pulling at this narrow band of leather, forcing it up between the swell of her buttocks. 'Now, if you will breathe deeply, I guarantee that you will begin to realise the purpose of this garment.'

Amelia shrugged and, resting her hands on her hips, did as Jenny suggested, filling her lungs as far as the garment would allow. The bodice immediately rode up, dragging the leather between her legs with it and exerting an exquisite pressure on her already stirring clitoris.

She gasped and squeezed her pelvic muscles, enclosing the leather in her succulent folds. 'Oh, Jenny,' she whispered hoarsely. 'I, I see what you mean!'

Mrs Featherstone laughed and, stepping back into the closet swiftly returned with a pair of matching leather elbow gloves and thigh boots. 'Here, put these on and you'll nearly be ready to go.'

Making no protest this time, being too filled with excitement to feel self-conscious in front of Mrs Featherstone, Amelia happily obliged, pulling on the boots and gloves. She jumped to her feet and, tugging the pins from her hair, shook it out until it framed her bare shoulders like a dark, luxurious blanket.

'I'm ready when you are,' she breathed, excitedly licking her lips. 'I don't care what happens next, so long as I continue to feel this good.'

Jenny chuckled and, taking Amelia's hand, led her out of the room and along the hall to the room at the end. She paused on the threshold. 'Now, Amelia, there's one thing I feel I must say to you before we proceed. I want you to promise that you will do your best not to be shocked by what you see inside. I know it will seem odd, frightening even, after what you've told me of your marriage, but I assure you that it is all for a good purpose.'

Amelia nodded quickly and then followed her into the green room. Nothing, not even Jenny's assurances, could have prepared her for the actual reality of it. All normal household furniture had been stripped from it and replace by what seemed to Amelia instruments of torture, similar to those she had seen during her last hours at Beechwood House. She swallowed hard, finding it difficult to distinguish between that terrifying image and the one she was currently presented with.

The usual comfortable features Amelia had come to expect of Jenny's home were absent and in their place were crudely carved benches, two unfinished tables and various stools dotted around the capacious room. She noticed with a shudder of disgust that the same type of wrist restraints Lord Carterall had so lovingly toyed with were in evidence here, hanging by silver chains from the walls, while what looked like a pair of stocks stood by the far window.

Amelia stepped over the bare floorboards and leant back against the wall, trying with difficulty to catch her breath within the confines of her restrictive garment.

'Come come, child,' Jenny laughed, tugging at her arm and guiding her further into the room. 'As I said before, there is nothing for you to fear in here. What is contained in this room is solely for your pleasure, isn't that right, Richard?'

Amelia followed her gaze across the room to where a man hovered, his face a picture of guilt. She bit her lip and, feeling his eyes raking over her and focusing on her naked pudenda, looked about her for an appropriate place to hide herself from his view, embarrassment suddenly returning to plague her.

'I, I'm sorry, Mrs Featherstone. I know you don't like me being in this room. I –'

'Enough!' She turned back to Amelia. 'I've told him a hundred times that this place is only for the use of my young ladies, and yet he still insists on coming in here. Why, look how he's distressed you! What shall I do with him, Amelia?'

Amelia shrugged and, despite her precarious state of undress, found herself switching her gaze again to the man who, by now, had moved closer to them. She ran her eyes appreciatively over him. Of a good height, perhaps six foot, he was dressed informally in a loose brocade waistcoat and breeches, while his mousy hair hung free just above his shoulders, framing a not unpleasant countenance.

'I, I don't know what you should do, Jenny, but please do something.' Her voice dropped to a whisper. 'Remember my current disadvantage!' Jenny smiled and squeezed Amelia's arm. 'I think it's up to you now to punish him for the embarrassment he's caused you. After all, this was meant to be a private affair.'

'But how?' Amelia enquired in all innocence. 'This is your place –'

'Here.' Jenny strode across the room, tore a cat-o'-nine-tails off the wall and shook it at Amelia. 'I think you should use this. I give you permission to punish him on my behalf and, believe me, he's had this coming for a long time!' She returned her attention to the man. 'You there, Richard? I think it's the table for you.'

'But, ma'am,' he protested, falling on to his knees before her, his hands clasped together above his head. 'I beg you not to be so cruel, I –'

'I said,' Jenny growled between clenched teeth, 'get on the table!'

Amelia's mouth dropped open when she observed Richard shake his head and then obediently do as she asked, lying face down on the table.

'Come, child. Help me to secure his arms and legs.'

Amelia remained where she was for a few moments, numbly observing Mrs Featherstone busying herself with attaching a wrist restraint to Richard's left arm. She didn't know what to think, whether to feel shocked or even disgusted, but she soon found herself moving towards the table, a delightful pounding growing in her groin as she stumbled forward.

'Jenny –' she began, only to stop short when Mrs Featherstone flashed her an annoyed glance. Without saying another word, Amelia began to do up the restraints on her side of Richard's body, stepping back to survey her handiwork less than a minute later. She noticed how he pressed his cheek against the coarse wood while his eyes pleaded with hers.

'Be gentle with me, my lady,' he whispered. 'I ain't that bad a fellow. I just like to look –'

'Be quiet. I think we've heard enough.' Jenny rounded the table and indicated for Amelia to follow. 'Now, dear, which is it to be, the cat-o'-nine-tails I have here or one of these beauties?'

Amelia blinked at the sight of the six whips strapped to the wall, each one a foot longer than the last. She swallowed hard. 'You expect me to beat him?' she enquired, aghast.

'Why, of course. He's caused you pain and so should be punished. What other way is there?'

'I, I don't know. I never have liked violence –'

'Oh please, my lady. Beat me, beat me until I come!' Richard wailed behind them.

'See, he wants you to do it. He knows he deserves it. How much more encouragement do you want?'

Amelia shrugged, her hands closing round the base of the cat-o'-nine-tails. She looked over her shoulder at the bound Richard and shuddered when she felt her nipples tighten at the thought of doing what she requested. Would it be such a bad thing? After all, Richard himself had asked, begged her for it.

'All right, I'll do it,' she announced, setting her jaw and returning to the table. Bending towards him, Amelia unceremoniously grasped the waistband of his breeches and, with a force which she didn't know she had, managed to jerk them down around his knees, revealing the smooth orbs of his buttocks.

'Ah,' she breathed, running a finger over their quivering surface, urging the kindling fire in her groin to ignite and envelop her. 'So firm. It is indeed a shame to besmirch them with this lash . . .'

She straightened up and, raising her hand, hesitantly flapped the whip on to his bottom. Richard hardly struggled at all this first time, only a dull whimper issuing from his pursed lips.

'Harder!' Jenny scolded behind her. 'You must do it harder. Beat submission out of him. Only then will you be able to gain your satisfaction.'

Amelia nodded and, taking a deep breath, sent the cat-o'-nine-tails crashing down on to his buttocks, a loud smack ringing out in the room. Almost instantaneously, excitement began to brew in her belly, kidnapping her groin, the leather band sliding back and forth between her legs as she slowly circled the table. Encouraged by this, she began to hit him again and again, barely pausing for breath, before sending the next blow spiralling down.

With every blow she struck, Richard writhed against his restraints, bucking and banging his forehead against the unpolished wood while incoherent syllables

171

streamed from his lips. Witnessing this, she could hardly believe the depth of sensation which grew inside her. What a change this was from being subjugated by men! Why, with every lash she afforded him, Amelia sensed her clitoris stirring and growing until it pressed painfully against its stiff leather enclosure, urging her on, reminding her of the urgency of her own need.

'Oh, my lady,' Richard cried, his buttocks jiggling with every forced word he managed. 'I'm sorry for embarrassing you!'

Amelia was hardly aware of his pleas by now, so carried away was she. The tension which had troubled her for weeks was finally beginning to ebb away, leaving in its wake a yearning for satisfaction.

Caught up with her crescendoing excitement, Amelia stepped up the tempo of her blows, ignoring the angry weals which were quickly developing over his buttocks. She merely slapped the stinging sweat from her eyes and carried on whipping him with a fervour so strong it was as if her very life depended on it.

'Enough!' Jenny eventually shouted, catching Amelia's arm as she raised it to inflict yet another hit on his sore bottom. 'Do you wish to make him unusable?'

Amelia stared at her with wild eyes, breathing heavily. Eventually her senses returned to her and she dropped the whip.

'Oh, Jenny, can't you take this off?' she gasped, indicating her leather construction. 'I'll surely die if I don't get some relief soon!'

The older woman glanced at the struggling Richard and chuckled. 'So will he if we don't release him. Why don't you get him to do it for you?'

Amelia thought a moment and, deciding that as she'd come this far she might as well continue, quickly nodded and swiftly undid his restraints, allowing him to sit up. She eyed his rampant erection jutting from between his legs and smiled, wrapping one arm around his neck and dragging him closer until his face was buried in her cleavage.

172

'Would you really like to please me, hmmm?' she whispered, reaching between them and grasping his cock, one finger skimming the edge his slick glans.

'Oh yes, my lady. I, I'll do anything —'

'Good —' Amelia stepped back from him, picking up the whip and pushing its handle between her legs where she ran it back and forth '— because I need you now. I want you to untie me and, and suck me until I come.' She fell back against the wall, thrilling shivers running up her spine as she observed Richard drag his lean body from the table and approach her, a broad grin decorating his features.

'Anything you wish, my lady,' he whispered, reaching between her and the wall and quickly untying the ribbons holding the leather g-string in place, 'I shall gladly do.' He dropped to his knees and, grabbing her by the hips, buried his face in her groin. His lips immediately found her erect pleasure-node and, drawing it into his mouth, he furiously sucked and nibbled at it, catching its silver tip now and again between his teeth.

'Oh my God,' Amelia cried, thrusting her pelvis towards his foraging mouth. 'Don't stop, Richard, please don't stop!' In her fury, she wound her fingers in his hair and pulled his head closer still, urging his face even deeper into her dewy crease. Teetering on the edge of orgasm, that heady finish mere seconds away from bursting within her, the strength inexplicably left her knees and she slumped against Richard. He fell backwards on to the floor, dragging her with him and, seeing his chance, entered her slick channel with a velvet thrust of his hips.

Amelia felt his thick cock riding up inside her, filling every inch of her, finally setting off that release which had been so long in coming. She shuddered uncontrollably, her vagina closing erratically around his questing prick, encouraging him on to his own, joyous conclusion until only the sound of their mutually laboured breathing remained as evidence of their ecstatic coupling.

'How can I ever thank you?' Amelia asked many minutes later, gratefully accepting the silk wrap Jenny offered her.

The older woman shrugged. 'It was my pleasure just to see you realise that which you have been missing all this time.'

'I certainly did that.' Amelia shivered, remembering the overwhelming sense of power she had experienced whilst whipping Richard. She found it amazing that she had been able to keep this facet of her nature locked inside her all this time. But then, she supposed she had Lucas's repression to blame for that.

'My suspicions about you were right, you know.'

Amelia raised her head. 'Suspicions, ma'am?'

'Why, yes.' Jenny chucked her under the chin. 'I always knew that deep down inside you were a commanding sort of girl. Why, I'll wager, there will be no stopping you now.'

Amelia smiled knowingly, already looking forward to the next time when she would get a chance to test out her new skills.

Chapter Fourteen

'*I* still don't think this is wise, m'lord,' Fran mumbled, catching Lucas's arm and trying in vain to draw him away from the window. In the hour or so he'd been sitting in the carriage, he'd seen various comings and goings from the other houses, but nothing from the particular one he was interested in.

'I do not care what you think,' he said continuing to stare at the row of smart porticoed townhouses opposite. 'No one is making you stay. You are free to go whenever you want.' Lucas cast a brief glance over his shoulder in her direction and noticed with satisfaction how she sank back against the seat, pouting. No one, not even Fran with her stimulating charms, was going to stop him finding out the truth of his wife's whereabouts. 'Exactly as I thought,' he chuckled, returning his gaze to the Little Piazza. 'Don't want to risk losing that necklace I promised you, eh?'

Of course he knew where Mrs Stevens's residence was – he was staring at it – he just had to make certain that this really was where Connie was staying. It wasn't that he distrusted Lady Boughby's confession – he knew he'd chosen well the moment to pose the question – he just had to make sure that she hadn't written to her daughter to warn of his impending arrival since then.

This was one of the reasons why he'd waited so long before even contemplating going in seach of his wife. By his conspicuous absence, he'd hoped to give Connie, and Amelia for that matter, a false sense of security in the belief that he had no idea where they were.

Judging by the apparent normality surrounding the residence he was currently observing, this certainly seemed to be the case, a fact which only added to the sense of anticipation already building in him.

'It's not that at all,' Fran protested behind him. 'I just don't want to see you wasting time when you should be getting that money for Paul.'

Lucas sighed and swivelled round to face her. He took her by the shoulders and looked deep into her hazel eyes. 'How many times do I have to tell you. I have no intention of paying that particular debt. I had in the beginning, but not now. If your friend thinks he can exact payment by the threat of violence, he's sadly mistaken. He obviously doesn't know who he's dealing with for, if he did, he would stay as far as possible away from me.' He smiled and touched her cheek. 'I think it's he who should be frightened, not me, don't you?'

'You don't know what he's like, m'lord. He's got Lennard with him and they mean to teach you a lesson.'

'Oh do they? Well perhaps I'll have to have a word with the local bailiff then. I'm sure he'll be able to sort them out. It should be most enjoyable watching the pair of them swing!'

Fran gasped and twisted away from him. 'Please, m'lord, don't say that. They mean no harm –'

'I'm certain they don't. Why are you so interested in their welfare anyway? Surely you don't imagine yourself in love with one of those brutes?' Fran coloured but remained silent. 'Well?' He demanded catching her arm. 'Do you?'

'I suppose you should know. Paul's my husband.' If Lucas was taken aback by this acknowledgement, he did not show it. Instead he moved his hands to rest at the base of her neck and dragged her back round to face him.

'Ah, so that's your game. You keep trying to get me to pay up with these supposed fears of yours for my safety, while in reality you simply want the money for yourself.'

'No, that's not it at all,' Fran protested, her fingers digging into the soft flesh of his palms as she tried to disengage herself from his grasp. 'I'm simply worried about what he'll do, what will happen to him if he carried out his threats.'

'Your class amazes me, it really does. I am certain that this sense of loyalty you all seem to be imbued with is no good for you at all. I'd forget about this Paul if I were you.'

'But you don't understand what I'm trying to say, m'lord. He could be dangerous.'

'Oh, could he? Well, what has he promised to do? He'll certainly have to think of something spectacular to achieve his aim for there's no wedding for him to disrupt this time.' Lucas's gripped tightened when she didn't answer. 'Tell me. What has that illiterate oaf said he'll do now? I need to know so that I may at least be on guard in case he's foolish enough to carry out his threats.'

'He didn't tell me, but I know he's got a pistol with him.'

'Oh is that all?' Lucas suddenly let go of her, laughing. 'Then I have nothing to worry about. As I said before, it is he who should be concerned, not me.'

Fran rubbed her throat furiously as if trying to erase the memory of his touch. 'I still don't think you should take this so lightly, m'lord.'

'Enough! If you carry on in this puerile fashion, you risk incurring my displeasure,' he warned, turning back to stare out of the window. 'Believe me, it won't be hard to find a replacement for you around here. Is that what you want?'

'No, m'lord. You know it's not. No man –'

'Aha!' Lucas announced, interrupting her, his eyes

177

glued to the sight of Connie alighting from a carriage and hurrying into one of the townhouses. 'You won't be able to escape me for much longer, dear wife!'

He settled back against the seat and, with a triumphant smile, tapped his walking stick on the floor. As the carriage started to move off, he turned to Fran grinning. 'I do so hope that you won't mind sharing your quarters, my dear, for very soon I promise that you will have a new room-mate.'

Amelia swapped the confines of the townhouse for the open space of the garden. Choosing a well-trodden path which led her away from the house and through a small wood at the far end, she closed her eyes and immersed herself once again in her pleasant memories.

Though a week had passed since her first experience of flagellation, the recollection of it was as fresh as if it had happened only a few hours before. Every moment of every day since then, she had found herself turning again and again to that momentous event, re-creating it on the lavish stage of her mind, its thrill barely dulled by the passage of time.

Never before had any one event captured her imagination like that one had. Why, just thinking about it now sent a hot flush sweeping over her, urging her fingers to explore the flower of her womanhood.

Amelia ducked behind the security of a large oak tree at the bottom of the garden and quickly drew up her skirts. Surely no one would see her if she indulged herself here, in the garden? Her hand slipped across the firmness of her stomach and hovered over her already erect clitoris, its silver tip protruding above the bristly crease of her sex-lips.

How she longed to experience again the potent exhilaration of humiliating a man. Now that she had tasted its delicious strength, she knew that her desires would never be simply satisfied in the future. Of that she was certain. With Jenny's help, she'd been able to open the door to one of her deepest, darkest desires, one which she knew she would now need to indulge at every opportunity. And one which certainly put what Lord Carterall had proposed into perspective.

Although she was glad that she hadn't stayed to witness first hand his plans for her, she no longer remembered that particular scene with the fear and loathing she once had. Now only a sense of delicious curiosity filled her when she thought of how she might pay him back for the anguish he'd caused her at the time.

Amelia gasped when she heard the sound of a twig break a few feet away and, hurriedly dropping her skirts, peered round the edge of the trunk to find the source of this unwanted intrusion. Narrowing her eyes, she spied Richard being led deeper into the wood by a girl she'd never seen before.

Seeing him again set a fire burning between her legs and she found herself silently following the couple, hiding behind this tree or that in an effort to escape their notice. Coming to the end of the wood, she just caught a glimpse of them as they disappeared arm in arm into an ivy-clad pergola.

Creeping along the outside edge, Amelia found a discreet break in the ivy and, pressing her eye to the gap, found that she was presented with a perfect view of the couple. Richard held the girl in his arms, his mouth covering hers. Amelia swallowed hard, a delicious throbbing overtaking her groin when she observed him move his lips to the generous orbs of her breasts. Coaxing one of them out of its restraints, he brought its rigid tip to his mouth, his lips completely enclosing it, much to the delighted sighs of the girl.

Unable to deny the steadily growing excitement which rose within her at this simple scene, Amelia groaned and immediately slapped a hand over her mouth, fearing that her lack of control had given her away.

The girl straightened up and, roughly pushing Richard aside, looked about her. 'Who's there?' she demanded, resting her hands on her hips. 'If it's you, John, I swear I'll skin you alive this time!'

Amelia shrugged to herself and, lowering her head, moved towards the nearest opening, ready to accept her punishment. Instead, she found herself greeted by laughter from the girl and a shocked expression from Richard.

'Why, Lady Beechwood, I presume.' She dropped a quick curtsy. 'I'm Amy and I believe you have already met Richard here.'

Amelia found herself colouring at the inference. Was nothing secret in this establishment?

'I, I'm sorry to interrupt you –'

'Interrupt us? Admit it, you were spying, and I'll wager that you liked what you saw. Hmm? Well, did you?'

Amelia slowly nodded. 'Yes. I, I saw Richard and after last time I –'

'Ah, I see. You wish for another experience with the ever-obliging Richard here, do you not?'

Amelia cast him a quick glance and, seeing his faint, knowing smile, nodded again, but with more enthusiasm this time. 'I wish to learn more about – him. I find his condition – fascinating.' She shivered, shifting uneasily as she considered the endless possibilities this situation afforded. 'But out here? Surely –'

'Ah that's where you are wrong, my lady. You see, at Mrs Featherstone's, nowhere is out of bounds, including this secluded garden. Now, if you desire it, we can go somewhere even more private.'

'But Jenny – Mrs Featherstone? She wouldn't be angry about us doing something behind her back?'

Amy chuckled and, taking Amelia's hand, led her further along the pergola until they came to a small wooden hut at the end.

'Of course not. She'll see this for what it is, an impromptu lesson, and will expect you to make the most of it. Now, are you game or not?'

Amelia didn't even stop to think, but eagerly followed Amy into the hut. They took a seat on a bench propped against the far wall while Richard made light work of removing the heavy shutters from the windows and allowing the burnished glow of sunlight to flood into the small chamber.

'Over here,' Amy commanded when he'd finished. 'My lady requires your services!'

'What do you intend him to do?' Amelia asked excitedly, opening her thighs and enjoying the sensation of her slick, heavy lips parting at the same time.

'Why don't you wait and see?' Amy laughed, tossing back her loose coppery hair before pushing up Amelia's skirts to reveal the whiteness of her stockings. 'You might just enjoy it!'

Richard approached her, his hands clasped in front of him in an image of supplication. 'Be gentle with me, my lady – I'm still smarting from the last time –'

'Be quiet!' Amy snapped. 'Her ladyship hasn't come here to listen to your whining. Now, on your knees!'

He shrugged and without another word, slowly lowered himself before Amelia. He stared up at her with plaintive eyes.

'What is it that you require of me?'

Amelia smiled, beginning to understand what Amy intended for her. She leant back against the hard seat and spread her thighs even wider until she felt she would split in half if they moved another inch.

'Well, Richard,' she breathed, licking her lips. 'You could start by using that ever-efficient tongue of yours on me like last time.'

Richard nodded and immediately pushed his face into her lap. Arching her back, Amelia thrust her hips towards him, offering him complete access to her ripe sex. He wrapped his arms around her waist and eagerly pressed his face to her ebony pleasure-mount, his tongue licking its way down from her pert clitoris to the luscious lips nestling just below.

Amelia couldn't suppress a shiver when his tongue slipped in between their juicy folds, tickling, teasing its way towards her tight, inviting channel. 'Oh yes,' she groaned, grabbing the back of his head and pulling his face even closer. 'That's it. Do me with your tongue!'

Richard responded by flicking his tongue in and out of her moist quim, lapping up the succulent juices which gathered there while pushing even closer in order to allow greater penetration.

Amelia came quickly with a sharp intake of breath, her body quivering and shuddering in time with her excited sex. Once the exquisite feeling had subsided, she twisted away from Richard's inquisitive mouth and returned her gaze to Amy. 'Hmm, that was good, but I feel I need much more than that.'

The red-haired girl nodded. 'I thought as much. Richard, if you please?' She pointed towards Amelia again.

'But, mistress,' he panted, a clearly defined bulge straining at the fabric covering his groin. 'I, I –'

'Enough of what you want. You are here to please us, not yourself. Now, Lady Amelia wants you to lie here, in her lap.'

Amelia raised her eyebrows as she observed Richard slowly get to his feet and lie across her legs. She struggled to keep him there, having to spread her legs once more to stop him sliding off, her pooling love liquid, accumulated from her previous orgasm, spilling freely out of her. Eventually achieving the right position, she couldn't help gasping when she sensed his thinly clad erection filling the space between her thighs.

She reached under him and, deftly undoing the buttons on his breeches, allowed his throbbing member its freedom. When she felt its hot, pulsating length brush her bare thigh, its wet tip skirting the delicate skin there, she sighed. Needing no encouragement from Amy, she grabbed his rigid shaft, moving her hand down to clasp his nob, her palm covering his clammy glans.

'Now, Richard,' she breathed, running her other hand over the seat of his breeches, enjoying the sensation of his buttocks clenching under her touch. 'Have you been a good boy and steered clear of the Green Room since my last visit? Or am I going to have to punish you again

182

on behalf of Mrs Featherstone?' Amelia moved her fingers back to clutch the base of his cock and then, with slow deliberation, began to run them up and down its length.

'No, I haven't, my lady! I couldn't help myself. I –'

'Enough!' Amy interrupted him, bending to take one of her damask slippers off. 'I cannot believe that you could disobey your mistress's instructions yet again.' She winked at Amelia and pressed the shoe into her hand. 'Here,' she said sternly. 'Flog the very life out of him while I watch. I want to hear him scream.'

Amy rose and, crossing the short space to the other side of the hut, ducked down into a squat and pulled up her skirts, her fingers immediately disappearing under the layers of her petticoats.

Amelia swallowed hard and returned her attention to Richard who lay quivering in her lap, contented groans emanating from his lips. Suddenly letting go of his cock, she passed the slipper into her right hand and brought it down hard on to his rigid buttocks. Richard instantly cried out: a mixture of pleasure and pain which sent a spasm of delight straight to Amelia's groin. She groaned and, squeezing her thighs together, imprisoned his prick between them before striking again, the leather sole of the slipper connecting sharply with his haunches.

'Please, my lady . . .' Richard begged, raising his buttocks up to meet her next blow and then swiftly lowering them afterwards, his penis moving smoothly back and forth between her thighs.

'Yes, Richard?' she breathed through clenched teeth. 'Do you wish me to beat you more? Like this? And this?' Amelia felt perspiration break out on her forehead and a sense of power fill her with every blow she gave him. Only after she had afforded him a dozen more strokes did she briefly pause to catch her breath. Rasping heavily, she glanced across the hut and noticed how Amy now lay on her back thrusting her fingers in and out of her wet orifice.

This sight, combined with the pleasure she was

already experiencing as a consequence of Richard's punishment, sent her quickly tumbling to the edge of orgasm. Unceremoniously pushing him from her lap, Amelia gave Richard no chance to compose himself, but quickly joined him on the dirt floor, driving her dewy crevice down on to his upstanding member. She wildly threw back her head, several pins flying across the chamber, allowing her own dark tresses to cascade down her back, as she rode him furiously.

'Oh, dear God!' she cried, rhythmically squeezing her pelvic muscles, drawing him deeper and deeper into her honeyed recess with every frantic movement she made. Richard forced his hips up, matching her frenetic pace, his hands clawing at the ties on her bodice, seeking out the quivering mounds of her breasts.

'Yes, oh yes, that's it!' Amelia fell back on to her hindquarters shaking uncontrollably, her vagina twitching in time with her cleaving thighs as she came, this second time far exceeding the first joyous spasms she'd experienced.

As the orgasm slowly died away, leaving a delightful heat in its wake, Amelia crawled off Richard and, ignoring his cry of disappointment, knelt at his feet. While she rested there, panting and struggling to regain control of her breathing, she observed Amy quickly scramble across the floor and, mounting his still erect cock, finish the job that she herself had begun.

Amelia closed her eyes but not her ears to their passion and, when their contented moans filled her consciousness, she savoured the intense feeling of satisfaction which enveloped her – a satisfaction she instinctively knew had only been possible as a consequence of what Jenny had taught her about herself.

Connie took a deep breath while her maid tied the last ribbon on her new stays. They were certainly tighter than anything she had been used to before but she was willing to go through with the discomfort they caused because she had been assured by Clarissa that they were all the rage.

In the days since it had been announced that they'd been invited to the Lord Chancellor's party, a noticeable shift in emphasis had taken over Clarissa's personal household. One of the main changes was that her maid's tasks and Connie's, for that matter, were now extended to dressmaking in an effort to make certain that she and her niece stood out among the amazing array of fashion likely to be present on the night.

'It is breathtaking to be sure,' Connie whispered, twirling around in front of the full-length mirror. She wore a ruby gown of the finest silk, its fully panniered skirt extending two feet on either side of her slender hips.

The bodice was decorated with rows of horizontal pleats in the shape of small fans of the same colour, while the skirt was edged with sprays of roses fashioned out of darker silk. The edging of her chemise which formed part of her decolletage and the fall of lace at her elbows had been starched until they were as stiff as a board.

Her golden hair had been liberally powdered and drawn back from her forehead over small, sausage-like pads to create the essential height fashion required, while the ends were caught in scarlet ribbons and teased into a delicate fall of curls at the base of her neck.

Connie purred contentedly as she took in this new, expensive image. She had certainly never dreamt of being able to wear anything like this when at home, let alone having an occasion which afforded such grandeur there, and she knew she only had Clarissa to thank for such an opportunity.

'Where is my aunt?' she asked Julie while she slipped into a pair of six-inch-heeled shoes she'd also been assured were de rigueur among the fashionable set.

'I believe she's awaiting you in the drawing room, my lady.'

Connie nodded her approval and, picking up her matching mask, left in search of Clarissa.

She found her sipping sherry with Sir Mandeville. They both turned in her direction, the shock visible on the gentleman's face despite the black velvet mask he wore.

'But, my dear,' he beamed, rushing over and raising her hand enthusiastically to his lips. 'Beside your aunt, you are the most enchanting creature I have ever had the good fortune to set eyes on.'

Connie coloured slightly at his compliment and pulled her hand away, suddenly finding his attention rather too familiar.

'Oh, Aunt, I cannot tell you how excited I am at the prospect of tonight!' She smiled at Clarissa as the older woman struggled to her feet, her movements hampered by the powder-blue silk she wore.

'Well I must admit that I too feel somewhat overwhelmed by it all, my dear. We must remember to repay Sir Mandeville for his kindness. After all, if not for his influence we should not have received invitations at all.'

'Oh, it was nothing,' he smiled, taking Clarissa's arm and leading her over to the door. 'Call it a pleasure on my part. It is payment enough to see the joy on your two lovely faces. I'm just sad that I was unable to find a suitable escort for your niece, ma'am.' He winked at Connie over his shoulder.

'Oh I shouldn't worry about that, Mandeville.' Clarissa laughed, disengaging herself from his grasp and helping Connie to lace up her mask, then turning in order to allow her to return the favour. 'If I have learned anything at all about her during her short stay, it is that she won't be long in finding suitable company for this evening's festivities!'

The drive to the Lord Chancellor's residence wasn't a long one, a fact which Connie was very grateful for, the carriage being rather cramped with their extended skirts. By the time the footmen helped her out, her legs were aching from the lack of space and she took the opportunity to stretch them while the servants helped out her aunt and Sir Mandeville. She glanced up at the imposing building before her and couldn't help but feel awe.

A blaze of golden light shone from each of its nine front-facing windows, each one providing Connie with a limited view of the splendid interior of the townhouse and its occupants. Due to the warmth of the evening, each window was open which, in turn, allowed myriad voices to drift across the pavement to her, the pleasing sounds of laughter and muffled conversation filling her ears.

One particularly high-pitched voice caught her attention and, looking upwards, Connie made out a woman leaning from one of the top-floor windows.

Narrowing her eyes, she saw that she held a bottle of wine in one hand while holding back the gentleman beside her with the other. He was obviously trying to wrest the bottle from her much to the woman's delight, if her excited squeals were anything to go by.

'Ready, my dears?' Sir Mandeville joined her then, taking her arm along with Clarissa's and guiding them up the small flight of marble steps and into the house. As soon as they had been announced, Connie pulled her arm away from Sir Mandeville and, professing a longing to meet the other guests on her own, left him to her aunt's company. There was something about the way he'd looked at her that night which had made her feel uncomfortable and she had decided that the less time she spent in his company the better, especially if she was going to truly enjoy this unique opportunity to mix with such a fashionable set of people.

She accepted a glass of wine from a passing servant and went immediately into the next room where she found a capacious dance floor thronging with people. Though not a connoisseur of the art herself, she stayed long enough to watch those couples who were brave enough partake in a lively gavotte before she ascended to the next floor.

During the next hour or so, she met a great many

people and quickly received the impression that, had they not been forced to do so through politeness, most wouldn't have even deigned to speak to her, due to her father's lowly position in society. Upon reflection, Connie wasn't that shocked by these people's thinly veiled snobbishness. She saw it only as a confirmation of what her mother had been saying for years about their family's lack of social stature, in spite of their many titles and obvious wealth.

In the past, Connie had always assumed that Lady Boughby was just being foolish. Now, in light of this unequivocal evidence to the contrary, she would have no choice but to believe her in the future.

'Can't get away so easily, my dear,' a familiar voice intoned behind her. A hand caught her arm, turning her round to face the speaker. 'I'm sure you knew that it would only be a matter of time before I caught up with you again.'

Connie caught her breath as she stared up into the masked face of Sir Mandeville. Perspiration had made his make-up run, causing ruby streaks to form over his cheeks and chin.

'Why, sir,' she laughed, trying to ignore the sudden unease brewing in her belly, 'where is Aunt Clarissa? I cannot see her anywhere.'

He shrugged, casually leading her through the room, inclining his head to those guests he knew.

'I suspect she has found her own amusement by now, my dear. Something which I think you and I should do forthwith.'

Connie stopped in her tracks and, trying unsuccessfully to pull her wrist free of his grasp, stared at him. She was rather disappointed to see that he displayed no sign of intoxication but rather seemed resolutely in command of all his faculties.

'Sir – please let me go. I, I am certain that you will have no trouble finding someone more ... amicable to your advances than I.'

Sir Mandeville smiled broadly at her attempt to brush

him off, his grip on her arm remaining steadfast. 'Oh no, my dear. You will not get away so easily. Your dear aunt has told me of your current enforced abstinence from things sensual and I mean to remedy that situation this evening, in this very house. Why, my old friend the Lord Chancellor has even offered me the convenience one of his bedchambers for the purpose.'

'No!' Connie cried, secretly hoping that someone in the room would hear her plea and come to her aid but, much to her growing terror, even those immediately surrounding them seemed oblivious to her discomfort and continued their conversations unabated. 'Please let me go. Can't you see that, besides the fact that you are my aunt's lover, I am unwilling?'

He threw back his head and laughed. 'You say that now but I can assure you that once you have sampled what I have to offer, you will quickly understand Clarissa's liking for me. Now, are you going to accompany me upstairs willingly –'

'You heard the lady.' A deep voice drowned out Sir Mandeville's, its tone full of menace. 'I believe she has already told you her answer, has she not?'

Both Sir Mandeville and Connie turned in its direction, their eyes falling on the tall, athletically built figure of a masked man standing behind them, his fingers lightly resting on the hilt of his sword. 'Do I need to remind you of that fact, sir?'

Sir Mandeville's eyes widened in shock, his mouth falling impotently open. When he regained his composure some seconds later, he gave a hurried bow to the taller man and without another word, left them alone.

Connie turned to her saviour and smiled, offering him her hand. 'How can I thank you, sir, for your kind intercession? I don't know how you managed it for Sir Mandeville is indeed an important man, but thank you all the same.'

'Please, there's no need. Any gentleman would have come to your aid in such circumstances. As for that insect, well, he probably just realised he would stand no

189

chance at all against my duelling skills. Now, may I introduce myself? Lord Dendrith at your service.' He sank into an elaborate bow and then raised her hand to his lips.

Connie involuntarily squeezed her sex when she felt his lips brushing the smooth skin of the back of her hand and noticed the strength in his grip. By the time she had retrieved her hand she found that she was shaking and in need of refreshment.

As if reading her thoughts, Lord Dendrith procured a drink for her and then led her out of the overheated room to a small balcony at the rear of the residence.

Connie was grateful for the coolness of the evening air as she leant against the balustrade and looked out across the ornate garden. Ripples of relief washed over her and she tried to think of something appropriate to say to this intriguing stranger.

'It is indeed a beautiful evening,' he whispered, his breath tickling the skin at the base of her neck. 'Much like you, my dear.'

Connie gasped and turned round to face him. She found herself pinned between his lean body and the balustrade.

'I, I am Lady Constance –' she began, stopping when she sensed another kind of hardness pressing into her through the layers of her skirts. She looked up and met his chestnut eyes, the intense look in them connecting with something deep inside her. She fidgeted slightly as she sensed wetness begin to build up between her legs. How different this was from the feelings she experienced just a few minutes ago with Sir Mandeville. 'You are indeed a flatterer, my lord. I suspect you say that to every lady,' she managed at last, gulping down the remains of her wine and trying to seem unaffected by his proximity.

'Not at all,' he said with a mischievous grin, his arm snaking round her waist. 'Only those I wish to bed.'

Connie swallowed hard and fluttered her eyelashes, her heart suddenly thundering in her chest. 'Is that so?

May I say that you are exceedingly forward, my lord? You hardly know me –'

'I can think of no better way of introducing ourselves can you?' Before she had a chance to answer, he lowered his head and, covering her mouth with his own, pushed his tongue past the obstruction of her lips. Connie immediately softened in his arms, enjoying the sensations his tongue created as it explored the moist contours of her mouth. His hand slipped down to cup one of her breasts, his fingers pinching and squeezing its nipple until she was ready to scream with excitement.

As suddenly as he'd kissed her, Lord Dendrith let her go, stepping back and adjusting his cravat. He held out his hand to her. 'Come, let us leave this place for a more amenable location.'

'No,' she breathed heavily, remaining where she was. 'I cannot go with you – I would be missed.'

Lord Dendrith raised his eyebrows, 'Here then?' He indicated the hard floor of the balcony and Connie laughed.

'Of course not, don't be silly. What I meant was that you could come back to my room. Just let me make my apologies and secure the carriage. I'll meet you downstairs where it is to be hoped no one will see us leave together.'

'Is it possible for you to do this?'

Connie shrugged. 'I'll tell Aunt that I've got a headache that's all.' Seeing him slowly nod, she pushed her way back onto the crowded room and, mindful not to bump into Sir Mandeville again, went in search of Mrs Stevens.

She found her some twenty minutes later unashamedly reclining on a settee with a gentleman, her arms entwined about his neck. Clarissa looked up almost guiltily when Connie told her of her plan to leave.

'Are you sure? I would be happy to return with you if you aren't feeling well enough to journey alone, or Sir Mandeville even. I'm sure he'd be only too pleased to oblige –'

'I'm certain he would,' Connie replied crossly,

remembering his advances. 'No, I'll be all right. I'll just have the carriage called and one of the footmen can take me home and then return for you later on.' She glanced briefly at the gentleman who was eyeing her with interest, before returning her gaze to Clarissa. 'I should hate to ruin your evening, Aunt.'

Chapter Fifteen

*T*he carriage ride back was a strange affair for Connie. Even though the stranger sitting opposite would shortly be sharing her bed for the first time, she neither felt the need nor the desire to find out more about him beforehand.

It was the oddest thing, but she just couldn't help feeling that they'd known each other for a long time. She supposed that this was one of the reasons why she'd felt there was little need for any more of an introduction than they'd already had.

Connie glanced in his direction, noticing how he lounged nonchalantly in the cramped seat opposite, his legs stretched out towards her while his gloved hands rested on the silver handle of a walking stick in between them.

She wondered briefly if he felt the same about her, but judged by the self-satisfied look on his face that he was probably just congratulating himself on engaging her affections so easily.

The carriage pulled to a halt outside the Little Piazza and, after a moment's confusion with the hem of her skirt when it got caught in the door, the pair of them hurried into the building.

After dismissing the footman, Connie took Lord

Dendrith's hand and began to lead him up the stairs towards her room. On reaching the first-floor landing she turned towards him, her fingers immediately going to the ties on his mask.

'Not yet, my lady,' he breathed, pushing her hands away. 'Let us keep them on for the moment. Who knows, they might just lend something to our enjoyment.'

Connie thought a moment and then nodded her approval. 'Why yes, I should have considered that. Although I long to see what you look like, and I suspect you me, it will certainly give us something to look forward to later on.'

She giggled and, catching his arm, tugged him across the hall until they stood outside her bedroom door. She turned back and threw her arms round him, grinding her pelvis against his while his hands closed round her narrow wrist. 'It won't be long now, my intriguing lord,' she whispered. 'I just have to send my maid away and then we'll be all alone. You wait out here and I'll call you in a minute or two.'

'Make sure that's all it is!' Lord Dendrith laughed, planting a kiss on her forehead then releasing her and leaning against the nearby wall.

Connie found Julie smoozing in the armchair beside her bed. She roused her and managed to get the maid to leave after allowing the woman to divest her of her gown. Once Julie was safely out of earshot and she was attired only in her underclothes, Connie opened the door and beckoned Lord Dendrith into the room.

In the pale light of the tapers dotted around the walls, he looked even more mysterious to her, a fact which sent an exciting shiver down her spine. Lord Dendrith took Connie by the shoulders and pushed her roughly back against the wall.

'My lord!' she gasped, the breath wrenched out of her by the suddenness of his movement. 'You *are* eager!'

He smiled, his hands tearing at the ribbons of her stays. 'Yes indeed,' he whispered. 'I am eager to sample your delights, fair lady. It has been a long time.'

194

'Oh?' she questioned, giggling with relief as the constrictive garment was torn from her body by his experienced hands. 'I cannot believe a man of your ... stature should have to look very hard for company.'

'Can't you?' Lord Dendrith ripped the coarse cotton away from her chest baring her ample breasts in one, sharp movement. He immediately bent and, fixing his mouth to one of her peachy nipples, began to suck on it with the fervour of a new-born babe.

Connie sighed, her hands lightly resting on the back of his head as wave after wave of pleasure raced through her, his tongue tantalising her sensitive teat while his teeth gently nibbled at its base. She spread her legs, urging the moisture already coating her puffy, turgid lips to ooze down from them to paint the space between her thighs.

'Take me now, my lord, fill me with your magnificent cock,' she mumbled, pulling him back up to face her. She craned forward and tried to kiss him, her hands moving down to the ties of his breeches.

'You're in no position to give orders now, my dear.' His tone was no longer friendly but tinged with anger as he caught her wrists and held her arms above her head. 'You have to learn that you satisfaction rests solely in my hands.' He drove his knee between her legs, spreading them even wider than before, his free hand fumbling under her skirts. Connie groaned with delight when his fingers eventually found her slick hole and pushed their way inside her yearning orifice.

'Yes,' she breathed, licking her lips and keeping her gaze fixed on his face. 'Do whatever you wish, my lord. Your pleasure is mine.'

'That's more like it,' Lord Dendrith growled, the whites of his eyes sparkling in the semi-darkness. 'Just what I want, a woman who knows her place!'

He began to move his fingers in and out of her, his mouth descending to cover hers, his tongue surging into her, seeking out the tightness of her throat. Though she was certain she would choke, Connie opened her lips as far as she could, urging his tongue on in its delightful exploration, shivering wildly when it met with her own.

Already Connie could feel orgasm building within her, its heady rush developing into an almost painful throbbing in her groin until, crazy with desire, she began to rock her hips back and forth against his probing digits. She squeezed herself around them as culmination burst within her, sending her slumping back against the wall.

'Please – don't – stop!' she groaned, shaking uncontrollably, her arms pushing wildly at his restraining hand.

Lord Dendrith swiftly scooped her up in his arms and carried her over to the bed where he threw her face down on to the mattress.

In the few seconds it took for him to rid himself of his breeches and frockcoat, Connie tried to push herself up but he rejoined her before she had a chance to do so properly and his hands marshalled her into the correct position for accepting his passion. His weight forced her face and breasts down against the bed while he pulled her legs up over his, hooking them around his thighs as he smoothly entered her.

Connie groaned, her hands moving to protect her head as she felt him shift his full weight on to her, his hands bearing down on her shoulderblades as he began to pump in and out of her.

The penetration was so deep that almost instantaneously she could feel orgasm rise again within her. She used her legs to drag him closer to her, arching her back and pressing her buttocks against his thrusting hips.

Lord Dendrith drew his prick out of Connie's vagina until only its slick tip remained embedded within her before quickly plunging it back in, the sharp sound of his thighs slapping against her buttocks echoing throughout the room.

'Yes!' Connie cried, clenching her internal muscles around his hardness, holding him within for as long as possible, before allowing him to withdraw for the next, surging stroke. With every frenzied attack he made on her slick receptacle, she was pushed further and further into the mattress, the sensation of her hardened nipples rubbing against its roughness adding to her escalating excitement.

She moaned as she came, her legs falling away from Lord Dendrith's, her mouth opening and closing in a silent scream at the very same moment as he removed his hands from her shoulders. He fell forward on to her, his seed pumping high into her, his weight forcing her deeper still into the mattress.

Connie struggled for breath under this added pressure, her shoulderblades already beginning to ache from the force his hands had exerted on them. She tried to crawl away from him, but found herself firmly under his semi-clad body.

Connie sighed and resigned herself to waiting, an awful sense of *déjà vu* sweeping over her at the familiarity of this situation. As she lay there, waiting for Lord Dendrith to release her, it suddenly dawned on her what the cause of this unexpected unease was.

She shivered, hardly believing that it could be true and, when he finally granted her wish and crawled off her, she immediately pushed herself into a sitting position and watched him with terrified eyes as he tore at the restraints of his shirt and waistcoat.

Lord Dendrith carelessly tossed his clothes into the heap already created by his discarded breeches and frockcoat. Connie caught her breath when he turned back to her, his hands immediately going to the ties of his mask.

'I wouldn't even bother,' she said with remarkable control. 'All I can say is that I must have been blind, deaf and dumb not to have recognised you earlier.'

He smiled and, silently releasing the mask, swiftly grabbed her arm.

Fran stretched out in the big bed, her left arm flopping into the empty space beside her. Running her hand along the untouched sheets, she cursed and pushed herself up.

'Damn him!' She lit a nearby candle and swung her legs over the side of the bed, knowing she'd been a fool to believe the marquess when he'd said he'd only be gone a short while.

Picking up her coarse nightgown from the floor and dragging it over her head, she went to the window and gazed out over the Piazza. No lights shone across the way and no sound emanated from the taverns and alehouses bordering the square. At that time in the morning, it seemed that even Covent Garden slept.

Fran turned away from the window and returned to perch on the end of the bed. He was probably disporting with her at that very moment.

She made to pour herself a comforting glass of wine from the bottle on the chest of drawers beside the bed but stopped dead when she heard the unmistakable sound of metal scraping in the lock. Slamming the bottle down, she jumped to her feet and excitedly went to the door.

'Ye have returned, m'lord. I knew you would –' The greeting died on her lips when she wrenched it open and was confronted by the sight of her husband bending at her feet, a hammer in his hands. 'Paul!' she gasped, stepping back in shock, the colour draining from her cheeks.

'None other.' He scrambled to his feet and pushed past her into the room with Lennard following close behind. 'You looked surprised, Fran. Expecting someone else, perhaps?' He chuckled to himself as he threw on to the bed the bag he'd been carrying and faced her. 'And how's my darling little wife then? Been keeping it warm for me have you?' He tried to give her a hug but Fran only pulled herself away.

'What are you doing here, Paul? How did you know I was staying at this particular inn?'

'Easy. Me and Lennard just used our brains and asked about. You and his lordship make quite a distinctive couple you know. As to your other question, well, we've come to teach his lordship a lesson and you are going to help us.'

'Never!' Fran crossed the room and pulled on the fur-trimmed robe Lucas had bought her the day before. 'I told you I wanted no part of it before. What makes you think I've changed my mind now?'

Paul smiled and approached her, his arms out-stretched. 'I thought you didn't want to see me get hurt.'

'I don't . . .'

'Well then, tell me where his lordship is and we can surprise him before he has a chance to stop us.'

'No!'

Paul grasped the neckline of her wrap and fingered its mink edging.

'Hmm, mighty fine indeed, but, you know, I could get you one of these if he paid up. Perhaps something even better.'

Fran slapped his hand away. 'I don't care what you can or cannot get. Just don't do this Paul, you'll be killed, I know you will . . . he ain't worth it.' She ran to the bed and threw herself face down on it, secretly hoping that her attempt at melodramatics might change his mind.

'Your tears won't sway me, my girl. I'm afraid I'm set on it. Now, are you going to tell me where he is, or am I going to have to allow Lennard here to have his way with you? You know he's been itching to do it for ages.'

'You wouldn't!' Fran dragged herself up to face him, her heart sinking when she saw the determination in his eyes. He sat down beside her, taking some of her hair in his hands and lovingly smelling it.

'It would certainly be a shame, for I couldn't half do with some loving myself, and who better to do it with than my wife?'

Fran swallowed hard, switching her gaze first to the leering Lennard and then back to Paul. She knew he would make good his word if she didn't comply with his wishes and, though she was loathe to admit it, she would rather give up the marquess than be subject to his friend's oafish lust.

She wrapped her arms round Paul's shoulders and kissed his forehead. 'You still believe me when I say that I like you, despite my desire for the marquess, don't you, Paul?'

He met her eyes. 'Aye, I do, darling. I know this thing with his lordship is just a passing fancy for you. When you grow tired of him I know you'll just move on to someone else, but I don't care any more, Fran. I know none of them mean anything to you. So long as you are happy to stay my wife, that's enough for me.'

'You really mean that?'

He nodded enthusiastically.

She clasped his head and pulled his face down to rest against her chest, his nose wedged snugly in the crease between her breasts. 'I should be happy to tell you what you wish to know, but first get Lennard to leave us for a while and I'll show you just how much of a wife I can be.'

Paul jerked his head up. 'You're not fooling?'

'Does it look like it? Go on then, before I change my mind,' she urged, laughing.

Fran watched him usher the taller man out of the room and then sank backward on to the mattress. If memory served her correctly, her charms would be enough to delay his departure until the morning. That, at least, would give the marquess a chance to leave the blonde haired girl's house before Paul and Lennard caught up with him.

'Let go of me, Lucas!' Connie shrieked, wrenching her arm away from him. 'I –'

'So glad you're happy to see me,' he replied sarcastically, 'and there I was expecting you to be over the moon at our sudden reunion.'

Connie slid from the bed and getting shakily to her feet, walked over to her dressing table where her powdering gown hung on the back of the chair. Quickly putting it on and securing it about her waist, she moved back towards the bed and stood staring down at the supine marquess.

'So, what is it that you want, or is there any need for me to ask?' she managed after a few moments' silence while she regained her composure.

Lucas smiled and crossed his arms behind is head. 'No, I don't think there is, you know.' He cast a lazy glance in her direction. 'May I compliment you on your good taste earlier? I must say that I have never seen you look so alluring as you did tonight. The town obviously has a good effect on you, my dear.'

'Unlike you!' she snapped, anger engulfing her. 'I see that it hasn't improved you one jot. I cannot for the life of me understand what it was which made me want to get involved with you. Perhaps Amelia was right about you after all.'

'Can't you? If I recall correctly, it was the lack of stimulation which drove you into my arms in the first place, a fact which seems to be continuing here. Why, you acted tonight as if you hadn't been fucked in a month.'

'Don't flatter yourself, Lucas. I have known others since we parted –'

'Oh I don't doubt it. I've long since known how promiscuous you are, Connie dear. I just don't think you've had anything remotely near to what I just gave you.'

'Hmm!' Connie sniffed and turned away, disgusted by his arrogance. 'I think there has been enough said on that score. Now, would you please leave. My aunt will soon be returning and I can assure you that she will not take kindly to your presence here.'

'Oh won't she?' a voice whispered beside her. Connie looked back to see Lucas standing there. He wrapped his arms round her waist and pulled her against him. 'How unfortunate for you.' He ran his lips up her neck to pause at her earlobe which he nibbled almost affectionately. 'There is one way you could make me leave before she returns.'

'No!' Connie tried in vain to pull away from him. 'I won't do it no matter how much you threaten me. I'm not my mother you know – one who gives in at the slightest sign of trouble.' She smiled bitterly. 'There is no point in trying to deny this fact either, for it is obvious that it was Mama who gave this address away. Other than me, she was the only person who knew that this was where Amelia had come when she first ran away. Now, I don't know what bargaining tool you used in order to obtain this address from her, but it won't work with me. Of that, I am certain.'

'Oh it was no bargaining tool, my dear.' Lucas's hand slipped inside the loose folds of her powdering gown searching out one of her breasts. 'I simply reminded her of that which we once used to share before she wed your father.'

'What?' Connie pushed against his arms with all her might and finally managed to break free of his grasp. She raced over to the window where she stood leaning on the sill with her back to him.

For several seconds she said nothing, only the sound of her own panting filling her ears as the shock of his admission sank in. But then, when her senses came back to her, she whipped around to face him again, shaking. 'Are you saying what I think you are? That you and my mother –' Connie broke off, unable to say the appropriate words. Lucas took great delight in finishing the sentence for you.

'Were lovers? Yes. Why do you think that she was forced into marriage with someone as low on the social scale as John? You witnessed the truth of his position this evening, I believe.'

'You bastard!' Connie growled. 'I thought my father was your best friend.'

'Oh he is. Do not doubt that.' Lucas sauntered across the room to join her beside the window. 'Who do you think it was who convinced him of the worth in saving your mother's reputation?'

'How noble of you,' Connie sneered. 'So my father

was coerced by you into taking your leavings? I don't suppose it should surprise me. I never did think him a very strong man.'

'It was hardly that. He saw the advantages in marrying your mother, and her family were quite happy to accept his suit after the scandal Amelia's father had already caused them.'

'So, does that mean ... am I ...' Connie raised her eyes to his, her throat suddenly going dry as she contemplated the most damning thought of all. To her disgust, Lucas only laughed at her anguish.

'Don't be silly, child. Do you think I would have allowed our liaison to take place if I thought you were in any way related to me?' He shook his head. 'No, my dear, my relationship with your mother stopped the day they announced their engagement.'

Connie focused her gaze once more on the open window where she stared down into the cobbled road below. 'I still cannot believe it ...' she mumbled almost to herself as she witnessed Clarissa's coach draw outside.

Lucas suddenly pushed her aside and craned his head out of the window. 'Is that your aunt? Well, is it?' he demanded, catching her by the arms and shaking her violently.

'Stop it, Lucas, stop it! Yes it's my aunt. Why, you're not afraid of what might happen when you are discovered, are you?'

The marquess ignored her question. 'Tell me where she is and I'll leave it at that. Just tell me where my wife is and I'll overlook the small matter of you taking her virginity before me.'

'Oh, that's it, is it? You are here out of a longing to avenge your bruised pride instead of any actual concern for what might be happening to Amelia. Well, if that's the case –' Connie stopped short as she heard footsteps hurrying up the stairs just beyond the door.

'You, my lord, had best hide or we will both incur my aunt's wrath.' Lucas made no move to do as she requested but, folding his arms across his bare chest, turned towards the source of the disturbance.

'I'm not going anywhere, my dear. Let it not be said that I run away from my battles.'

Connie shrugged and went back to the bed where she sank on to the mattress in defeat and awaited her aunt's anger.

The door opened and Clarissa entered the room carrying her shoes in one hand and a candle in the other. She went straight to where Connie reclined and bent over her. 'Are you all right, my dear? I was most concerned for your welfare when you left.'

'Yes, Aunt, I am fine,' Connie replied, avoiding her eyes and staring up at the ceiling instead.

'I must say that I am surprised you are not tucked up in bed. I should have thought it would be the best thing in the circumstances –'

'That, my dear lady, is my fault I'm afraid.' Lucas stepped forward from the shadows and bowed, an erection clearly jutting from between his legs, its slick, splayed tip gleaming in the subdued light.

Clarissa's lips stretched into a smile as she cast the candle's glow over his nudity. 'So niece, there was no headache after all. Why, I do declare, you are a woman after my own heart! I shall disturb you no more –'

'Aunt –' Connie scrambled from the bed and ran to her side. 'I might as well tell you about this man for he will not leave until he knows the truth. This is Lord Beechwood, Amelia's husband.'

'Is it? My goodness.' Clarissa turned back, her gaze falling on his prodigious organ once more. 'Then both she and you are indeed lucky women. Now, may I suggest that we convene again downstairs in, say, an hour or so, where we may discuss this most delicate of situations in more suitable surroundings?'

'You mean you are not angry?'

'No, of course not,' she laughed. 'Should I be?'

'I just thought you wouldn't appreciate me bringing a man here.'

'That would be rather hypocritical of me, I think, considering that I have my own guest waiting for me.'

'Is it Sir Mandeville?' Connie asked, deciding that if it was she'd rather remain in her bedroom until he left.

'No, dear, and you needn't worry. He won't be visiting us again. I have made sure of that.'

'But how –'

Clarissa tapped her nose. 'Surely you know by now that I have an uncanny knack of knowing everyone else's business? However I must admit that this little discovery tonight has certainly foxed me. Now, I shall see you two later downstairs where I will tell his lordship exactly what he wants to know about his estranged wife. In the meantime, I suggest you enjoy yourselves, for I am sure that my guest is beginning to tire of his own company.'

'But, Aunt –' Connie began, catching her arm, trying to stop her leaving.

'I'm sorry, dear. I know how much Amelia means to you, but when she came to stay here I told her quite plainly that I would not stand between man and wife. That is a promise I intend to keep. No matter what you feel about his lordship, he is her lawful husband. Now, do as I suggest and I'll see you two in an hour. Good evening.'

Connie reluctantly shut the door and turned back to Lucas, nausea overtaking her at the triumphant expression on his face.

Chapter Sixteen

Amelia put the last of the pins in her hair and went down to share breakfast with the other girls. She met an alarmed Jenny on the stairs.

'What on earth is wrong?' Amelia asked with genuine concern, having come to look upon the older woman as a friend as well as mentor in the short time she'd been in residence at the school. 'Are you unwell?'

'No, dear, it's nothing like that. This, I'm afraid, concerns only you.'

'What do you mean?' A shiver ran up Amelia's spine as Jenny led her across the hall towards the drawing room. 'What's happened? Is it Connie or Mrs Stevens?'

Jenny stopped outside the door and patted Amelia's hand. 'You have a visitor, dear.'

'A visitor?' Amelia considered this for a moment, her eyes widening as an awful thought entered her mind. 'Surely you don't mean –' She broke off, unable to say his name.

'I'm sorry, Amelia. We tried to keep him out but he was most insistent that he saw you. When he threatened to report my establishment to the local magistrate I had no choice but to agree.'

'It's all right,' Amelia said, straightening up. 'I know only too well just how demanding my husband can be.'

The sense of fury which swept over her then was stronger than anything she had experienced since leaving Beechwood House. It went straight to her stomach, twisting her intestines into knots, a testament to the anguish Lucas was still able to cause her despite their separation.

'How dare he try to disrupt my life again?' she demanded as much to herself as to Jenny. The fact that he should turn up here, in London, only confirmed her worst fears: that after all this time he still considered her his wife, still considered her his property. 'What am I going to do? I simply cannot allow him to return me to the life I've spent all this time trying to escape.' Amelia blinked and stared at Jenny, suddenly knowing what the answer was. The older woman smiled, chucked her under the chin.

'You are going to go in there and face him like the woman I know you are. This shouldn't be such a daunting task now, especially in the light of what you've recently discovered about yourself, should it? Well?'

Amelia slowly shook her head. 'I suppose I've always know that this moment would come. I just didn't think it would be so soon.'

'Exactly, and I believe you are ready finally to face the truth about your relationship with him. Now, compose yourself, my dear, for he won't wait much longer.'

'I know,' Amelia whispered, moving towards the door.

'Give him hell. You owe it to yourself to do that at least. Show him that you are no longer the girl he knew, but a woman who knows what she wants out of life, one who isn't prepared to put up with his arrogant ways any more, no matter what he threatens.' Jenny smiled and gave her a reassuring hug. 'I know that the memory of what has passed between you must still be terribly fresh in your mind, but you've got to put that aside when you confront him. Who knows, he might not be as angry as you imagine. Why, he might just be glad to have found you at long last.'

'I very much doubt that,' Amelia mumbled, her arm

trembling as she reached for the doorknob, 'but I'll do my best not to give in to him. After all, I've got too much to lose by returning to Beechwood House.'

Lucas barely moved at her entrance, preferring it seemed to continue inspecting one of the many paintings which graced the walls of the room.

Amelia was rather perplexed by his reaction, or lack of one, to be precise and, for a moment, she didn't know what to do as she stood there holding open the door. However, it didn't take her long to realise that this was probably a ploy on his part to undermine her composure and she was determined that this time she wouldn't give him the satisfaction of knowing he'd annoyed her.

Quietly shutting out any unwanted eavesdroppers, Amelia moved into the centre of the room and rested her arms on the back of the small two-seater settee which stood there. 'Why, I do declare,' she laughed, trying to sound unconcerned, 'that this must be the first time I've known you not to have anything to say, my lord.'

Lucas turned and faced her than, his expression surprisingly placid. Amelia swallowed hard and gave in to the urge to take a good look at him to see if he was as she remembered. His familiar brown hair hung in a tangle about his shoulders while a crumpled shirt was carelessly shoved into the waistband of a pair of grey silk breeches. Amelia caught her breath, wondering how he could still look so attractive, despite such dishevelment.

'I am silent through shock, madam,' he said gravely. 'I never thought I'd see the day when you of all people would count bawds and whores among your friends.' He shook his head but made no move towards her. 'All I can say is that you've sunk in my estimation.'

'Oh please, save your sermon for someone else!' she spat, finally giving in to the anger which had been steadily growing inside her since hearing of his visit. 'I care not what your opinion of me is. Why, you could hate me and it wouldn't bother me, so little do I value it now.'

Lucas screwed up his mouth in mock indignation. 'My, you are bitter, aren't you? I wonder what's caused this ill feeling you seem to have towards me.'

'I think I have every right to be bitter, don't you, after the way I've been treated at your hands, my lord!'

'No, I don't actually. Your recent behaviour has only confirmed that I was perfectly correct in treating you the way I did. You've no idea of the embarrassment you've caused me as a consequence of your absence.'

'Oh haven't I? Well let me tell you that your discomfort is nothing compared to what I've suffered since I was forced into marriage with you and before, even. If you have come here with some notion to return me home, you are sadly mistaken –'

'You know, wife, I find you changed,' Lucas said with a perplexed smile. 'You seem much more ... antagonistic than I remember.'

Amelia raised her head defiantly. 'There are many things you don't know about me, my lord. I can honestly say that I am not the person you left back there in the hands of that brutal friend of yours. Since we've been apart, I've managed to shed the effects of your contaminating influence and realise, once and for all, what I want, need, out of life.'

'Oh really?' He licked his lips but still made no move. 'Now that is a point I would definitely like to put to the test.'

'Don't toy with me, Lucas. If you think that I will submit to your will this time, you are very much mistaken!

'Am I?' he asked in the sweetest of voices. 'I wouldn't be so sure about that if I were you.'

Amelia met his eyes then and shivered when she saw the unmistakable fire of desire in them. 'That's what you think. One of the most important things I've learnt since I ran away is that I don't have to do anything I don't want to. I'm my own woman now –'

'Is that so? Well, I'm sorry to have to disappoint you, my dear, but you don't honestly expect me to allow you to remain in this questionable company, while I return empty-handed to Beechwood House, do you? I wouldn't be a very good husband if I did, would I? What on earth would my friends think if it became known that I couldn't even control my own wife?'

With a speed which both shocked and caught her off guard, Lucas suddenly lurched forward, catching Amelia's arm, pulling her towards him over the back of the settee.

'Unhand me . . .' she cried, struggling to wrench her wrist from his iron grasp, frightened by the strength in it. 'You have no right to use such force with me!'

Lucas didn't answer but, keeping hold of her, rounded the couch until he was standing beside her and her right arm was cruelly twisted behind her back.

'I have no right? I'll tell you about rights!' He pulled her ruthlessly backwards against him and, letting go of her arm, slid his around her waist. 'The only rights which count are mine as your lord and master,' he whispered, the warmth of his breath tickling Amelia's ear. She gasped, the potent, masculine scent of him filling her nostrils, reminding her of pleasures past, as he dragged her even closer until every contour of his muscled body was pressing into her back.

Amelia shivered, his proximity causing a pounding to grow in her groin. She felt his hand on her neck, stroking, teasing the downy skin there, leaving goosepimples in its wake, till it moved on to grasp her chin, pulling her face backwards until her eyes met his.

'How clever you must have thought you were when you escaped Carterall,' he mumbled, trailing his lips across her forehead. 'You should have known I'd come looking for you.'

Amelia shrugged, twisting her head from side to side in an effort to avoid his gaze. His hand held her firm, forcing her to bear his attention for as long as he wanted.

'I, I knew I had to try for my own sanity's sake.'

'Speaking of which, are you aware that I could have

you locked up for such an outrage? Why, if I so choose I could have you committed this very day.'

'Your idle threats do not frighten me, my lord. I think I would rather reside in a madhouse than with you!'

Lucas burst out laughing, his grip slackening slightly. 'You know not what you say, madam, for if that indeed happened you'd soon wither without the caress of a man. Of that fact, I am certain. You and Connie, it seems, are equal on that score.'

'Oh are we? I think not.' She resumed her assault on him then, digging her nails into the pliant flesh of his arms, twisting her hips this way and that while she thrashed her legs about. 'I demand that you let me go this instant!'

Lucas ignored her plea. 'Why, the proof is staring you in the face as we speak.' He released her as suddenly as he had trapped her in his arms. 'Just look around you now, at this establishment. Why would you be staying here if it were not so?' Amelia staggered away from him, her head spinning wildly as the blood rushed back in. 'Face it, Amelia, ever since you left, you've been trying to reproduce that which only I can give you.'

'No. That is true of my cousin perhaps, but not me,' she breathed, bumping into a nearby table, a wave of heat consuming her as it dawned on her that this was by far the most plausible explanation for her actions since leaving Beechwood House. 'I'm here because this was the only place left for me to stay. At least I have friends here who make no demands on me –'

'And what about your home?' Lucas demanded, stalking her determinedly, forcing her to retreat even further into the room. 'No one made you leave it. You could have always returned.'

'And risk the "punishment" your friend so looked forward to inflicting on me? Though I now understand his particular motivation, I can honestly say that I believe I took the correct decision in running away. Why, I swear that it makes me shudder when I consider what I would have become had I stayed.' Amelia shook her head. 'No,

Lucas, I'm sorry to say that if being married to you means becoming some sort of dolt with no will of my own, then I should rather be a widow.'

For one brief moment, when she saw the harsh glow of anger replace the desire in his eyes, Amelia thought he was going to strike her. She stepped back defensively, only to realize with a sinking heart that there was no more room for manoeuvre. She was snugly pinned against the side of an armchair.

'So,' Lucas breathed, while he licked his lips and cast his eyes once more over her, 'you wish to be a widow? Well, before anything as drastic as that happens, I think it's my duty to remind you of what you'd miss if that was indeed the case, don't you?' He didn't give her a chance to answer but grabbed her shoulders and propelled her backwards over the arm of the chair.

Amelia tried to rise, to tidy her skirts which had billowed up above her knees as she'd tumbled into the seat, but the force Lucas exerted on her was too much for her to overcome and she remained pressed into the cushions.

'Lucas, let me up this instant!' she demanded, stretching her arms up towards his face, trying to catch hold of it.

'Oh no, my sweet,' he leered, his free hand moving to one of her exposed ankles. 'I have waited too long for this reunion. Do not deny me the pleasure of it now.' Amelia felt his fingers tracing a line up her calf, the warmth of them tantalising her, causing goosepimples to form on her skin under the thick silk of her stockings.

When she sensed her love juices building in her quim a few seconds later, she suddenly realised that she'd lost this particular battle of wills. If only she had been able to outwit Lucas this time, how different things would have been. She would certainly have enjoyed demonstrating to him just what she had meant when she had said she'd changed! Now that only seemed a distant fantasy, for once again it looked as if her husband had got the better of her.

212

Lucas purred contentedly, his fingers slipping under her starched petticoats and skirting the ebony edge of her pubis. He hovered nearer to her and, resting his knee on the small triangle of upholstery visible between her legs, grasped a fistful of her skirts and yanked them clear of her groin.

'Good lord!' he exclaimed, unable to hide his surprise when he stared down at her uncovered sex, his eyes focusing on one particular spot: her pierced clitoris. 'Well, well, well –' a broad grin swept across his features as he regained his composure '– you certainly are a mystery, my dear.'

Amelia swallowed hard and, to her relief, managed to shrug her shoulder away from his restraining hand. She made to pull herself up but stopped dead when she met his eyes, saw him shake his head.

Not to be put off, Amelia raised her chin and addressed him as calmly as she could. 'My lord, have you not subjected me to enough this day? Must I undergo an intimate interrogation from you as well?'

Lucas's lips twisted into a sardonic smile. 'When we married, I never imagined you would present me with so many . . . interesting diversions. Obviously I was way off the mark on that score. However, I shall enjoy making up for that miscalculation at a later date. For the moment though, let's just see exactly what this little addition does for you, shall we?'

Without hesitating, he thrust his hand into her groin, a finger and thumb closing round her silver tipped pleasure-node. Amelia sucked in her breath and dug her fingernails into the palms of her hands while she fought the urge to push her pelvis up to meet this calculated exploration of his.

Lucas took hold of the ring and began to slide it back and forth, rotating it in small circles between his fingers, tugging, pulling at her clitoral head until it grew hard.

'Please,' Amelia breathed through clenched teeth, rolling her head from side to side. 'No more. I don't think I can take much more!'

Lucas ignored her plea and continued to stimulate her sensitive organ until she was forced to give in to her need and began to rock against his touch.

'You like that, don't you, Amelia?' He increased the speed of his finger's movements, wildly twisting the ring back and forth. 'Tell me how much – how much you want to come.'

When she didn't answer straight away, he stopped what he was doing and stared down at her. Amelia flopped back against the seat, her chest heaving, perspiration forming on her brow with the swift approach of orgasm.

'Don't do this to me now, Lucas. Don't be so cruel.' She met his stern gaze and suddenly realised that there was only one way to satisfaction for her. The question was, was she prepared to pay the price?

'Well?' he enquired, carelessly examining his nails.

'No! I won't give in –'

Lucas resumed his assault on her senses, the fingers of his other hand sliding into her wet valley and beginning to pump in and out of her tight, lubricated channel, their movements matching exactly the rhythm of those already teasing her clitoris. 'Oh please –' Amelia opened her thighs as wide as they would go and pressed her sex in his direction, offering him even easier access to it. Any doubts left in her about how much she wanted him were swiftly swept away by the strength of an inexplicable desire to have his long, wide prick inside her, instead of the fingers she was currently enjoying.

'Take me, Lucas,' she screamed, suddenly not caring how desperate she sounded. 'Fuck me properly. I want to feel all of your cock in me!' She stared up at him with wild eyes, waiting for him to do as she demanded.

'So you want me now, do you?' he enquired, leaning over her until his lips were only an inch from hers. 'Is it really me you want, or would any stallion do?'

Amelia frowned and pounded her fists against the chair. 'This is agony, Lucas, and you know it,' she exploded, consumed by frustration. 'Will you do as I ask

– please?' As if to tempt him, she raised her torso slightly and pressed her mouth against his, her tongue seeking access between his rigid lips.

'Enough!' Lucas withdrew his hands from her groin and, pushing her roughly back down on to the seat, clambered over the arm of the chair to kneel astride her, trapping her arms under his legs. 'I've heard about enough of your needs. I think it's time you thought about mine, don't you?'

Amelia's mouth fell open in shock as she watched him slowly undo the buttons on his breeches and free his ample member. It sprang towards her, its foreskin retracted to reveal the mottled, plum-coloured glans. As she stared at it, a gleaming bead of liquid appeared on its tip and she swallowed hard, returning her gaze to his face.

'Oh my God, Lucas. You can't mean it.'

He smiled knowingly. 'Can't I? If I recall, the last time you indulged me, you rather enjoyed it. Why, if you please me well enough, I might even allow you your own satisfaction this time.'

'How magnanimous of you!' Amelia tried unsuccessfully to wiggle her arms free but the weight of his frame kept them firmly in place.

'Now, do I need to force you? It makes no difference to me but a little wifely compliance would certainly be an appreciated gesture on your part.'

Amelia's natural instinct was instantly to refuse his command but, as if she needed reminding of the precarious position she now found herself in, a sudden spasm tore through her cunny. She gasped, her back arching in silent recognition of the heightened state which continued to envelop her groin and which she knew she was in danger of losing if she didn't do as he asked.

'All right,' she said quietly forcing herself to say the words. 'I will do as you ask, but only if you promise to make me come afterwards.'

'It will be my pleasure.' He thrust his groin towards her, the jewelled tip of his cock brushing the smooth

215

surface of her mouth, coating it with the first essence of his excitement.

Amelia licked the thick liquid from her lips, enjoying its salty flavour, before craning her head towards him and accepting him into her mouth inch by inch. She vaguely heard him sigh when she began to run her tongue up and down his shaft, circling its pulsating warmth, coating it with her own, sensuous saliva while at the same time savouring the masculine taste of him.

Lucas grabbed the back of her head and pulled her face towards him, forcing her to take all of him into her mouth until her teeth closed gently around the base of his prick.

Amelia swallowed hard, unable to suppress a shiver when he withdrew his prick almost completely out of her mouth, only to plunge it straight back in, his knob slamming into the back of her throat. She kicked her legs violently against the arm of the chair, a moan rising in her chest as desire brewed in the pit of her stomach one more, renewing the urgency of her own need.

As if sensing this frantic state of hers, Lucas moved one of his hands from her head and, fumbling behind him eventually found her pert little pleasure-bud. While continuing the assault on her mouth, he began to manipulate her clitoris, focusing attention on her ring as he had only minutes before.

Excitement quickly rose again to command her groin, sending streamers of stimulation through her. She squeezed her internal muscles vigorously, pumping her hips back and forth, mimicking the cadence of her oral stimulation as she sucked harder and harder on his rigid organ.

Lucas's breath came in harsh rasps as he pushed himself again and again into her mouth while his fingers worked at her. With a loud shout, he suddenly wrenched his member from her a few seconds later and collapsed forward on to her, his hand immediately leaving her clitoris to clutch his cock as it pumped his seed all over her chest.

Amelia twisted frantically underneath him, her mind racing at the thought that she might be left on the verge of orgasm yet again. Lucas sighed, his hot breath brushing her neck, and shifted slightly to one side, giving her the chance she'd been yearning for.

She dragged her right arm from underneath him and pushed it between her legs, her fingers easily continuing where he'd left off. 'Yes,' she sobbed, breathlessly pinching and kneading her own pleasure-nub, rolling it between thumb and forefinger. 'If you won't finish me off, you bastard, I'll have to do it myself. Oh!' Amelia came with a sudden jerk of her body, her sex fibrillating only the once.

Amelia sank back against the chair in disappointment, wondering why she had gone to so much trouble for such a feeble orgasm. This was the first time her culmination had been anything but satisfying and she knew what the cause of this was: Lucas and his attempted dominance.

'You look puzzled, my dear,' he interrupted Amelia's thoughts as he rolled off her and got to his feet. 'Could it be that your own ministrations weren't enough for you?'

'I don't know what you mean.'

'Come, come, you cannot fool me. What you just experienced is nothing like what I remember of your reactions.' He pushed his shirt back into the waistband of his breeches and then held out his hand to her. 'I wonder if this is because I denied you that which you truly craved – the pleasure of my cock in your cunny?'

Amelia sniffed and remained where she was.

'Save your egotism for your admirers, my lord. You are the reason it wasn't so good for me this time. I'd forgotten how stifling your arrogance can be!' she cried on the verge of tears, easily remembering how she had begged him to take her only a few minutes before.

Instead of the embarrassment she'd expected to feel as a consequence of this painful memory, Amelia was rather surprised to sense anger brew once again within her. It burned its way into her consciousness, a searing reminder of the humiliation she'd just suffered at Lucas's hands.

As Amelia silently observed him stride to the door, a triumphant bounce to his step, she shivered, her anger quickly metamorphosing into a longing for revenge as strong as her recent desire for him.

Well, if he thought that she would now willingly return with him to Beechwood House just because she'd openly admitted her desire for him, he was going to be sorely disappointed. On that score, Amelia was resolute.

She swung her legs over the arm of the chair and struggled to her feet, a sense of wicked delight coursing through her when she thought of how she would greet him when he came to call on her again. She was determined that next time she would be ready and waiting for him, ready to demonstrate exactly what she'd meant when she said she had changed.

Connie stared across the busy road at the house, her mind frantically searching for a suitable way of introducing herself to its household.

While she observed the steady stream of fashionable couples strolling past it, blissfully unaware of what went on behind its grand exterior, she realised that she had to act soon if she was going to give Amelia any time at all to prepare for her husband's reappearance.

Stepping off the pavement, she was forced to jump back on to the curb when a liveried carriage trundled round the corner and swept past, just inches from her. Connie gasped, not so much from being startled by this near collision, but from the fact that she had immediately recognised the coat of arms emblazoned to its door.

Retracing her steps back across the pavement, she sought refuge in the doorway of a nearby house and, praying that its occupants wouldn't mind her brief sojourn on their property, she observed the carriage as it drew up outside the house.

One of the liveried footmen accompanying it hopped

down from the driver's seat and hurried into the building while the other opened the carriage door in preparation to receive its owner.

This could only mean one thing – that Lucas had beaten her to it and reached Amelia before she'd had a chance to warn her.

Connie turned to leave, only to pause when she noticed Lucas emerge from the house and nonchalantly descend the steps carrying his frockcoat over his arm.

She narrowed her eyes when she spied his untidy appearance and deduced that he must have gone straight to Mrs Featherstone's after leaving her, instead of returning to his own lodgings to wash and change, as she'd hoped. This would certainly explain how he's managed to get here before her.

A couple of spots of rain splashed on to her face and, glancing up at the angry sky, she pulled her quilted cloak tighter round her. She'd already failed Amelia once that day, she certainly wasn't about to let her down again so soon.

Connie shrugged. Perhaps by offering her support now, in what was surely Amelia's most needy time, it would go some way towards making up for her earlier deficiency, as well as letting Lucas know that she wasn't going to stand idly by and allow him to walk all over her friend.

Carefully dodging the parade of carriages and wagons which thronged the road, Connie precariously made her way across it to the pavement opposite, where she briefly tidied her dress before carrying on.

She approached Lucas, calling his name, but he didn't answer. He seemed to be too engaged in an altercation with three rough-looking men to hear her.

Connie blinked when she observed him raise his hand as if to strike the tallest of them, only to be stopped in his tracks when his opponent pulled a pistol from the waistband of his breeches and pushed it into Lucas's face.

Connie gasped, her hand flying to her neck. As she

stood there gawping, she was suddenly filled with the urge to go to her lover's aid even though she knew that, in reality, there was little she could do.

The other two men also pulled out pistols, one clambering up into the driver's seat to subdue the groom and one of the footmen, while his companion pushed the barrel of his pistol into Lucas's back and forced him and the other footman into the carriage.

The remaining man took hold of the door and, looking furtively about him, suddenly rested his gaze on Connie. Smiling broadly, his eyes sweeping appreciatively over her from head to toe, he crooked a finger at her, indicating for her to join him beside the carriage.

For a moment, Connie was too shocked to move, but she regained her composure and began to walk slowly towards him, trying to fathom out why he should be interested in her. Could he be planning to kidnap her too?

'Be you his lordship's bit of skirt?' he leered as she approached him warily.

'I beg your pardon?' Connie stumbled, hardly believing his familiarity, his rudeness.

'Be you the one in Covent Garden?'

'It is true that I am staying in Covent Garden for the time being.' Connie longed to demand to know what was going on, but the appropriate words refused to form in her throat.

'Well, know this. We three here have captured his lordship for nonpayment of a longstanding debt of fifty guineas. Now, do you know his wife?'

Connie nodded. 'Yes I do.'

'Good, you had better tell her what you saw today and say that, if the debt ain't paid, she'll never see him again.'

'What?' she coughed, choking on the vehemence of his threat.

'That's right girly. If someone don't pay up, then his lordship will end up deader than a doornail. Do you understand? Someone will contact you later in Covent

Garden to tell you where to leave the money.' The man cocked his hat in her direction and then, without another word, clambered into the carriage, slamming the door behind him.

Connie leant against a nearby lamppost as she watched the carriage roll off into the distance. She knew she must see Amelia immediately and, ignoring her shaky legs, she crossed the pavement and climbed the steps of Mrs Featherstone's house.

Chapter Seventeen

'My dearest cousin, what can I say other than that I've failed you as a friend?' Connie cried, looked pleadingly at Amelia.

'Damn him! In only a few minutes he's already caused chaos to my feelings, my situation – how dare he do this to me again? Who does he think he is?' Amelia said almost to herself while taking Connie's hands and drawing her close. Her frown quickly changed to a smile when she met the younger woman's eyes. 'Despite my anger, I am well aware who is to blame for all this. This is entirely Lucas's doing and you have nothing to reproach yourself for, my dear. Even if you could have warned me in time, it wouldn't have stopped him coming here would it?' Connie shook her head. 'Very well then, dry your tears and come have some tea with me. Lord knows, I could certainly do with some!'

'What are you going to do now, Amelia?' Connie asked once they were both settled on the sofa.

'I know what I'm not going to do!' Amelia declared, taking a gulp of her drink. 'If Lucas thinks that I am going to return to Beechwood House just because he has turned up here demanding my compliance, he's got another think coming! I've travelled too far to give up everything I've achieved.'

'Why, Amelia,' Connie chuckled. 'I don't think I've ever seen you so fired up, not even before you married Lucas. What on earth has happened to increase your enmity towards him? Surely it can't simply be your separation.'

'No, it's what I've learnt during it which has changed me. Since coming to this place I've discovered a new life, one which I know is right for me, one where I'm allowed to make my own decisions. I simply cannot allow him to ruin this like he did my previous one.'

'But how are you going to stop him? You know what power he has, the lengths he'll go to achieve his aims.'

Amelia shrugged, knowing that this was the hardest question of all.

'And what of Lucas anyway?' Connie continued. 'Can you honestly say that you hate the sight of him?'

Amelia shivered when she remembered the thrill Lucas's proximity had caused her just a few minutes before. 'Perhaps not, but I have certainly gained new skills with which to deal with his arrogant ways. If only there was some way I could get him at a disadvantage, I know I'd be able to show him that I'm not so weak any more!' Amelia got to her feet and began to pace the room. This conversation was leading into areas she would rather remained hidden. But, as of old, Connie seemed able to prise even the intimate of thoughts from her. When she realised that there was no longer any point in skirting round the truth, she stopped in her tracks and stared down at the younger woman. Perhaps if Connie knew how she really felt she might be able to think of a way out of this distasteful situation.

'All right, I'll tell you something. I never could keep anything from you, could I, cousin?'

Connie shook her head, smiling.

'What happened this morning has only confirmed what I've suspected for a long time. Despite what he's done to me, the indignities he's forced upon me, I cannot deny that I want Lucas more than any other man I have ever met. And yet, even the thought of living with him again fills me with terror, for I know nothing in him has changed.' She turned away, a blush of shame painting her cheeks while she waited for Connie to scold her for being so proud.

'I understand what you are saying and I really wish that I could help you as I did on the eve of your wedding, but I'm afraid that in this you are most definitely on your own.'

Amelia turned back sharply, raising her chin. 'I am only too aware of that, Connie. That's why all this is so hard for me, but you can rest assured that, despite this, I will do all in my power to make sure I don't suffer the same sorry outcome as last time. Believe me, something drastic will have to happen to make me –'

'I'm afraid it already has,' Connie said quietly.

Amelia's eyes narrowed when she observed the concerned expression covering Connie's features. 'What do you mean? Has something happened to Lucas?' she asked, fear gripping her heart. 'If it has, I think I have a right to know.'

'He's been kidnapped.' Connie's words rang out in the room.

'What? What did you say?' Amelia caught a nearby chair for support as this news sank in.

Connie lowered her head. 'I observed it not half an hour ago as he was leaving this place.'

'And you waited this long to tell me?' Amelia bent down and, grabbing Connie by the arms, began to shake her. 'You stupid, thoughtless child! Didn't it cross your mind to tell me straight away? That time is of the utmost?'

'Stop it, Amelia, stop it!' Connie managed to wrench herself from her grasp and fall down on to her knees, sobbing. 'I didn't know how to tell you after you expressed your abhorrence for returning to Lucas so vehemently. I, I didn't think you'd care.'

'You didn't think I'd care? Well you are wrong, my girl. Terribly wrong. Even though I have no desire to return to the life I once had with Lucas, the fact still remains that I want him desperately,' she blurted out without thinking. 'Why, in the light of what you've just told me, I believe it's now my duty to put aside the feelings of rancour I have for him as my husband, and focus on my desire for him as a man, so that they may give me the motivation to effect his safe return.'

Amelia went to the window and pressed her flaming cheek to the cool glass. At least Connie hadn't seen fit to press her further about her sudden change of heart. Right now, the last thing Amelia wanted was to explore the feelings which lurked in the dark recesses of her mind, the ones which prompted her to make such rash decisions and which lay at the root of her turbulent relationship with Lucas.

'I'm sorry, Amelia,' Connie whispered several minutes later, eventually breaking the silence which had descended on the room.

'No, it is I who should apologise.' Amelia moved back to where Connie crouched on the floor and helped her to her feet. 'You only did what you thought best and, in your shoes, I suppose I should have done the same thing.' She sighed. 'Now, tell me what it was which made you come to this conclusion.'

Connie nodded slowly and described the disturbing scene she's just witnessed outside. 'The man said that Lucas owed him fifty guineas and that, if you didn't play it, something dreadful would happen to him.'

'I see.' Amelia pressed the back of her hand to her forehead while she tried to sort out the muddle of thoughts and emotions which filled her mind. 'And you say that he will contact me at Clarissa's? Well then, there is nothing more to it. We had best repair to your aunt's. Perhaps she will know what to do.'

'Take this pistol and watch him, Fran,' said Paul moving towards the battered door of the small, cupboard-like room. 'We'll be in the next room seeing to his servants. If he gives you any trouble, don't hesitate to yell.'

Fran jumped to her feet and followed him to the door. 'You trust me that much?'

225

Paul touched her chin and smiled. 'I trust you as much as them.' He hooked a thumb over his shoulder. Fran stood on tiptoe and observed Lennard and a man she didn't recognise busily tying up the footmen. Lucas's driver already sat on the straw-covered floor, bound and gagged. 'You aren't about to scupper my plans, are you, my dear?'

'No it's just that –' She turned back and glanced at Lucas who was sitting against the large wooden support which dominated the tiny chamber, his hands secured behind his back to its base. 'Must you be so . . . cruel?'

'Cruel? He don't know the meaning of the word. I tell you, no mercy is to be shown him!' Paul glared down at the gagged Lucas. 'Not until his wife coughs up the money, anyway. Perhaps then he'll learn to pay his debts. Now I'm going to have me a rest. I leave him in your capable hands.' He gave her a quick kiss and then left them alone, closing the door behind him.

Fran pushed the barrel of the pistol into one of the pockets of her skirt and, getting down on to her hands and knees, began to crawl towards Lucas, a broad smile stretching her ruby lips.

When she reached him, she placed a finger against her mouth while she loosened his gag enough to push it down around the base of his neck.

'See, I tried for your sake, my lord,' she whispered, nibbling his ear. 'I tried to get you some comforts but Paul wouldn't have it.'

Lucas jerked his head away from her. 'That blackguard will hang at Tyburn for this outrage. Upon my life, I swear it!'

'Shhh, do you want to alert them out there?' Fran cautioned, fear gripping her at this threat. She was only too aware of the substance behind his vehemence. 'I shouldn't even have loosed your mouth. If they find out –'

'To hell with them,' Lucas growled, keeping his voice low. 'I care not about them. You could untie me and give me your pistol –'

226

'No, I wouldn't do that to Paul –'

Lucas shrugged. 'Your loyalty is admirable but it is futile, my dear. He will pay with his life whether you let me go or not. Surely it would be more humane to let him die by the pistol rather than the noose?'

'Please don't talk like that. Paul is only doing what he thinks is right. If you had paid up in the first place none of this would have happened.'

'Me give in to violence? Never! I think that it's about time you realised the value of my friendship and stopped worrying about that oafish husband of yours.'

'I can't, m'lord. I love him!'

'Oh please,' Lucas scowled. 'Not another one taken with romantic notions? Believe me, you'll save yourself a lot of pain if you forget about him now while he's still alive!'

Fran shivered at his words, suddenly realising that, no matter how strong her yearning for the marquess, her real allegiance was with the man she loved, her husband. It was up to her now to make sure that no harm came to him, even if it meant crossing Lucas and possibly even risking death for herself.

Fran smiled and, shuffling closer, slid her hand down his front to rest on the waistband of his breeches. 'Now, m'lord, what shall we do to amuse ourselves until that pretty little wife of yours comes up with the money?' Her fingers easily undid the ties and slipped inside the smooth fabric to cup his balls.

Lucas caught his breath, his legs twitching when she began gently to knead him, delighting in the sensation of the sensitive skin firming against her fingers.

'There, you like that, don't you, m'lord?'

Lucas didn't answer but pushed his tongue between his lips and flicked it over their succulent surfaces, coating them with saliva. Fran covered his mouth with her own then, her tongue meeting his and snaking round it.

Dragging her hand out of his breeches, while at the same time pulling her lips away from his, Fran sat back on her legs and carefully removed the pistol from her pocket. After placing it on the floor beside them, she quickly undid her bodice, her hands scooping her breasts out of their restraints until they hung, unfettered, over the line of her stays.

'I want you to mount me now!' Lucas ordered, craning his head forward, his lips urgently seeking the mottled tip of one of her exposed nipples.

'Not so fast,' Fran giggled, her hand once more inside his breeches, easing out his rock-hard cock. 'This, for once, is going to be at my pace.' Grasping the thick shaft, she began to pump her hand up and down, working the tight skin back and forth, her fingers rising now and again to skirt the violet edges of his glans. Hearing the soft moans which escaped his mouth, she found his lips again, her tongue foraying deeper into the honeyed depths of his mouth, seeking out the tightness of his throat.

Fran lifted herself on to her knees and, feeling the silky wetness lining her already pouting sex-lips, clambered over his legs to straddle his erection.

Raising her head, she stared down at him and smiled, her hands raising one of her breasts up level with his mouth, enabling him to take in its rigid tip. She couldn't help shuddering at the delightful sensations his tongue created as it brushed, tantalised, toyed with her nipple, while his moist lips encircled her areola.

'Oh yes, m'lord,' she sighed, finally lowering herself on to his awaiting prick. 'That's just fine for me!' Fran squeezed her pelvic muscles, drawing his hardness even deeper into her well-oiled recess until she could feel his knob pressing at the very entrance to her womb.

Letting go of her breast, she grabbed hold of his shoulders and began to move, sliding her dripping sex up and down the solid rod of his penis, shivering as she ground her pudenda into him.

Lucas, breathing through clenched teeth now, raised his legs to meet her pumping hips, the flushed orbs of her buttocks slapping against their tensed muscles.

'Faster!' he commanded, is eyes alight with a fierce glow. All he could do was gently rock his pelvis in time with her ever-increasing movements, but this was enough to send Fran's excitement crescendoing.

She gritted her teeth as glorious streamers of sensation rose from her groin to envelop her abdomen, her breath coming in sharp gasps as she pushed herself frantically up and down on his cock, searching urgently for release.

'Oh, my lord!' she cried, falling against him as orgasm exploded inside her, her sex twitching wildly, its muscles clamping around his prick, forcing his culmination to erupt at the same moment as her own.

Fran slumped over Lucas as his seed spurted high into her vagina, his cock pulsing wildly within her. She pressed her lips to his moist forehead, and pushed back a long, chestnut strand of hair from his eyes as she sensed his thrusting legs gradually slow to a halt underneath her and then drop back on to the floor.

A few minutes later, when the ecstasy of their coupling was just a fond memory, Fran crawled off him, her contentment suddenly tinged with regret. Despite the longing she still felt for him, she knew that this would be the last time she'd get a chance to indulge her passion.

'You may have the money as soon as you wish,' Clarissa smiled, indicating for both Connie and Amelia to take a seat at the dining table. 'It is the least I can do.'

'Thank you, ma'am.' Amelia slid into the stiff, oak chair opposite. 'I hate to give in to extortion, but what else can I do?'

'You really are serious about this, aren't you?'

Amelia frowned in the older woman's direction. 'I don't understand what you mean.'

Clarissa poured red wine into three glasses and passed them to her guests before answering.

'You'll have to forgive me, my dear, but I must admit that I find your sudden concern for your husband difficult to understand. Didn't you run away to escape him?'

'I did indeed, ma'am, and I too find my reaction hard to fathom, but when I think about him being held to ransom by these men, it just makes me shudder. I know Lucas has treated me appallingly in the past, as he has everyone else, but, even so, he doesn't deserve such an end as this.' She shrugged, taking a sip of her wine. 'I suppose that in a matter as grave as this, I must forget my enmity towards him and concentrate on doing my duty as his wife.'

Connie squeezed her hand as if to lend support to her inexplicable change of heart. 'I agree with you, but don't you think it a bit hasty to have already decided to pay the ransom?'

'No. What other choice do I have? We don't know where Lucas is being held, or even if –' She broke off, her voice rising to a hysterical pitch.

'I know, dear –' Clarissa reached across the table and patted her shoulder '– but you mustn't think of such a possibility until you know it's true, otherwise you'll just fall into a fit of melancholy. Now, about that money –' Clarissa was interrupted by the footman and, after disappearing for a few minutes, she returned with a younger woman following closely behind.

In spite of the fact that the woman was wearing a gown made of the finest shot silk, Amelia recognised her immediately as the serving woman from the inn at the crossroads where she'd first met Lucas. She shook her head, hardly believing that such a coincidence was possible, until it dawned on her why this woman was here.

She jumped up from the table and, pushing her chair to one side, confronted her. 'I've seen you before, wench!' she cried, her eyes reluctantly taking in Fran's silky, fawn-coloured hair and her beauty.

'Amelia, please.' Clarissa stepped between them and guided her away from the scowling Fran, back to the table. 'I understand your anger but, no matter what you think of her, this woman has information about Lucas which I think you should hear.'

'I don't want to –'

'Oh I think you will, if you care to listen, that is,' Fran interposed, staring at Amelia.

'How dare you speak to me in such a manner? Do you know who I am?'

'Certainly I do, your ladyship, and if you don't want to become the widowed Lady Beechwood, I'd let me speak if I were you.'

Amelia bit her lip, cutting off the retort which was rising to her lips. 'Very well, proceed.' She rested her head in her hands.

'Right then. Paul thinks that I'm here only to deliver the ransom note.'

'Paul?' Amelia questioned.

'You are correct in thinking that you've seen me before, m'lady. Only then you were in a more compromising position I think.' Amelia coloured but said nothing. 'Well he's my husband and he's the one who's holding his lordship. Anyway, he thinks I'm on his business this day but I've my own plan for I fear for his life too.'

'And so you should,' remarked Clarissa, pouring herself another glass of wine. 'I can't see him escaping this easily even if Amelia does pay the ransom.'

'You've hit the nail right on the head there, ma'am. 'Luc– his Lordship has made it plain to me what he intends for Paul once he's free.'

'Oh has he? And why should he confide in you? How is it that you've gained his confidence?' Amelia demanded, staring at her.

Fran grinned. 'Well, m'lady, I believe I supplied him with that you denied him when you ran away. So I know what I'm talking about. If I don't do something, Paul will surely die.'

Amelia coloured slightly. 'Your loyalty to your husband is admirable, but why should it be any concern of mine?'

'Because if we do this my way, neither of our men will get hurt.' She smiled cunningly and leant across the table

231

towards Amelia. 'And it might just be the chance you are waiting for.'

'Chance?' Amelia frowned. 'What chance? I'm afraid I don't follow you.'

'Don't tell me you wouldn't like to get your own back on Lucas for all he's done to you?'

'What?' Amelia gasped, hardly believing what she was hearing.

'Oh yes, m'lady. I know what's happened to you since you married him – the whole village does. Why, at one stage, I was even to be part of your humiliation but you ruined his lordship's plans by running away.' Fran leant back and glanced at Connie and Clarissa. 'Now, you can't tell me that you have no desire to get your revenge on him?'

'Well, I, I –' Despite her embarrassment at discussing such a thing with this woman, Amelia knew that she was right, that she'd give anything to get a chance to show Lucas the error of his ways. She just didn't like being reminded of the fact, especially by someone she hardly knew. 'I suppose you are right, but how can this be so? From what you've said, my husband is in danger and I don't think we should do anything which could jeopardise his life.'

'You don't have to. If you do this my way, you could have your revenge on your husband and I would get mine back. It's simple.'

'Oh yes?' Amelia raised her eyebrows. 'What's the catch?'

'There ain't one really. I just want you to promise that you'll do all in your power to make sure that, once free, his lordship doesn't come after Paul.'

'And pray, how am I going to do that? I'm hardly on bargaining terms with Lucas after the embarrassment I've caused him these past weeks.'

'That's what you think now.' Fran picked up the bottle of wine and, gulping down the last of its contents, winked at Amelia. 'I think you'll change your mind once you see how your husband is being kept!'

Chapter Eighteen

'*A*re you sure this is wise?' Amelia asked, catching her breath as she pulled the satin breeches up over her hips and tied them tightly round her slim waist. 'I mean, what is anyone going to think if they catch us dressed like this?'

'Oh stop moaning,' Connie scolded. 'Just look on this as a unique chance to shed the constrictions of our stays for a few hours.'

Amelia tucked her lawn shirt into the breeches and, picking up a ribbon from the dressing table, tied her raven hair into a ponytail at the nape of her neck. When Fran had suggested they wear men's clothes, she had instantly refused, so shocking was the idea, but after much cajoling from Connie and Mrs Stevens, she eventually realised that their usual attire would only hamper their efforts.

Amelia turned round in front of the mirror, sliding her hands down over the silky fabric, admiring the way it stretched over her pelvis, emphasising the gentle curves of her hips and the swell of her thighs. She was certainly beginning to appreciate Connie's enthusiasm for the male garb.

'There, how's that?' Fran pushed Amelia out of the way and moved in front of the mirror. 'Do I look the part?'

'You certainly do,' Amelia replied tersely, still not used to the woman's forwardness, 'though, what for, I should hate to guess.'

Fran raised her eyebrows, her eyes meeting Amelia's in the mirror. 'I know I offend you, your ladyship, but I can't be any other way.'

Amelia softened a bit and smiled. 'I'm sorry, Fran,' she sighed. 'I suppose I'm just anxious about what is to take place tonight. You are certain that your husband and his men will be asleep, or at least off their guard when we get there?'

'Quite certain. That idea of yours to take some ale with me went down well with Paul and his accomplices. Why, once they heard you were ready to pay the ransom, they couldn't wait to start drinking! It is to be hoped that by the time we arrive, they'll be so merry that they won't notice me tinkering with their pistols.'

'And if they're not?'

'Then we put your other idea into action.'

'But how will I know when to do it?'

Fran turned back to face her. 'You'll know sure enough, believe you me. Now stop all this fretting.'

'I hope you are right for I shudder to think what would happen if I got it wrong. It could be dangerous –'

'Oh fie to that,' Connie chirped, taking Amelia's and Fran's arms in hers. 'The danger's the most exciting part. I simply cannot wait to get started. Nor you, Amelia, I suspect. Pray, what will you do with Lucas when you get him on his own?'

Amelia shrugged, a shiver of delight running down her spine when she considered the possibility of Lucas finally getting what had been long due to him. 'I couldn't say at this stage, Connie, but, rest assured, I shall not be lost for ideas when the time comes.' Amelia pulled out of her grasp and went over to Clarissa who had been watching them lazily from an overstuffed chair in the corner.

'Thank you, ma'am, for the use of these ... clothes. I don't know where you got them all from, but they are magnificent!' Amelia squeezed her pelvic muscles as she spoke, enjoying the sensation of the cool fabric riding up between her moist vaginal lips. 'But, on a more serious note, I believe Connie has spoken to you about the safeguards we wish you to employ on our behalf.'

Clarissa nodded. 'Don't worry. If you haven't returned by this time tomorrow I will not hesitate to contact the authorities, you can be assured of that.'

'Thank you, for none of us really knows what will happen this night. Now there is one more thing I must ask before we leave, although I feel rather embarrassed to do so.'

'You want to take the fifty guineas with you.'

'Why yes, how did you know?' Amelia asked in surprise. Clarissa tossed a small purse into Amelia's hands.

'Call it female intuition if you like. I was going to offer it to you even if you didn't ask. You might need it after all and, if you don't, I know I can rely on you to bring it safely back into my care.'

'Thank you for your confidence, ma'am. I won't let you down on that score.'

Amelia joined the others and followed them into the hall, her heart skipping when she heard the horses' hooves on the cobbles outside.

Connie clutched at the waistband of Amelia's breeches as they stumbled along together in the darkness, searching for the thin crack of light which denoted the tumbledown shed that Fran had assured them was where Lucas was being held.

Amelia stopped abruptly and, straightening up, rubbed her aching back.

'What are you doing?' Connie demanded in a hoarse whisper, bumping to a halt behind her.

'I'm beginning seriously to doubt Fran's reliability, that's what!' Amelia had thought it odd when Fran had told them that a cowshed on the edge of Kensington gravel pits was Lucas's jail. Now, she was beginning to wonder if all this wasn't simply an elaborate ruse on Fran's part to get back at her for the contempt she had afforded her when they'd met at Clarissa's.

'Don't give up now.' Connie grabbed Amelia's waist again. 'Let's carry on a little bit longer.'

Amelia shrugged and resumed her precarious journey through the night, pulling Connie along with her.

For what seemed like hours, they trudged slowly through the darkness, Amelia beating back with her riding crop the dense undergrowth which clutched at her ankles, until she spotted the faintest of lights flickering through the branches.

'I think that's it,' she whispered in relief, suddenly stumbling, dragging Connie with her towards the source of the light. Breathing heavily, Amelia pressed her face to the cowshed's rickety wall and peered into the gap between its slats.

Three lamps hung from the beams supporting its thatched roof, casting a warm glow over its sparsely furnished interior, making the straw which covered the floor shine like highly polished gold. Amelia then spotted Fran in the shed creeping along the far wall on tiptoe, being careful not to disturb the slumbering figure of a man just inches from her feet.

'Right,' Amelia whispered, taking Connie's hand and leading her quietly round the side of the building. 'Fran's inside. I think we can follow now.'

'Are you sure?' Connie questioned, suddenly timid. 'We haven't given her much time.'

Amelia shrugged. 'She's had plenty. Now come on.'

Finding the ill-fitting door was easy enough but opening it certainly wasn't and Amelia found herself having to push her shoulder against the splintering wood. The door refused to move at first, remaining resolutely stuck in the frame but then, when Amelia was about to give up in desperation, it unexpectedly gave way under her force and flew open, sending her reeling into the centre of the cowshed.

'Hey, what's this?' A puzzled, sluggish Paul rubbed

his eyes and struggled to his feet, pointing his pistol at Amelia with shaking hands. 'It's not Lady Beechwood, is it?' he slurred, swaying slightly.

Amelia raised her chin and took a deep breath, drawing in scents of hay and dung, refusing to be intimidated. 'That is correct.'

'Fran!' He raised his eyebrows when his wife stepped forward from the opposite corner. 'What are you doing here?'

She sighed. 'You might as well know. We've come to release his lordship.'

'Have you? You there. You might as well come in too.' He frowned at Connie who was standing in the doorway. 'Well, come in and shut the door behind you!'

She did as he commanded and joined her cousin in the middle of the shed. Paul stepped forward and wrenched the riding crop from Amelia's hand, tossing it away out of reach. 'So, you thought to cross me, did you?' He glanced in the direction of his men who had also been woken by this untimely entrance of Amelia and were hurriedly clambering to their feet.

'We were doing it for your own good.' Fran tried to touch his arm but he shied away from her touch, nearly overbalancing in the process.

'Were you?' He shook his head, quickly regaining his equilibrium. 'I should have know that you couldn't be trusted. Obviously your lust speaks louder than your conscience! Now, get over there against the wall all three of you!'

'Paul –' Fran cried, in one more desperate attempt to calm him down. 'It's true –'

'Shut up, I don't want to hear it. Just get over there.'

'Paul's men stepped towards the women brandishing their pistols. Amelia looked from Connie to Fran and then back to Connie and, seeing the determination in their eyes, suddenly nodded.

'Now!' she shouted, the loudness of her call making Paul jump.

In one, well-calculated movement, each of them

rushed at him, tearing at the pistol in his hands. Paul's friends, taken aback by the suddenness of the women's movement, stood motionless for a second or two. By the time they realised what was happening and made a move to help Paul, Fran had already wrested his pistol away and was pushing it against his chest.

'I think it should be you who gets back against the wall, don't you, Paul? And tell these oafs of yours to do the same.'

He hesitated at first, glancing at Lennard and his companion as they hovered just out of reach, waiting for his next command. Then he shrugged and nodded. 'Boys, drop yer pistols.'

Paul backed away from Fran to lean against the wall, while his men let go of their guns and reluctantly joined him.

'What do you intend now? To turn us over to the magistrate so you can go off with his lordship? A cosy little threesome is it to be?'

Fran smiled and, keeping her pistol pointing at his chest, leant forward and dropped a kiss on his forehead.

'Don't be daft, you silly man. I told you I love you. No, we are just rescuing Lucas for her ladyship here, and then perhaps you can stop all this nonsense.'

'You know I can't. Besides, do you honestly think that his lordship is going to forget this quickly?'

'Paul –'

'This is no longer in my husband's hands,' Amelia interrupted. 'I'm taking over now.' She glanced at Fran and, noticing the pistol she was clutching, shivered. 'You can get rid of that as well. It frightens me!' Amelia swept her gaze round the interior of the shed and frowned. 'Where is he, by the way?'

Fran tossed the pistol into the straw beside her. 'He's in that room all tied up,' she whispered, hooking a finger over her shoulder. 'Do you want me to release him?' Amelia thought a moment and then smiled wickedly.

'No, Fran, I don't think I do. Let us just leave him where he is for the time being. Now –' she turned to

Paul '– sir, I believe I have something which has been owing to you for some time.' She reached into her pocket and pulled out the purse of money Clarissa had given her.

'You are very kind, your ladyship,' he whispered when she pressed it into his hands. 'If his lordship had paid up –'

Amelia held up her hand. 'Yes, I am well aware of who is to blame for all this and I promise you that he'll get what's due to him presently. Now, you and your men may leave whenever you wish.'

Amelia stood back as they gathered their things together and then headed for the door. Fran followed them, turning to Amelia when she reached it.

'God bless you, ma'am, I'll never forget what you've done for us this day.' Without another word, she too disappeared into the night.

'You might as well untie them, cousin,' Amelia remarked, her eyes sweeping over the vision of Lucas's bound and gagged servants as she unhooked one of the oil lamps from the rafters. 'And once you have done that, pray join me in the other room. Who knows, I might just need your help.'

Excitement rose within Amelia as she strode across the shed to the flimsy slab of wood which stood between her and her husband. Roughly pushing it open, her heart leapt into her throat when she set eyes on the pitiful sight of Lucas crudely tied to a stanchion in the centre of the small room.

'Well, well, well,' she said, bending to release his gag. 'This is certainly a unique experience!' Lucas shook his head and stared up at her, relief clearly visible on his face.

'My word, I must say that you have the most appropriate timing, my dear, and in such fetching garb too? I had wondered if you would come to my aid.'

'Did you now?' Amelia asked, getting to her feet and staring down at him. 'After what you've done to me, you are lucky I'm here at all.'

'Come, untie me so that I may assure that blackguard's safe passage to the nearest gallows,' Lucas demanded, ignoring her last comment.

Amelia shook her head. 'I do not think you are in any position to give me orders now, do you? Fran and her husband will be well out of reach by the time I allow you your freedom. Oh, Lucas, if only you had paid your debt in the beginning none of this would have happened!' Lucas tugged at his restraints, kicking his legs about on the floor.

'All right, I get your point, Amelia. Now untie me. This jest has gone far enough.'

'This is no joke, my lord. Why, I find that I rather like the commanding position I now find myself in.'

Connie joined her then, an amused grin stretching her lips when she too stared down at Lucas. 'Here,' she whispered. 'I thought you might be needing this.' She pressed the discarded riding crop into her cousin's hands. 'What are you going to do with him?'

Amelia shrugged. 'Well, I just don't know, Connie. He could certainly do with being taught a lesson. What do you think?'

'I think this foolishness has gone far enough,' Lucas interrupted, glaring up at them, while pushing even harder against the rope binding him to the support.

'I don't think he has any right to complain, do you Connie?'

'Why, no. I think he should be asking for our mercy. Certainly not scolding us!'

'What?' Lucas shouted. 'If you think that I –'

'First, I think he needs to be in a more accessible location, don't you?' Connie nodded and left the room briefly, returning in the company of Lucas's head groom, Marcus, and his footmen.

'What is it that you wish us to do, my lady?' Marcus smiled, catching sight of his master on the floor.

'I command you to untie me!' Lucas cried. 'You'll never work for me again –'

'Silence!' Amelia snapped. 'I'm afraid that his lordship

has temporarily lost his wits and does not know what he says.'

'I see.' The men looked at each other, smiling to themselves. 'We are then happy to serve you in this matter, ma'am,' one of them said, moving towards Lucas. 'What is it that you would have us do?'

'What do you think Connie? One of the beams?'

'Oh yes, please!'

Amelia watched with satisfaction as the three men untied the rope binding his hands to the pole and, easily overcoming his vociferous struggles, dragged him out into the main chamber of the cowshed, his flailing feet kicking up clouds of dust behind them.

'Up there would be fine.' Amelia pointed to the ceiling. 'Tie him to that beam.'

When they had done this, Amelia stepped towards Lucas and inspected their handiwork. Still bound at the wrists, Lucas's hands were firmly attached to the unevenly cut length of wood and, though his feet rested on the floor, they had bound his legs and he was unable to move more than a few inches in any direction.

'Excellent. You've done your work well, gentlemen. You may go and fetch his lordship's coach now.'

'Leave and you hang for this outrage!' Lucas swung his body in his servants' direction, only to be cruelly stopped in his tracks by the rope securing his wrists.

'I think I shall leave too,' Connie whispered, glancing at Lucas with a wry smile. 'I should hate to spoil your moment of glory after it's been so long in coming.' She moved over to Lucas and, raising his chin with a finger, stood on tiptoe to give him the lightest of kisses. 'Enjoy, cousin, but don't be too harsh with him. It would be a pity if you totally ruined this!' She moved her hand down to his groin and briefly cupped his balls through the fabric of his breeches, a groan issuing from Lucas's pursed lips when she swiftly withdrew it and left the two of them alone.

'So, husband, we are at last by ourselves. I wonder what we should do?' Amelia smiled and, lightly bending the riding crop between her hands, circled him, pausing only to admire the soft swell of his firmly muscled buttocks before facing him again.

'Amelia, untie me. This is madness. I should hate to have to punish you for more than you already deserve.'

'Promises, promises,' she laughed, shaking her head. 'Methinks it is you who deserve the punishment and not I, for it seems that you have far more to repent. I think that it's about time you learnt to respect me.' She inched closer to him and began to undo the pearl buttons on his shirt.

'You are enjoying this, aren't you?' he asked, craning his face towards her, seeking out her lips. Amelia looked up from her task and smiled, resisting the temptation to afford him his desire.

'Of course. Now, save your feeble kisses for later, my lord. You may find that they are all you are able to give after I've finished with you!'

Without another word, she pushed her hands inside his shirt and ran them over the swell of his chest and down across his firm stomach to the waistband of his breeches. Quickly undoing them, she grabbed either side and ruthlessly pushed the thin fabric down over his thighs, revealing the evidence of his arousal. His erection sprang towards her out of its dense bed of auburn curls.

'Ah.' She licked her lips, returning her gaze to Lucas's face. 'I see that what I promise is not so distasteful to you as you make it out to be, husband.'

Lucas shrugged as far as his bonds would allow and pushed his hips towards her. 'I'll forgive you if –' he began.

'Enough!' Amelia shook her head. 'As I said before, you are most certainly not in any position to give orders, nor even suggestions right now. So I'd save my breath if I were you, and accept your fate like the man you keep professing to be.'

Moving round to his back and knotting his shirt out of harm's way, she pressed her thinly clad body next to his. Lucas gasped. Amelia reached in front of him and firmly took hold of his cock, sliding her hand up and down its thick shaft. He began to buck against her touch, working his cock back and forth within the circle of her fingers, his breath becoming more and more laboured with every frantic surge forward he made.

'Ah yes,' he rasped, his bottom bumping back against her groin. 'Just a little while longer and –'

'That's enough for now I think.' Amelia let go of his manhood and moved a safe distance away from him. She delighted in the sight of him writhing.

'Christ, but you've got to release me. I'll loose my mind if you don't.'

'Will you?' she asked, lightly tapping her cheek with the crop. 'Perhaps you'll now understand what you put me through every time you denied me culmination?'

'Yes, yes,' he growled. 'I understand. Just frig me, Amelia, that's all I ask –'

'That's all? Hmmph! I think even that's far too much, considering what you've made me suffer in the past. No, Lucas. I'm afraid you are going to have to experience much more before I ever consider allowing you to come.'

She moved nearer to him again, pressing the riding crop into the crease of his buttocks and running it back and forth. Lucas shuddered with delight and, thrusting his buttocks towards her, presented her with a splendid view of the tight oval of his arse. A sudden longing filled Amelia and, gritting her teeth, she ruthlessly pushed the wide end of the whip into that enticing orifice.

Lucas immediately stiffened and, when she started to twist the whip to and fro within the ring of rigid muscles, threw back his head in silent ecstasy. Bending towards him, she rested her chin on his shoulder, her hand still moving the whip between his buttocks. 'Do you like this, Lucas? Does it thrill you as much as when you did it to me on our wedding night?' she enquired, her tongue flicking over his earlobe.

'Stop,' he panted, wrenching his head away from her face. 'This is too much to take, just too much!'

'Oh, tsk, tsk,' she scolded, swiftly withdrawing the

end of the crop from his arse. 'Afraid that your famous control will fail you now?'

'No,' he breathed, shaking his head. 'No, it's not that at all.'

Amelia suddenly grabbed a fistful of his hair and, jerking his head back, pressed her lips to his cheek. 'What is it then? Tell me now!' Tugging harder on his hair, she pulled his face back even further until his Adam's apple strained against the skin of his throat.

'My – control – is greater than you can ever imagine,' he managed, gasping for air.

'Well then, I think that it is about time I really put that facet of your personality to the test, don't you?' Without another word, she let go of his hair and raising the crop high above her head, brought it down as hard as she could on to the quivering flesh of his buttocks. Lucas started, a groan escaping his lips, every muscle of his body tensing, as if in readiness to receive the next blow.

'Oh my, Amelia. You can't do this,' he murmured, craning his head over his shoulder, trying to catch her eye. 'I never thought my actions could make you ever consider doing this.'

'Didn't you? Well believe it, Lucas. They did and, by God, I will!' she joyously shouted, hitting him again. The delicious sense of control this action afforded Amelia was greater than any orgasm she'd ever had at Mrs Featherstone's and, as a consequence, it spurred her on to even greater heights of flagellation.

Amelia struck again and again at his already shining orbs, putting everything she had into the blows she afforded him, taking even greater delight when the initial anguished cries Lucas emitted quickly metamorphosed into ones of delight.

Excitement raged in her groin at the sight of the strident angry weals her ministrations caused all over his pliant, white flesh. She spread her legs, sensing her love juices spilling out of her gaping orifice and coating the tops of her thighs, preparing her for the invasion she knew was yet to come, while she once again concentrated her attention on his haunches.

'Have you anything to say to me?' she breathlessly demanded, the rhythm of the blows she inflicted on him creating a steady cadence which disturbed the silence of the cowshed. 'If you don't answer me Lucas, I might just grow tired of this – and stop.'

'Please don't,' he cried, shaking his head. 'I'll do anything you say. Just don't stop. I couldn't bear it if you did. I apologise for everything I've put you through since we married. I know it was wrong – it was just my foolish way of imposing my will on you. I know now that you deserved better than what I gave, have given you.' The stream of words which flowed from his lips astounded Amelia for, despite the ferocity of the beating she continued to give him, she'd never imagined that it would yield such an abundant crop of responses as this.

Lucas twisted and gyrated under her punishing ministrations, his hips working back and forth while his breath was wrenched from him in sharp grunts.

'Oh, Amelia,' he shouted as he suddenly came, his cock pumping, arcing its milky load on to the floor. 'You are indeed changed!'

She instantly stopped hitting him and, burning up with a sudden heat herself, tore her shirt off, before returning to examine her handiwork. In the golden light of the lanterns, Lucas's buttocks, criss-crossed by sharp weals, glowed brilliant red.

Tracing one of them with her finger, she noticed how he stiffened at her touch, and she suddenly felt rather guilty for being so eager with the whip, despite the obvious enjoyment they had both gained as a result of it.

Kneeling behind him, she pressed her mouth to one of his buttocks, her tongue brushed over the throbbing orb, tracing the outline of one of the weals she had created. Lucas moaned softly into his chest when her tongue went further, tickling, following the downy skin from the crack of his arse up to the base of his spine.

'Oh Christ, Lucas,' Amelia gasped, falling back on to

her knees. 'I never imagined you could afford me such pleasure! If only I'd realised this a lot sooner, how different things would have been.' She wrapped her arms around his slim waist and buried her face in the small of his back. 'Now, if you could just treat me like an equal, I know we could be so happy!'

He made no sound or movement at her plea, but remained stock still within her grasp, his chin resting squarely on his chest.

Quickly regaining her composure, Amelia got to her feet and walked back round to face Lucas, her unfettered breasts jiggling as she moved. He raised his head and wearily studied her, his face flushed and sweating, his eyes glued to her semi-nakedness.

'W– what further indignities have you in mind for me now, wife?' he quietly asked, his voice trembling slightly. 'Have I not paid enough for my pride? Isn't my acceptance of my own guilt enough for you? Must you command my complete humiliation as well?'

Amelia smiled and wound her arms round his neck, her hardened nipples pressing into the thick bed of hair decorating his chest. 'You misjudge me, Lucas, for I am not like you. I know when a punishment is warranted and when it is not.' She licked her lips. 'I believe you've learnt your lesson now, have you not?' He swallowed hard and then nodded, his lips seeking hers. 'Very well then.' She ignored him and, reaching between them, tweaked the head of his cock, urging it once more to stiffness. 'I think it's about time we did this properly as man and wife, don't you?'

She pulled away from him and, smiling, slowly undid the restraints on her breeches until she stood before him, naked.

A smirk stretched his sensuous lips. 'I, I had forgotten just what beauty you possess, Amelia. It seems that I have been very remiss and overlooked many things these past weeks.'

She returned to him and, swiftly releasing his wrists, stepped back, her own desire still raging within her.

Though the longing to be possessed by him was so intense, it verged on the painful, Amelia used all her self-control to stop herself making the first move, wishing instead to make this the first test of her husband's willingness to change.

Lucas vigorously shook his arms before stepping forward and snaking one round her naked waist while his other moved to rub at his inflamed backside. 'Why I do declare there's a devil in that wrist of yours! I swear I'll not be able to sit down for a week! How on earth shall I explain this to my friends?'

'Oh I'm certain that you'll think of a suitable answer. You are, if my memory serves me correctly, the master of deception.'

A pained expression covered his features. 'Is that how you really see me?' Amelia looked away, suddenly finding it hard to keep her eyes on his. 'Well, then I am very sorry. Perhaps I can make it up to you, starting with now?

Very slowly, almost imperceptibly, the marquess manoeuvred her backwards until she was pinned between his body and the coarse wooden wall, his revitalised erection pressing into the firmness of her stomach. He caught Amelia's face in his hands and lowered his head until she could feel his luxuriant breath caressing her lips. He moved one hand from her waist and eased it to her slippery cleft, his fingers curling upwards to part her swollen lips and enter her secret place.

Amelia caught her breath as he pushed them high into her vagina.

'And now, my dear, will you tell me what you require of me?'

She met his eyes, her mouth forming a gasp as his fingers pressed even further into her until she was certain they were brushing the entrance of her womb.

'Surely you don't need to ask?' Amelia breathed, her gaze never leaving his face.

'After tonight, I am loath to misread your desires, my

dear, lest I incur yet more of your anger.' He smiled mischievously. 'Although a most enjoyable experience, I'm not quite sure my extremities can take such punishment again so soon!'

Amelia chuckled, suddenly realising that this was the first time she'd been able to display anything other than shock and indignation in his company. Perhaps things had changed after all.

'I want you to take me, Lucas,' she said slowly, meeting his eyes. 'I'll go mad if I don't come soon!'

Lucas smiled and unexpectedly withdrew his questing fingers. Sweeping his arms under her buttocks, he raised her up until her hips were level with his. Amelia snaked her arms round his shoulders and, clasping his waist with her thighs, lowered her trembling quim on to his waiting prick. As its pulsating length filled her, its wide tip pushing apart the sensitive walls of her sex, Amelia tightened her grip on his waist, dragging him even closer.

Lucas clutched her back and, pushing nearer, pinioned her firmly against the wall. He started to move, his forceful thrusts pushing her repeatedly against the splintering wood. Amelia rested her face against his shoulder, her teeth closing on the tautness of muscle, while he clasped her moist sex around his questing cock.

Urgency crept into her consciousness, creating currents of pleasure which rose from her groin and swept through her in wave after wave of growing excitement. She hugged him even tighter to her and began to bob up and down, meeting his powerful movements with equally frantic ones of her own.

Sensing her building response, the marquess, his breathing becoming increasingly laboured, surged more quickly into her, his knees knocking against the wall while he threw his full force behind every, potent thrust.

'Oh, Lucas, yes, harder, harder!' Amelia cried, gritting her teeth. She moved her hands to the back of his head and pulled his mouth to hers, her tongue entering that moist cavern at the precise moment orgasm exploded in her vagina.

Uncontrollable shudders coursed through her, making her grind her buttocks into the marquess's hands while her lips opened in a silent scream. She pressed her face against his, enjoying the feel of his early morning stubble scraping against her cheek as he too reached climax.

'Oh, Amelia,' Lucas panted, propelling his pulsing member into her one last time, 'how I've misjudged you all this while. I swear I'll never underestimate you ever again! I know now that you are the only woman for me!' Amelia felt his burning seed filling her just before her legs gave way and she sank down into the straw, exhausted from her own joyous conclusion.

She lay quietly on the ground for what seemed like hours, only the sound of her own laboured breathing engaging her attention as she struggled against the tiredness fast sweeping over her. Her eyes were just closing when she became aware of the faintest of noises, a presence beside her. Amelia rolled on to her side and looked straight into the eyes of Lucas. She started, noticing the remorseful expression filling them.

'What is it?'

'What can I say, Amelia? How can I make up for the pain I've caused you these past weeks?' He reached out and touched her hair. 'If nothing else,' he murmured, inching closer, 'this night has proved just how much I need you, how much we need each other.'

Amelia allowed him to draw her into his arms and shivered when she sensed one of his hands roving down over the smooth curve of her hip. 'I cannot deny that I have thought that too.' She raised her face to his and tasted the sweetness of his lips before continuing. 'But I must confess that I find it hard to accept this sudden change in you, husband. How am I to be sure this isn't another trick on your part, that once we return to Beechwood House you will set Lord Carterall to his vile task once again?'

Lucas chuckled, his hand lightly caressing her ebony-haired pleasure-mount. 'Oh, I think that after the skills you so readily displayed tonight, my dear, you'd be able to give him a run for his money! As to your other concern, all I can do is once again beg your forgiveness. I know that in the short time that we have been married, I have gone out of my way to prove my dominance over you. I suppose I really had this coming for the outrages I have forced you to bear simply because of my damned pride.'

'Yes, you did, but what a way to show you the error of your ways!' She giggled and, twisting round in order to face him, shuddered at the look of desire in his eyes.

Perhaps returning to Beechwood House with him wouldn't be so bad after all. So long as Lucas remembered that in pleasure's daughter he'd finally met his match, Amelia was certain that everything would eventually work out well for them.